CROSSROADS

Also by Belva Plain

THE SIGHT OF THE STARS

HER FATHER'S HOUSE

LOOKING BACK

AFTER THE FIRE

FORTUNE'S HAND

LEGACY OF SILENCE

HOMECOMING

SECRECY

PROMISES

THE CAROUSEL

DAYBREAK

WHISPERS

TREASURES

HARVEST

BLESSINGS

TAPESTRY

THE GOLDEN CUP

CRESCENT CITY

EDEN BURNING

RANDOM WINDS

EVERGREEN

Crossroads

Belva Plain

DELACORTE PRESS

DOUBLEDAY LARGE PRINT HOME LIBRARY EDITION

This Large Print Edition, prepared especially for Doubleday Large Print Home Library, contains the complete, unabridged text of the original Publisher's Edition.

CROSSROADS
A Delacorte Press Book / December 2008

Published by Bantam Dell
A Division of Random House, Inc.
New York, New York

Delacorte Press is a registered trademark of Random House, Inc., and the colophon is a trademark of Random House, Inc.

ISBN 978-1-60751-316-2

Printed in the United States of America
Published simultaneously in Canada

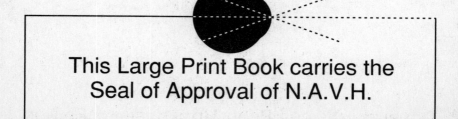

This Large Print Book carries the Seal of Approval of N.A.V.H.

CROSSROADS

Junctions

❧

"Envy is natural to man."
—HERODOTUS

Chapter One

If the gray clouds in the sky had not suddenly split apart and released an explosion of rain, Jewel Fairchild would have chosen to walk back to the train station on the shady road between two walls of green shrubs and trees. It was really amazing that such peace and quiet could exist not many miles from the crowded streets where she lived and worked. But had this entire day not been amazing?

Cassandra Wright, the owner and CEO

of Wright Glassworks, had been riding her horse and, having come too close to a fence post, had hurt her leg. She would have to stay at home for a few days—an unheard-of occurrence at the Glassworks, where her dawn-to-dusk work ethic was legendary. Her efficient secretary had spent most of the day on the phone, as Mrs. Wright was directing the business from her home. (Even though Cassandra had been married twice, she insisted on being called Mrs. Wright because Wright was the name of her ancestors and her business, and the politically correct Ms. was way too trendy for her taste.) When it was discovered late in the afternoon that an important paper required the CEO's signature, Jewel, who was a receptionist at the Glassworks, had been summoned by her supervisor and told to hand-deliver the document to Mrs. Wright's home. Although to call the place a "home" was to understate so totally the grandeur, the dreamlike other-worldliness of it, it was almost funny.

Of course Jewel had known that Mrs. Wright and her family wouldn't live in a hut, but she'd never seen anything like what she'd seen today. Now, as she leaned her head back on the seat of the car in which the Wright family gardener was driving her back to town, she went back over every moment of the last few hours, trying to fix them in her memory forever.

First there had been the train trip out of Wrightstown, the busy city that was named for the glassworks that gave it its reason for being. Cassandra Wright didn't live near her business—of course not. She lived out in the country where the air was pure and the nights were quiet. There was a special spur off the main train track with a station at the end that serviced the area. Jewel had walked from the train station—it hadn't started raining yet—and after about fifteen minutes, she'd approached a big white house gleaming in the gray gloom of the day.

Inside the house everything gleamed too. A woman who identified herself as the housekeeper had answered the door and led Jewel into the foyer, where she had a quick impression of glossy furniture, silk, crystal, and photographs in silver frames. Light sparkled from a chandelier above her; on a wall opposite a sweeping staircase there was a huge painting by some artist with a French name. The housekeeper had said the name, but Jewel had been too busy taking in all the splendor to register it.

The housekeeper led her through a series of hallways and rooms—more rooms than anybody would think one family could use. In the main hall a clock chimed like music. A rare treasure this clock was, according to the housekeeper. But by then Jewel was beginning to realize that the word "treasure" described everything in this place.

At first she was too overwhelmed to do more than stare. But slowly, a need started to grow inside her to touch what she was seeing. As the housekeeper hurried her along, she dug a foot into the carpet to feel the depth of the silky nap; she allowed a finger to trace the back of a richly brocaded chair. If she could have, Jewel would have inhaled all of it; she would have done anything, anything to take all this gleaming beauty inside herself, to own it, just for one second.

* * *

There was only one object in the place that did not seem to gleam. Actually, she wasn't an object, she was a young girl, and she was sitting on a sofa reading a book. She, her book, and the sofa were all in the library, which was where the housekeeper had brought Jewel.

"You can wait in here and I'll get Mrs. Wright . . . ," she'd started to say to Jewel, but the girl had looked up and the housekeeper had realized that they were not alone. "Oh, I'm sorry to disturb you, Miss Gwen, I didn't see you there," she said. The girl didn't seem surprised that she'd been overlooked. "This is a person from the glassworks come to give your mother a paper to sign," the housekeeper went on. "I'll put her in the sitting room."

"It's all right," the girl said. "Let her stay." Her voice was light and soft and there was a trace of something in it that Jewel wanted to say was snooty. She looked at the girl; this was Gwendolyn

Wright, Cassandra Wright's daughter—
her adopted daughter. In Wrightstown,
the fact that Queen Cassandra had
adopted this girl made her something of
a celebrity, or at the very least, an object
of curiosity.

It only took Jewel a second to pass
judgment on her. "Miss Gwen," she decided, was dull. Her face wasn't exactly
homely, but it was just like the faces that
you see on the street when you walk
around a city or go to a mall, and would
not recognize if you were to see them
again. Her hair was red, but not a vibrant shade, it was rather washed-out.
Her eyes were a nondescript brown. The
only bright things about her were the
gold bracelet glinting on one arm and
the gold wristwatch on the other. She
looked up at Jewel and nodded. "I'm
sure Mother will be along any minute,"
she said. She hesitated as if she was
going to say something more, then
changed her mind. Two pink spots
flared in her cheeks and she looked
down at her hands which were folded
in her lap. And there her gaze stayed,
while the silence in the room grew from

being merely uncomfortable to down-right insulting.

She didn't even offer me a glass of water! Jewel thought indignantly. *I may not have been raised in a big house with clocks that are treasures and pictures that were painted by people whose names you can't pronounce, but even I know that's no way to treat a visitor in your home. Where are her manners?*

As if she'd heard the unspoken rebuke the girl finally looked up. "Please sit down," she said. She smiled awkwardly.

She's shy, Jewel thought. *So shy she's tongue-tied.* The realization was a surprise. The girl was wearing hundreds, maybe even thousands, of dollars' worth of jewelry, and she lived in a palace! How could you be shy with all of that? But the two pink spots had now turned crimson and were spreading across Gwen Wright's plain face.

I guess it's up to me to help us out, Jewel thought. She smiled her own wide, welcoming smile; she had a beautiful mouth and perfect teeth and she knew how to use them. A picture of the face she saw each day in the mirror flashed through her mind. Unlike Gwen Wright's drab tresses, her own hair was a shimmering mass of ebony waves. Her wide blue eyes—really they were closer to violet—were fringed with thick lashes, her complexion was porcelain white, her nose was as beautiful as her mouth, and as for her figure . . . well, let's just say she'd never had any trouble attracting boys. Her beauty was her talisman, which was why it always came to mind when she needed extra confidence. Not that she needed any at all to talk to this dull, tongue-tied girl who was glancing longingly at the book good manners had forced her to put aside.

"What are you reading?" Jewel asked, to break the ice.

"*Le Petit Prince* by Saint-Exupéry." She pronounced it with the same nasal accent the housekeeper had used when saying the name of the artist who had painted the picture in the foyer.

"That's French, isn't it?" Gwen nodded. "Do you speak it?" Another nod. Jewel was starting to get annoyed. She was willing to do her best to keep a conversation going, but a little help from

Miss Gwen would have been nice. After all, she was the one who had had all the advantages—she even spoke French, for heaven's sake! But it was as if it was Jewel's job to smooth things over for her, and it was Gwen's right to be taken care of. Jewel was willing to bet she got away with this kind of thing all the time.

Then miracle of miracles, the mute one spoke. "I'm going to Paris, you see, so I need to bone up on my French. Hence Exupéry."

Her lack of enthusiasm made Jewel even more annoyed. *I've never been anywhere, not even to Boston or New York; she's going to Paris and she looks miserable about it.*

"I know I should be excited." Gwen seemed to read her mind again. "But the thing is, I'm going with Mother."

And that did explain some of Gwen's attitude. Jewel had a brief but vivid vision of the formidable Mrs. Wright, whose every instruction at the glass-works was carried out with every *t* crossed and every *i* dotted. The instructions were always graciously given, but they were obeyed in record time because no one could imagine what might happen if they weren't. Mrs. Wright was a stickler for order at home too, as everyone in town knew from her servants' gossip. Jewel tried to imagine what it would be like to take a trip with a woman who insisted that her mail must be sorted in a tray by the time she walked in the door from work, whose Christmas presents were wrapped and ready to be delivered by December first. Her decorations consisted of one wreath that was hung on her front door and one electric candle that was placed in the front window because, as she had famously decreed, more would be vulgar. No, Cassandra Wright would not be an easy traveling companion. On the other hand, she was taking her daughter on the trip of a lifetime! So what if she was a stickler for order and punctuality. Jewel would have put up with a lot more than that for a chance to see Paris!

"I'm sure you'll have a wonderful time," Jewel said politely. "Paris should be very . . . interesting."

"Oh, yes," Gwen said. "The trip will definitely be interesting." And for the first time Jewel thought she saw a spark of humor in the nondescript brown eyes. It vanished the next moment when Mrs. Wright entered the room.

Jewel had seen the woman at the glassworks, of course. She passed Jewel at the receptionist's desk every morning on her way to her own office, and always threw a "Good morning, Jewel" over her shoulder as she went by. Cassandra Wright never seemed hurried when she moved through a room, but you always knew she was going to get where she wanted to go. And woe to anyone who waylaid her. "Purposeful" was a good word for her; "regal" was another.

Seeing her here at home, she was still regal, but there were differences too. First, there were the dogs that bounded in at her side. One was a collie she called Missy and the other an exuberant mutt named Hank. Mrs. Wright made them both sit, and cooed "good dogs" in a tone of voice Jewel couldn't have imagined her using. Then there was the way the woman was dressed. At work she wore structured pastel suits that

were always in the latest style; the
tweed skirt and gray turtleneck she was
wearing at home had been softened by
wear, and she seemed softer too. Her
graying brown hair was tucked into her
signature chignon, but a few tendrils
had escaped around her face. Her high
cheekbones, chiseled mouth, and deep-
set, intelligent eyes all seemed gentler
somehow. Part of the reason might have
been the injury to her right leg and the
slight limp that slowed down her usual
brisk movements, although her posture
was still perfect; Cassandra Wright
came from the class that would have a
straight back in the coffin. And now, in
her presence, it was Jewel's turn to be
tongue-tied.

Fortunately no one seemed to notice.
The documents were produced and
whisked away by the housekeeper to be
perused and signed at Mrs. Wright's
leisure. Jewel was thanked for coming
out in such inclement weather as if she
had had a choice in the matter. Then it
was all over and Mrs. Wright was saying, "You can't possibly walk to the train
station in this rain. If Gwen had her

driver's license, she could drive you, but she won't be getting it for a week or two. Can you imagine? She's delayed it for two years! She already has her own car but she has yet to drive it."

"I don't like cars; they're dangerous," said Gwen. She seemed to have gotten even duller since her mother had come into the room. "Driving is too big a responsibility."

Her mother dismissed the statement with a shrug and turned back to Jewel. "I'll ask our gardener, Albert, to take you back to your home. It's too late for you to go back to work today. Albert is a very nice man and we've known him forever."

Chapter Two

As he drove Jewel home, Albert proved to be not only a nice man, but a talkative one. In the space of five minutes he had pointed out the stable where Mrs. Wright boarded her beloved horses, and told several stories about her prowess as a rider in her youth.

"You know Mrs. Wright very well," Jewel said, to say something.

"I've been with the Wright family for twenty years" was the proud reply. "And if I wasn't going to be seventy-eight this

month I wouldn't be retiring. Mrs. Wright
is the salt of the earth, let me tell you."
He looked at Jewel in his rearview mirror, as if he was waiting for her to chime
in with her own praise of the great lady.
But Jewel was thinking about the beautiful white house, now gleaming in the
rain, that was receding behind them.
The sense of well-being and pleasure
she'd felt while she was inside it was receding too—in spite of her efforts to re-
capture it.

When her supervisor had asked her to
take the papers to Mrs. Wright, she'd
felt like a schoolkid who had been given
an unexpected recess. Then she'd gotten a glimpse of a paradise she'd never
dreamed existed. Now the recess had
been canceled; she'd been politely ushered out of paradise, and was on her
way back to reality. Tomorrow she would
go back to her dreary job and smile and
be sweet because no one must ever
know how much she hated it. That was
what she had to look forward to. And
behind her in the white house was a girl
who complained about going to Paris

and didn't even appreciate her car enough to drive it.

Gwen Wright probably has more money in her pocket than I have in my whole bank account. I'll bet she doesn't know how much she has; she's never even counted it. I know to the penny how much I have. Because I have to know.

Albert broke into her reverie. "Did you see that mutt, Hank? Mrs. Wright took him in even though she has Missy, that's her collie that wins all the awards," he said. "Mrs. Wright can't stand to see any animal in trouble. That little stray showed up at the back door loaded with mange, and one of its legs was full of buckshot where some farmer had shot it up. Anyone but Mrs. Wright would have had the dog put down but she told that vet to do whatever he had to, to save it. I don't know how many operations it took, it cost the earth, but now that mutt lives in the house and it has a bed right next to Missy's, and Mrs. Wright doesn't make a particle of difference in the way she treats both of them. That's the kind of person she is." He paused, and once again, Jewel knew that was her cue to respond.

"Mmmm," she said.

That wasn't nearly good enough for Albert. "Look at the way Mrs. Wright took in Gwen when she was just a baby. That poor little thing was all alone in the world."

"Babies who are put up for adoption usually are."

"But that poor little one—"

"Oh, for Pete's sake!" she cut him off. "You feel sorry for Gwen Wright? Have you looked at the bracelet she has on her arm? Gold, with diamonds in it."

"Mrs. Wright gave it to her for her eighteenth birthday. That's my point, she's so good to Gwen . . . after everything that—" Suddenly he stopped short. He'd been intending to say more and he'd stopped himself.

"After what?" Jewel asked, her bad mood instantly replaced by curiosity.

"Nothing. Just . . . Mrs. Wright is a good woman, that's all." But that wasn't what he'd started to say.

"Because she wanted a baby and she adopted one?" Jewel baited him.

"There's nothing wonderful about that! People do it every day."

"But Mrs. Wright didn't want this baby. . . . She couldn't have!"

The words had slipped out, Jewel could tell. And there was no way she was going to let him clam up now. "What are you talking about?"

"It's not important."

"What do you know about Mrs. Wright and Gwen?"

"Nothing. That is . . . I don't really know. . . ."

"But there's something you *think* you know. What?"

"It's not like the Wright family confides in me. . . ."

"It's something wrong, something bad. . . ."

"It's not bad!"

But there was something suspicious about it. Jewel could smell it.

"Just drop it!" The old man was really upset now.

"Okay. But if you won't tell me, I'll start asking around. And in a town like this, you know someone will know something. It would probably be better if I heard it from you instead of digging up a lot of old dirt."

He seemed to realize the sense of that. She saw him gather his thoughts for a second, then he plunged in. "Mrs. Wright has had her own share of troubles. Life hasn't been as easy for her as everyone thinks. Her first husband died in a car accident—"

"Yes, I know about that!" Now that he'd started to spill his secret, Jewel wanted to hurry him along. "He was on a business trip in New Orleans. Checking on a glassworks outlet down there."

"It wasn't like that, not quite." Al paused. "The truth was, that man was no good. Most people didn't know it, because he was so friendly and likeable and he was on the boards of so many charities and all . . . but some of us who saw him up close . . . we had his number." He paused again. Would he never get on with it? Jewel bit her tongue. "Do you remember what he looked like?" he asked.

Jewel tried to dredge up an image in

her mind and failed. "I was only four when he died," she said.

"He had red hair. Not bright red, kind of dark. Like Gwen's."

It took Jewel a moment to grasp his meaning, then: *Oh, my god!* she thought, as icy prickles ran up and down her spine. "Are you saying . . . ?"

"I'm saying I don't know for sure. But all the servants in the house knew that man cheated on Mrs. Wright. He had been doing it for years. And the outlet in New Orleans was his idea and it never made any money. . . ."

"So if he did have a mistress down there . . ." Jewel's mind was reeling. "Did Mrs. Wright know her husband was running around on her?"

"I'm sure she suspected it, but I don't think she would have stayed married to him if she'd known for a fact."

"So she found out about the baby after his death."

"And she took it in. Her husband's illegitimate child."

"And she never told anyone."

"Just Gwen's nursemaid Mavis, and Mavis told me in strictest confidence.

Mrs. Wright wanted to protect Gwen from the humiliation—"

"She wanted to protect herself!" Jewel said. And it was astonishing how much she liked the idea of proud, regal Cassandra Wright forced to confide in the hired help and lie to the rest of the world.

"If she had really wanted to protect herself, she would have left Gwen with no one to care for her," Albert said hotly. "But taking her in was the right thing to do, and Mrs. Wright—"

"Yes, yes. She's a saint!" Jewel said, but her mind was racing. "Does Gwen know?" she asked Albert. "About her father?"

"Of course not. I told you, Mrs. Wright protects her. And you can't say a word about any of this. Like I said, I'm the only one Mavis told, and . . ."

She gave him an injured look. "Albert, I'm not that kind of person."

He seemed reassured—but only a little. "I wouldn't want anything to hurt Gwen."

"Of course not."

"You see, she's a good kid. But

she's . . . well, she's different. Yes, that's it. Different."

*   *   *

Different. The word kept repeating itself in Jewel's head for the rest of the ride home. *Yes, Gwen Wright is different. From me, anyway. She's eighteen and I am twenty-two. Her mother was a tramp who slept with a married man, and mine was a decent woman who got married and took care of five kids until she was so worn out she died. Now the tramp's daughter has everything a person could ever want, and I have to scrape by.*

So she was adopted. And there's a nasty story about it. And it's been kept from her so she doesn't know where she came from or who she was. Tough. But no tougher than the way I had it after Ma died and a half a year later Pop found another wife and then scooted off as far as you can go without dropping into an ocean.

Albert said Gwen's different, but what he means is she's special. So she shouldn't have to face life like the rest of us do. Well, who the hell decided that?

*   *   *

"Duffy Street—is this the place?" Albert asked. Jewel had been so busy with her thoughts she hadn't even noticed that they'd reached the city.

"Yes, here. Stop in front of the delicatessen. I live over it, on the third floor."

"Then here you go."

"Thank you. Good night, Albert."

"Uh . . . Jewel . . . ?"

"Mum's the word, Albert. I promise."

"Well then, good night."

Chapter Three

Jewel got out of the gardener's car and watched as the last vestige of her visit to paradise drove off. *Now you're back in your world, Jewel,* she told herself. *Here it is in all its glory—two flights of rickety old stairs up to the third floor and the owners are too cheap to have brighter lights. Be careful not to stumble and break your leg. Now you're in the apartment—so called—two rooms and a kitchenette—so called. Compare that with what you've just seen. The rugs like dark blue velvet, the fern plant in the cut-glass bowl on that little table. It looked like mahogany. It had to be mahogany, so dark and shining. . . . But now you'd better stop comparing, because if you don't it'll drive you crazy. Still, you will never forget the home where Gwen Wright lives, not until the day you die. You'll think about it before you go to sleep at night, and you'll daydream about it when you're awake. You'll dream about that house the way other women dream about finding their true love.*

There was a rocking chair in Jewel's living room—so called—the one new piece of furniture she'd bought for herself. She sat in it now, closed her eyes, and tried to let the back-and-forth motion soothe her. But it didn't work. Not tonight. She looked around her room in the darkness. She'd been so pleased with herself when she'd moved to Wrightstown; she'd been sure she was moving up in the world.

Wrightstown had been built on a river, like so many New England towns. The township had been founded before the

Wrights had established their world-famous glassworks—no one could remember what it had been called in those pre-glassworks days—but it was because of the glassworks that it had grown and remained vibrant while other small communities in the area had withered away. There were jobs to be had in Wrightsville, and because of that, other smaller businesses flourished there too. There were restaurants and movie theaters and a shiny new mall just a few miles away from the center of the thriving city. There were doctors and lawyers and dentists and teachers. There was even a theater that showed the occasional road show from New York as well as rock concerts and other special events. There were rich neighborhoods, full of gracious homes, that climbed up the hills that surrounded the city, and poorer neighborhoods with meager but tidy bungalows crowded near the railroad tracks. These were the homes that had been built for the employees of the glassworks a century earlier. Some of these old areas had fallen into disrepair in the seventies and the eighties and were now being rediscovered by smart young people who had graduated from college and were rehabilitating them. Wrightstown had its own college too.

Jewel had not come from Wrightstown. Her home was farther up the river, a smaller, meaner little community that had surrounded a textile mill in the days when Americans still manufactured their own fabrics, yarns, and threads. Jewel's father had come there from his family's failing dairy farm, a smart, angry boy whose anger came from the fact that he was smart and had wanted to go to college but he hadn't had the money. Instead he'd had to rely on his clever hands. The only work he'd been able to find in the dying textile town had been with a cabinetmaker. The shop where he worked was not a place that did the kind of custom work with fine wood that might have satisfied his soul. He built ugly, boxlike cabinets with cheap hardware to be sold to people whose kitchens and bathrooms were as drab as his own. He came home at night smelling of wood and sweat and machine oil. Jewel couldn't remember seeing him without sawdust in his hair, not even on Sunday.

Her mother had not been as smart as her father, but she had been a beauty. It was from her ma that Jewel had gotten her spectacular eyes, mouth, and hair. As a child, Jewel had watched her mother's beauty disappear as lines brought on by stress and worry etched themselves on her lovely face, first between the eyes, then under them; then finally the lines became trenches along the sides of her mouth, pulling it down until the smile that had once been radiant was a grimace. It was money, or the lack of it, that had robbed Ma of her youth and her pretty smile. Money made all the difference—always.

Jewel shifted in the rocker. A picture had come into her mind, one she didn't want but she couldn't push it away. It was just a snapshot of a moment that was over in a second—but it was one of those moments that can put a life on a certain course forever. It had happened at the end of the day, when her father had come home. As usual he was tired and out of sorts. Ma had served the dinner that had been cooked with an eye to a dwindling paycheck rather than taste and pleasure, and she had watched Pop's bad temper mount. And Jewel had watched her. Ma had looked at the children gathered around her table— more mouths than they could feed—and then she looked again at Pop. And her eyes were full of the kind of exhaustion that reaches down into the bones. It was as if she was carrying some burden that was so heavy that she was going to sink under its weight. And Jewel, who was way too young to know anything about the ways of men and women, nevertheless understood it. Because Pop's fatigue and bad temper had never interfered with his . . . well, Ma would have called them his needs. If anything, the urgency of them seemed to increase with his weariness—and his bad temper. And his needs meant more kids—nothing had ever interfered with that. Ma knew this was going to be another night of needs and as she looked at Pop and the children, she was beaten. Jewel jumped up to take the bowl out of her mother's hands and started serving the potatoes herself. That was how it had begun. That was how Jewel became one of those girls for whom the carefree years of childhood are a myth because they have taken on the job of helping.

Over the years, there was a lot of helping to be done, for, added to the usual household chores, there was always at least one person in the overcrowded little house who had some kind of physical ailment: a broken arm, or measles, or a bloody nose resulting from a boyish fistfight in somebody's backyard.

What Jewel remembered most was the ugliness of it all, the turmoil of clothing ready for the wash, of unmade beds and a cluttered kitchen where meals were eaten while everybody was in a hurry, going or coming and going again. Everyone in town seemed to have more money than Jewel's family had. Their houses had nice curtains on the windows and their girls went to school wearing nice clothes. Jewel wanted to be well dressed and well groomed. She never was. Her hands were rough from washing and cleaning; her beautiful hair was cut bluntly with scissors at home.

There was no time for a trip to a beauty shop, no money for a carefully styled coiffure or manicured nails tinted a shining pink.

One bright day, when she was eighteen, Jewel went walking alone beyond the town. She kept on going until she reached the farm country where cornfields bordered the road on either side, and as the wind rushed, the cornstalks swung. Clouds overhead clove the blue. She had heard in school the words "lapis lazuli." Was this it? And suddenly before her eyes, Jewel saw how the ocean must look as the sky arches over it. She saw enormous waves plunge through the vastness. Everything was alive. Everywhere and everything, from the ocean to the growing corn, to the birds that passed high overhead, all moving things going, going somewhere. Somewhere!

*　　　*　　　*

Jewel opened her eyes and stopped rocking. Now she was no longer eighteen, and she was going nowhere. Her life was empty and she had no idea how to fill it. Of course a man would be a solution, and she'd met quite a few attractive men who were attracted to her. But she hadn't loved any of them. Because the men who came her way were in the same predicament she was: working hard and not having enough to show for it. And she wasn't going to risk winding up like Ma.

She got up to pull down the shade. The rain and wind were bending back a scrawny tree that was just beyond her window. Beyond the tree was the endless dark. She turned away from the window; she was going to bed. One way to get rid of the pictures in her mind was to sleep.

*   *   *

Sleep was coming slowly. Too slowly. Jewel twisted and turned in the bed sheets, kicking them off and pulling them back. This didn't happen to her often—thank heaven—but tonight the pictures were stronger than her will; they kept on coming. Now she was back to that wonderful house and that nobody of a girl who didn't seem to belong there. Then she was in the car with Albert and he was telling her about Cassandra Wright's great secret. The secret from which Gwen Wright had been so carefully, lovingly protected. Protected as Jewel had never been. A thought joined the pictures racketing around in Jewel's brain. *I wonder what would happen if Gwen were to find out.* She tried to push the thought aside, but like the pictures it just kept coming back.

Chapter Four

The morning after the rainstorm dawned, as such mornings usually do, clear and achingly beautiful. But that was not the reason why Gwen awoke and knew she couldn't stay inside. The encounter with the girl who worked at the glassworks had upset her . . . only upset wasn't the right word. What Jewel had done—that was her name, Jewel—was send Gwen back to a place she had thought she'd left behind. It was a gray place, full of foggy emotions, which could engulf her if she wasn't careful.

When Jewel Fairchild had appeared in the library, Gwen had to keep herself from gasping. *She's so beautiful!* Gwen had thought. *Like a tropical flower, with that white skin and those blue eyes and that red, perfect mouth—I can see how red it is through her lipstick. Even her teeth are bright when she smiles, and her smile is delightful.* And a stab of an emotion Gwen recognized as her old nemesis, envy, had shot through her. And once again she rembered the day she'd turned five.

*   *   *

Gwen jumped up, went to her closet, and reached for her clothes. She was not going to think about her fifth birthday, not today, she told herself. But after a moment it was clear that blotting it out was going to be easier said than done. It was a part of her personality—maybe it was a curse—that things that had happened long ago stayed as fresh with her as if they had happened in the last five minutes. This was especially true with incidents from her childhood. And that fifth birthday still seemed to encompass everything Gwen had been as a child—all her doubts and angers.

She had known that her party was not going to be an elaborate affair; her guests were all from the public school that her mother insisted she attend and Cassandra would never have had the bad taste to outshine the other children's parties. Besides, she didn't believe in conspicuous displays. There would be no pony rides or hired clowns to help celebrate Gwen's fifth year and Gwen didn't expect them. However, she had expected that on her special day she would be the best-looking girl in the room. She was relying on her new dress to accomplish this feat for her—from an early age she had known she was not pretty. But her party dress was more than pretty; in Gwen's young eyes it was nothing short of magnificent. She had chosen it herself on a trip to Wrightstown's most expensive department store. She'd been attracted by the magic of the fabric—an iridescent silvery taffeta that shimmered with different undertones as the light caught the folds of the skirt; now they were blue, now they were green, and every once in a while there was a glint of red. The dress itself was plain in design, with small puffed sleeves tied with black velvet ribbon and a simple heart-shaped neckline; there were no ruffled frills, no lacy trim, nothing to distract from the material. Gwen had known instantly that she wanted it, but as usual, she hadn't trusted her instincts, and so she had pointed it out tentatively to her mother. To her enormous relief, Cassandra had appreciated it as much as she did. In fact, she'd seemed extremely pleased— to say nothing of surprised—with Gwen's choice. "It's perfect," she'd said. "How clever of you to have seen it among all those poufy dresses."

Swelling with pride, Gwen had watched as the precious garment was paid for, and packed in a box with the department store's name on the lid. She had carried it home in the car on her lap. And on the day of the party she had put it on confidently, knowing that she would be prettier than all the other girls.

There are times in our lives when the vision in our mind of how an event *should* unfold is so strong that it blocks us from seeing what is happening in reality. That was why Gwen didn't realize that her dress was not working the hoped-for miracle. True, none of the other little girls had mentioned it—as it always is with females, be they five or fifty, it was the other girls she wanted most to impress—but she had faith that given time and opportunity they would. Meanwhile she was being shunted more and more to the outskirts of her own party as the other, more sociable children congregated in the center of the living room. It was at that moment that a latecomer named Carol Anne Jenkins had walked in.

By the age of five, most children know who among them will be the winners in the battle for attention and popularity, and who will be the losers. Every one of Gwen's little classmates knew that Carol Anne was a winner. Not only did she have blond hair that fell naturally into long shiny curls, and large blue eyes, she took tap lessons and had once been asked to entertain at a variety show given by the Rotary Club. Adults loved her, and through sheer personal charisma she managed to be popular with her peers in spite of it.

Carol Anne was wearing a pink tulle dress. "Mama made it for me," she announced proudly. "And the petticoats too." There were three of them pushing up the skirt—liberally trimmed with ruffles—until it stood out from her waist at almost a forty-five-degree angle. Fake pink roses tied with pink satin bows were buried in and among the tiers of ruffles; more roses, ribbon, and white lace edged the bodice of the dress and the sleeves.

Years later Gwen would realize that the fabric was a slick synthetic and Carol's mother sewed for her because the family couldn't afford to buy ready-made, but at that moment at her birthday party, Gwen only knew that Carol Anne Jenkins had stolen her day. If Gwen had been asked what she was feeling she would have said, "I'm not enough." And she hated feeling that. In mounting anger, she watched as the other girls flocked around the thief gushing over the roses and the ruffles. Finally Gwen couldn't stand it anymore. She inched her way through the admiring throng until she was at Carol Anne's side, then as Carol Anne accepted compliments— compliments that should by rights have gone to the birthday girl—meek and mild little Gwen Wright reached out and yanked one of the golden curls as hard as she could.

Carol Anne began to cry, Cassandra and Gwen's nanny came rushing in, and by the time the adults had sorted out the different versions of the incident offered by the witnessing children, Gwen was already regretting what she'd done. She probably would have said she was sorry on her own, if Cassandra hadn't pursed her lips in the way that required instant obedience and said, "Gwen, I'm ashamed of you. Apologize to Carol Anne immediately."

All of Gwen's grievances came back to her, and iron entered her soul. She raised her head to look her mother in the eye and shook her head.

Cassandra was stunned. She couldn't

believe she was being defied. "I told you to apologize, Gwendolyn," she repeated.

This time Gwen whispered, "No."

She'd been ordered to go to her room while the other children were served cake and ice cream and sent quickly on their way home. After they were gone, Cassandra had come upstairs to see her. With stubborn pride Gwen had refused to cry and she had refused to explain herself. But like the superwoman she was, Cassandra had seen into Gwen's mind and understood what had motivated her.

"Jealousy is a particularly ugly emotion," she'd said, "especially for someone in your position who has so much. Giving in to it is nothing more than self-indulgence, and refusing to acknowledge what you've done is beneath you."

But Gwen still couldn't choke out the words "I'm sorry."

There was no way to tell her mother why. Perhaps at that age she didn't even know all the reasons herself. Years later she would understand that it hadn't just been the one party where she'd felt like she was "not enough"; she'd been feeling that all of her life. And the person who had made her feel that way—the person who was not going to get the satisfaction of an apology from her—was Cassandra.

*　　*　　*

Gwen had finished dressing. She was wearing her favorite outfit for early autumn; a flared corduroy skirt, and a light sweater with a flannel shirt tossed over it, in case there was a nip in the air. She could tie the shirt around her waist if the weather warmed. As a concession to the rain of the previous evening and the wet grass, she had pulled on an old pair of boots. She sat at the vanity table she seldom used, and briefly contemplated, then rejected, the idea of putting on some lipstick. She looked at herself in the mirror.

Obviously, she was as capable of jealousy today as she had been when she was five. And she didn't want to be. She agreed with Cassandra: It was a particularly ugly emotion when you had been given as much as she had. And she'd gotten better over the years. It had taken a truly beautiful girl like Jewel to bring on an attack of the devil voices that whispered that she was inadequate. Well, at least this time she hadn't reached out and yanked a handful of the shining blue-black hair that fell in waves around Jewel's face. But she had been unforgivably rude. She sighed. The sad part was, even though she couldn't control the devil voices, she knew why she was so vulnerable to them.

Chapter Five

Gwen had read once that the first five years of one's life were the formative ones and she knew this to be true. In that time, scars could be made on the soul that never faded. Or one could develop a belief in oneself that would last a lifetime. Gwen had collected . . . well, scars might be too strong a word; a better one might be insecurities. She wished she could say it had been no one's fault, but that wasn't true.

It had started when she was an infant.

She couldn't remember that time, of course, but she knew that was when she'd gotten the message that she was "not enough." That her mother, the most important figure in her life, had found her lacking in some way. How she had gotten that feeling Gwen couldn't have said, although she had pondered the question at great length.

Was it the fact that her mother did not do the daily chores of caring for her as other mothers did? But Cassandra Wright was not like other women; it was impossible to imagine her changing a diaper, or patiently feeding spoonful after spoonful of sloppy baby food into a tiny resisting mouth. Servants did such things for her and had since she herself was a child. Besides, Cassandra worked long hours at the glassworks, where her responsibilities were overwhelming. No one could have expected her to involve herself with the minutiae of child-rearing. From the beginning Gwen had understood that. Gwen had always been an understanding child.

She understood that her mother was not one for overt gestures of affection;

she did not expect Cassandra to throw her arms around her in a bear hug, to shower her with kisses, or to coo endlessly over her. Reserve had been bred into Cassandra's bones, and somehow Gwen had known that. So why did she feel that in some profound way she was a disappointment? Why did she feel that there was a barrier—thin as a silken veil but strong as steel—that sometimes descended when her mother was with her? It wasn't there all the time, but when it came she could feel her mother withdraw in a subtle way. Then Cassandra would hand Gwen over to Sarah—the nanny who had replaced Gwen's nursemaid, Mavis. Sarah would whisk Gwen away, and Gwen would know that once again she'd been banished.

Not that her mother was ever cruel to her. Cassandra rarely lost her temper; she was kind, and fair, and always generous. Still, children know when they are a source of joy. And Gwen knew there were times when she was not. And she wondered what was wrong with her.

*   *   *

She'd always known she was adopted. Cassandra had told her when she was very young. "You probably weren't old enough to understand what it meant," Cassandra said later—Gwen was seven at the time, and they were talking about it. "It probably would have been better if I had waited until you were more mature. But too many people around here knew about it, and you know the way they all like to gossip about us . . . the Wright family . . . and I didn't want you to hear it from anyone but me." She paused. "Of course, I knew how intelligent you were. I was sure if you had any questions you would have asked me."

But I do have questions, Gwen thought. *Lots of them. I just never felt like I could ask them.*

And then, because hope springs eternal, she asked her biggest one, "Why did you pick me?"

And still clinging to hope, she waited for her mother to say, *Because I fell in love with you the second I saw you.* Or, perhaps, *Because I couldn't imagine my life without you.*

"I had wanted children throughout my first marriage," Cassandra said.

Was it Gwen's imagination or was she speaking a little too carefully?

"And after he . . . my husband . . . died, and I saw you . . . it seemed like a golden opportunity . . . and . . ."

Gwen knew it wasn't her imagination; her mother, who always knew what she wanted to say, who was always so sure of herself, was stumbling. And hope died. "But it wasn't a golden opportunity," Gwen said slowly. "You made a mistake."

Her mother gave a little gasp. "No, Gwen!"

"You thought you wanted a child but you really didn't. It's okay, Mother. Everyone makes mistakes. . . ." She was trying to sound like a grown-up intelligent girl of seven, but her voice broke on the last word.

"That wasn't it. . . . It was . . ." And for a second Gwen thought her mother was going to say what it was. But then Gwen spoiled everything by starting to cry.

Cassandra dropped her reserve and got down on her knees to look Gwen in the eye. "Gwen, I've never ever regretted it!" she said. And then she added something that Gwen would ponder for years. "No matter how it started out, I am so glad I did it. Always remember that."

*   *   *

Gwen checked her face again in the mirror. Then she caught herself and had to laugh. *What are you hoping will happen?* she mocked herself. *You're still you. You haven't suddenly become a tropical flower.* Still she looked herself over carefully, her simple outfit, her lack of makeup, her hair held off her face with a clip. *You're enough. Grow up and believe that you're enough.* But the mind saying something intelligent like that and the heart believing it were two entirely different things.

*   *   *

Gwen realized that not all of her difficulties could be attributed to her mother's strange shifts in mood. There was a long-standing argument, she knew, about the influence of nature versus nurture on a child. And from the very beginning Gwen's nature had been . . . unusual. Ordinary experiences could trigger ideas and fantasies in her that didn't occur to other more . . . well, usual children. A case in point had been the Face in the Window Incident.

When she was quite small, Gwen had seen her own reflection in a window. When she'd moved in a certain way the vision of her face had vanished altogether; when she moved again it reappeared, but it was distorted. This had brought up thoughts that were slightly disturbing, but also fascinating. She'd tried them out on Nanny Sarah.

"How do I know I'm real," she asked the woman. "How do I know I'm really here?"

"What silly questions. You're a real little girl, and you're right here. Where else would you be? Now eat your lunch."

But Gwen couldn't let the subject drop. "But what if we're all just a part of a daydream some creature—one that's much bigger and stronger than all of us, like God—is imagining. What if it decides to stop imagining us some day and we all just disappear!"

This had brought on sputtering from the nanny about the Bible and good little girls not saying such things.

Later, Gwen overheard the nanny telling the cook about it. "She's an odd duck," the nanny said. She didn't sound as if she found it a particularly appealing trait.

Unfortunately there were other indications of Gwen's oddness. For a while she had become obsessed with words. "Why do we say it's a plate?" she demanded. "Why don't we call it spinach? Or a mud pie?"

"Because it's a plate, that's its name," her nanny had replied.

"But what if the name is wrong? In other countries they call it something else."

"Well, we're right here in the good old U.S. of A. So you don't need to worry your head about what foreigners might say."

"But what if they're right and we're wrong? Or what if everyone is wrong?

What if words don't mean anything?
What if nothing means anything?"

"Odd duck," said the nanny to the cook. "Just odd."

*　　　*　　　*

Gwen gave up on Nanny Sarah. But questions kept cropping up in her mind. And no matter how hard she tried to keep them to herself, she needed to talk about them. So the next time she had one of her odd-duck ideas she decided to take it to the place where children were supposed to get answers—or so she had been told. She took it to her school.

Gwen planned her presentation carefully; she didn't want her teacher, Miss Spencer, thinking she was odd. This meant she had to wait until an empty Land O'Lakes butter box was thrown into the kitchen trash. She retrieved her treasure on a Saturday and hid it until Monday when she brought it to school. Monday morning was show-and-tell time, and when it was Gwen's turn to speak she held the box out so the entire class could see it.

"There's a picture of a girl on this box," she began. Something about the seriousness with which she said it—or maybe it was just the fact that she'd brought an old butter box to show-and-tell—must have seemed funny to the other children, because they started to titter. Normally this would have been enough to send Gwen back to her seat, but need drove her on. "The girl is holding a box of butter that has a picture on it of a girl holding a box of butter," she went on bravely.

"Yes, you're absolutely right, Gwen. How interesting. Thank you for sharing that," said Miss Spencer. "Now does anyone else have something to—"

"But when does it stop?" Gwen broke in. "Does it just go on and on forever?"

"Does what go on?" asked Miss Spencer who was as bewildered as Nanny Sarah had been.

"The box!" Gwen said. The other kids were laughing out loud now. "The box and the girl, does it just go on forever with boxes and girls holding them? What does forever mean? And is there a bigger box that I can't see with a bigger girl holding it . . ." and then to her horror Gwen felt the treacherous tears stinging at her eyes, and, dropping the Land O'Lakes box, she ran out of the classroom.

"Neurotic," Gwen overheard Miss Spencer say to the school nurse after she had taken Gwen to the nurse's office to lie down for a little while. "The child is obviously having some serious problems."

"Are you going to ask for a conference with the parents?" asked the nurse.

"Would you want to be the one to tell Cassandra Wright her daughter is disturbed? I'm not touching that with a ten-foot pole."

And there it was. In addition to nurture and nature, there was another element forming the character of Gwen Wright when she was young. She was a Wright of Wright Glassworks, living in the vicinity of Wrightstown. If there was ever a definition of life in a fishbowl, that was it. Actors and politicians, who had, after all, asked for the scrutiny, did not live more public lives than Gwen and her mother did in their small world. Perhaps ordinary little Susie Jones could afford to be an odd duck; Gwen Wright could not. She was not supposed to have strange thoughts. She was supposed to be above all the petty emotions that plagued those less fortunate than she.

When bright and shiny Jewel Fairchild came into her home, Gwen Wright was not supposed to feel insecure because the girl was so amazingly beautiful. Gwen was not supposed to envy that warm and easy smile that said Jewel was one of those who never met a stranger while it took Gwen months and sometimes years to decide she'd made a friend.

Enough! said a voice inside Gwen's head. *If you keep on like this you'll think yourself into one of those gray fogs that take days to climb out of. Go out into the fresh air. Get away from yourself.*

She left the bedroom, walked quickly down the long hallway to the wide curving staircase. At the bottom of the stairs she was met by undulating fur as Missy and Hank surrounded her. She let them out, then brought them back to the kitchen for their breakfast. They polished off the contents of their bowls, and then, having recognized her outfit as the one she wore when she was going outdoors, tried to follow her through the back door. But Gwen held them back.

"Not this time, babies," she said. "Now, Hank, don't look at me like that. I'd take you with me in a minute, but I'm going up the hill and you know what you did the last time you came with me. I won't have you bothering my little guys, you know."

So she left the dogs, barking canine pleas and indignation behind her, and walked outside.

Chapter Six

❧〰〰〰❧

The land on which Cassandra's home sat was well maintained but not manicured. There was a long lawn in the front of the house, a row of red maples that protected it from the road, and flower beds lining the front path in which daffodils, iris, and peonies bloomed in the spring to be followed by zinnias, daisies, daylilies, hollyhocks, and phlox in summer. In back of the house itself was another lawn that gave way to the surrounding forest of the area. In the spring violets and lilies of the valley carpeted the ground under a canopy of branches. In the autumn that same ground was carpeted again with the gold, red, and orange of the fallen leaves. The trees were pruned for safety's sake but otherwise they were left to grow freely.

The house itself was the kind of structure that would have been called a stately home if it had been listed in a guidebook. The artwork and priceless antiques inside it were the results of collecting done by four generations of a family with impeccable taste and the wealth to indulge that taste. Quite simply, when you were in that home, you were seeing civilization at its best. But once you went outdoors you felt you were in the woods—with all the beauty and simplicity that nature had to offer. Cassandra and her family had the best of both worlds.

Behind the back lawn there was a hill. Halfway up it, beneath the oaks, the pines, and the thread of sunshine that seeped through a thickness of the undergrowth, there was a flat stump that provided a seat where one could comfortably settle down. This was Gwen's destination—her special place where, as everyone in the house knew, she was not to be disturbed. She'd been coming here since she was a child. Sometimes she came to read, usually classics that required concentration and peace, like books written by Dickens or Dostoyevsky. Sometimes she merely sat quietly, and watched the small creatures who lived there: the squirrels who barely disturbed the silence when they buried nuts, which they would find under the snow in winter. Or the chipmunks, who scurried in and out of their three-room apartments—one room for their babies, one for food storage, and the third one for what? Gwen had forgotten. It was because of these little creatures that she would not take Missy and Hank with her to her retreat on the hill; the dogs frightened them away.

Gwen sat on the stump and prepared to enjoy the silence and the air and the companionship of the squirrels. Instead, another memory flooded back. But this was one she welcomed. She never tired of reliving it.

*   *   *

It had happened when she was sitting
on this very stump—she had been six
years old. A man had climbed up the hill
to talk to her. His name was Walter Amburn, and Gwen would always believe
that he had changed her life.

Gwen had seen him before that day;
for several months he had been coming
to the house, mostly in the evenings, to
escort her mother to various events. He
was not a tall man—when Cassandra
wore her high-heeled shoes, she was almost his height. His best feature was his
hair, light brown and curly, although his
nose was a bit too big for good looks
and his eyes were too deep-set. But
there was something about his face—
something kind and humorous—that
Gwen liked.

She always knew when he was coming, because Cassandra's eyes would
flash in a way they never did normally.
Sometimes, when she was getting
dressed to go out with him, she would
look at herself in the mirror and she
wouldn't like the dress she had chosen

or the earrings, and she would change them at the last second—a phenomenon totally out of character for one as decisive as she. Then she would have to rush down the stairs in a clatter of high heels so she would not be late when Walter arrived—the rushing was also totally out of character. There would be an uncharacteristic note of excitement in her voice as she greeted Walter, told the maid to get her wrap out of the closet, and went out into the night with him. Sometimes his hand would be under her elbow guiding her gently down the front steps, sometimes it would rest for a second on the small of her back, also for guidance. And Gwen, young as she was, could sense that there was something special in that touch of hand to body.

There were times when Walter and her mother did not leave the house right away, when they only had plans for dinner in a local restaurant, or at the home of friends. Then Walter would take off his coat and Cassandra would lead him to the living room where they would have drinks in front of the massive fireplace and eat the little canapés the cook had labored over. Or they would take their drinks into one of the cozier rooms, the library or the sitting room. The sound of them, of their laughter and talk, would echo down the halls of the house.

Gwen had been introduced to Walter during one of these interludes. She had been told he was a special friend of Cassandra's and she had believed it. But she hadn't really talked to him—not until the day under the trees.

When he appeared there in her refuge, Gwen had looked at him, seeing once again the kindness in his face and the warmth in his smile. Walter Amburn radiated warmth, everyone seemed to feel it. Now he was bending over so that Gwen and he were eye to eye.

"I hope I'm not intruding," he'd said gently. "Your nanny said I might find you here. I understand this is your special spot."

Shy, Gwen had nodded silently.

Walter had looked appreciatively at the canopy of green branches overhead, the velvety moss, and the dappling of sunshine and shadow on the grass. "I can see why," he said. "May I sit down?"

Gwen nodded again, and in spite of his nice slacks and the possibility of grass stains, he settled himself on the ground next to her. He began talking to her, but not in the silly way that adults usually talked to children. Walter told her how the moss that carpeted the earth under them had grown, and he showed her how to tell how old a tree was. And before Gwen knew how it had happened she was telling him about the patch of sunshine a few feet away where the wild daylilies grew every summer and about the squirrels and the chipmunks she watched. She mentioned that she'd made up a story about this place that was so magical to her, and he asked her if she would mind telling it for him. It was a rather long and rambling saga, she would realize later when she got better at storytelling, but Walter had listened intently and thanked her when she was finished.

Then she asked him why he had come to sit under her trees, because it wasn't something adults usually did, especially when they weren't dressed for it.

"I thought we should get to know each other a little," he'd said, "because I'm going to be in your life for a long time. You see, I'm going to be marrying your mother. I hope that meets with your approval."

And Gwen had thought about the shine in Cassandra's eyes and the way she ran down the stairs to meet him. And she had thought about the way Walter had listened to her story. And she said, "Yes. I think that will be fine."

"Thank you," he'd said gravely. "That's a big relief to me."

*   *   *

It had been better than fine. The advent of Walter had been the beginning of a new relationship between Gwen and Cassandra. The chill Gwen had always felt had begun to warm; the distance had been lessened. Her mother was a happier person now, and the happiness poured over everything and everyone around her.

And then, out of the blue, came the

bedtime story. Gwen was never really sure how or why Cassandra decided that she wanted to read to her daughter every night. She suspected that in some way Walter had been behind it, although she didn't know that for sure. It would have been like him to point out to his wife that Gwen was a child who loved stories and Cassandra herself was a voracious reader. It was Walter's instinct to bring people together, and to bring out the best in them. Or maybe Cassandra herself was looking for something she and her daughter could share; maybe she felt the lack of closeness between them and was looking for a way to reach out. Maybe she was trying to expand Gwen's mind. Maybe it was a little of both.

The idea of Cassandra Wright cuddling up with her little daughter every night for a cozily domestic reading of a bedtime story was so impossible that Gwen had never even dreamed of such a thing. But one evening as she lay in bed and Sarah turned on the television that would lull her to sleep, Cassandra appeared in her room with a book in hand.

"I've brought a novel I thought we might enjoy together," she said as she snapped off the TV. "It's called *Heidi*. Your pediatrician says it's too advanced for a child of your age, but I'm not sure he knows how very bright you are. It was one of my favorite stories growing up, and in any case, I'm afraid I couldn't bear reading some of the pap they write for children these days."

So there were no rhyming kittens or fairy princesses saved by white knights for Gwen. She didn't care. The bedtime story became her favorite part of her day. Propped up against her pillows, bathed and bundled into her night-clothes, she would wait for Cassandra to come in—often dressed for an evening out—sit on a chair at the side of the bed, and read.

Gwen had no trouble following the story. She and her mother laughed together at Fräulein Rottenmeier; they sighed over the mountains of Switzerland together, and the wildflowers. For several weeks the only thing Gwen wanted to eat were grilled cheese sandwiches, and the cook had instructions to oblige her—after all, cheese melted on a chunk of bread over the fire was what Heidi and her grandfather ate.

The bedtime story had been a turning point; and over the next few years Gwen and Cassandra would find other interests and passions they shared. Gwen developed a taste for the classical music her mother adored: Beethoven, Schubert, and Mozart. They listened to Cassandra's favorite recording of *La Bohème* together and followed along with the libretto. Both mother and daughter had a deep love of animals, and a need for nature. They felt the same sense of loss when old trees were cut down and beautiful marshlands were drained for yet another ugly housing development. Both of them had a sense of justice and fair play. Cassandra understood Gwen's need for quiet and time alone; Gwen respected her mother's reserve and need for order. Perhaps it wasn't a perfect relationship—but where are those found? As far as Gwen was concerned it was much better than it once had been.

*　　　*　　　*

Of course she still had her scar tissue; that kind of thing never totally disappears, and there were times when she was angry—usually when she realized once again that she would never fit in with other youngsters her age. Those were the times when she hated being a Wright, hated her own quirky mind, and hated the superior being who was her mother.

"Yes, you're different," Walter said one day when they were having iced tea in his studio. Walter was an artist, very much in demand as a portrait painter. Gwen thought it was because he always seemed to find whatever it was that made his subject special and somehow managed to put that on the canvas. He had a gift for liking people. "I know being different isn't fun now, when all you want to do is be one of the pack, but you have to look at the bigger picture. Most of the world's great ones were odd ducks, as you call yourself. They couldn't fit in so they had to discover something else to get them through, some great passion. They became our geniuses, our poets and composers, our philosophers and scientists. I believe passion is what brings joy. Not always happiness, you understand, that is a toss of the dice, but joy will always come from finding what you love to do and doing it." He'd paused for a second and then he'd smiled his warm smile. "In any event, that's what this odd duck keeps telling himself."

Gwen had thought for a moment and then she said, "When you were talking about the great ones, you didn't mention business people like my mother. Do you think they can have a passion for what they do too?"

Walter had laughed. "Yes, of course they can; your mother is proof of that. She is a genius in the way she handles her company. I guess I don't think of including business in the great endeavors of the world, because I can't imagine doing what Cassie does every day. But I do respect anyone who can." He looked at her then. "And I hope you do too, Gwen. It' s very important to respect other people's passions."

It was Walter who had put into proper perspective the odd-duck notions Gwen had had as a child. "You're in good company," he said. "That question you asked about the butter box? What you were really talking about was the concept of infinity. Men have been puzzling over that one since the Greeks. As for questioning the reality of your own existence, a brilliant man in the seventeenth century named Descartes grappled with that. He came to the conclusion that the fact that he had the capacity to think enough to ask the question was proof that he existed. He said 'Cogito, ergo sum' meaning 'I think, therefore I am.' It's one of the more famous ideas in Western thought, so you see, you're on the same page with Descartes. Personally, I think you should be quite pleased with yourself."

When Walter said things like that to Gwen, it didn't make up for snubs on the playground or other children giggling when she said something they thought was weird. But it helped.

And when there were clashes between Gwen and Cassandra—and inevitably there were, because they were mother and daughter, and because each in her own way was strong—Walter was the one who made peace. Walter, who appreciated them both, could point out to Gwen that Cassandra was actually showing her affection when she seemed domineering and overbearing, and he could tell Cassandra that Gwen was merely being determined like her mother when she dug in her heels so stubbornly. There were times when Gwen couldn't believe how lucky they were to have Walter. She knew her mother felt the same way.

But then there were other times. Times when no matter what anyone said—including Walter—Gwen felt she was not pretty enough, or smart enough. Times when she felt . . . no, she *knew* she just wasn't good enough.

*   *   *

Gwen shifted her position on the stump and a chipmunk fled, frightened, into his hole. *Poor thing! I wonder what's going through his mind? Does he have a mind in the sense that I understand that?*

Does he think the way I do? Is it the same kind of process? I'm sure a biologist—a scientist with graphs and microscopes for measuring things exactly— would say no. But do the scientists have all the answers? I'm afraid I don't think so. If you look at it, that chipmunk and I are the same. We both want to be fed; if it's too cold or too hot we don't like it; we want to be comfortable. And we both get frightened. We are afraid of different things, but it is the fear itself that neither of us wants. We are afraid of being afraid.

So what does the chipmunk think about? When I was a child I used to ask that. I used to wonder why animals don't fight the way humans do. They do fight, of course, but it's for important things like food or territory or mating rights. I've never seen a squirrel go after a rabbit just to inflict pain. Come to think of it, I've never seen a squirrel fight a rabbit. At least, not here. I guess they have enough food and shelter here.

Why do people fight? Why do we say nasty things to each other, or behind each other's back? Or perhaps just stare and say nothing? Why do we want to hurt each other? And I'm not exempt from that. I get angry. God knows I get jealous. So what are we all thinking? Why do we do the things we do?

When a woman takes in a baby, does she do it because she wanted one so desperately? Was she happy because she got to make a choice? That's what most adoptive parents say—"I was lucky because I got to choose you and you were the perfect baby for me." *My mother has never said that. She cares for me, I feel it. But she's never said, I loved you from the moment I saw you. You were the only child I could ever dream of wanting.*

And what happened to the woman who gave birth to me? Why did she give me up? What about my father, did he agree that I should be given away? Did he even know about me? Are they still out there somewhere? Why am I thinking about this? Why does everything always lead me back to this question? Who were my birth parents, and what were they like? I can't help feeling that Mother knows something about them, *but she won't admit it. She doesn't even want to talk about it. If I were to ask her she'd say,* Gwen, why go into all of that? *Once when I pushed her about it, she said,* When I adopted you, I didn't see any reason to ask a lot of questions about your past. *But she was picking her words very carefully. Mother doesn't lie, not really, but when she's not telling the whole truth she's careful with her words. Or maybe I just want to believe she knows more than she does. Maybe it's just wishful thinking on my part.*

Such were Gwen's thoughts, and she did the best she could with them.

Chapter Seven

There was a big bay window in the back of the living room, Cassandra liked to take her early morning coffee there where she could watch the hill behind the house as it slowly came alive. So she had seen Gwen make her solitary journey to the place beneath the trees which had been her refuge since she was a child.

And in so many ways she still is a child. She is so vulnerable, so defenseless. She will let herself be intimidated by a flashy little piece of work like that Jewel Fairchild from the glassworks. That girl is all surface and show, but Gwen doesn't see that. She felt uncomfortable around her because Jewel is pretty . . . all right, she's more than pretty, she's beautiful . . . and she has confidence. The kind of mindless confidence Gwen will never have because she's too smart and sensitive. Even when she was ten months old, the first time I saw her . . . there was something diffident about her. As ironic as it was, I remember thinking that she reminded me of myself.

*   *   *

Cassandra turned away from the bay window. She didn't like to live in the past, but there were times when her mind went back. Back to her first marriage and her first husband. Back to the carnage she could still imagine after all these years . . . and to the opening sentence of the headline story in a New Orleans newspaper. A sentence Cassandra could still recite by heart: *After a horrendous collision between a car and a truck, after the shattering of glass, the roar and rumble and the screech of brakes, a man and a woman are dead tonight.*

The news had flown quickly from Louisiana to New England, and to Cassandra Wright. Her husband, whose last name no one could quite remember, was dead. He'd been in New Orleans trouble-shooting for the Wright Glassware outlet he'd opened there, and at the time of the accident he'd been giving one of the outlet employees a lift home.

The fact that such pain had fallen upon the Wright Glassworks family had not made it any more or any less tragic than any other people's disasters, but it certainly had made it a bit more interesting in Wrightstown. For Cassandra, the pain was not what people might have expected. In some ways it was less, and in others it was much more. Or, it would become so.

Her husband's name, the one that everyone forgot, was Bradford Curtis Greeley. Cassandra had married him for a variety of reasons; several of them, she had realized later, had not been good ones. But she was a woman who stood by her commitments and at the time of his death they had been together for ten years.

Originally she had married him because she loved him. But love for her in those days had not been a simple thing. From the time she had reached puberty her father had warned her against fortune hunters.

"You will be prey to them, Cassie," he'd said. "Your private assets are considerable—but it is the glassworks that is the rich prize. There are many unscrupulous men who would do anything to gain control of it."

It never seemed to occur to Father that he was suggesting that no man would pursue—or marry—Cassie for herself. Or that it would be so distasteful to marry her that it would come under the heading of "doing anything." But that was certainly the way Cassandra heard it.

"If only you had a brother," Father had sighed. And there it was, the big disappointment of his life. He did not have a son. There was no male heir to take over the running of the glassworks and protect dear little Cassie, who didn't have the brains to avoid allying herself with the grasping lothario of his nightmares.

"If your mother hadn't died so young . . ."

But Mother had died when Cassie was just a toddler, and Father had not remarried, and Cassie was an only child.

"I could structure a trust to handle your affairs but your great-grandfather and your grandfather were most specific about their desire that the glassworks not be managed by banks and trust officers."

Thank you, Great-Grandfather and Grandfather, Cassandra had thought.

But in spite of her attempts to see the humor in her situation, Father's warnings about fortune hunters had borne fruit. By the time Bradford came into Cassandra's life, she was twenty-eight years old, and not only single, but a virgin.

Her father hadn't trusted Bradford—even though he had hired the young man to head up the woefully dated sales division at Wright Glassworks.

"A bit too slick for my taste," he'd said of his new employee. "A bit too much of the snake oil salesman. Although that may be what one wants in a 'marketing man.'" Father had been suspicious of newfangled business disciplines and labels. "Give me a man who has come up through the production line," he liked to say.

But the sales for Wright Glassware were down across the country, and Bradford, who had a marketing degree from Harvard, had been highly recommended by several of Father's friends. Father had signed him on—reluctantly. And Cassandra had fallen in love.

Cassandra sipped her coffee and leaned back in her chair.

So think back now, since my mind is already headed in that direction . . . how could I have loved Bradford? Yes, he was interesting. He was an intellectual, or was that just a pose? He was charming and fun. But there was more.

Not only did he come from a family that was far more distinguished than mine, he'd mentioned a trust fund— oh, so discreetly—so I thought he had money. I thought a man who was independently wealthy wouldn't need to marry me for the glassworks. I fell in love with Bradford because I thought he was interested in me for myself. I fell in love with him because he laughed at my jokes. Because he was good-looking with his red hair, and his blue eyes. And face the facts, I fell in love with him because Father didn't like him.

But then she'd found out that while Bradford's family pedigree was indeed as long as he'd said it was, there wasn't any money. And knowing he was poor, all her father's warnings about fortune hunters had come back to haunt her. When Bradford asked her to marry him she said no. She kept on saying it for a full year.

So why did I marry him? Because Father had died after a horrible six-month battle with cancer, and for the first time in my life, I was alone. Because after Father was gone there was no one to run the glassworks, and I thought I needed a man to do it. Because Bradford could be very persuasive. Because I was twenty-eight and tired of being a virgin.

Not the best reasons in the world, but she'd built a marriage on them. And then Bradford had died. And as Cassandra was preparing to fly to Louisiana to bring the body home she had a phone call from a lawyer she'd never heard of whose office was in New Orleans. The man said he had handled Bradford's affairs in New Orleans. Cassandra hadn't known her husband had any affairs in New Orleans besides those that concerned Wright Glassworks. She and the man had scheduled a meeting for the next day.

And there she was, dressed in mournful black, sitting across a desk from a middle-aged lawyer whose voice was low and whose expression was very kind.

"You know," he said in an accent that had a slur of the South to it. "Your husband came to this city quite often."

"Yes, on business." There was something about the way the man was looking at her that made her uncomfortable. She heard herself start to offer an unasked-for explanation. "The outlet here in New Orleans was his idea, you see, and I'm afraid it wasn't doing very well. My husband felt an obligation to oversee it personally, to be hands-on. . . ."

The man opposite her had shifted his eyes away. He couldn't look at her.

"But . . . there is something else you wanted to tell me," she said slowly. "Some other reason why he came here so often . . ."

There followed a silence that she had never forgotten. Mr. Robichaud had lowered his glance to the floor, then raised it to the bright light beyond the windows, and speaking with obvious difficulty, he said, "Life is not always what we expect, is it? Every one of us has to learn that in some way, sooner or later."

"With all due respect, I think I've learned that lesson . . . especially recently." She drew in a breath. "Please, Mr. Robichaud, tell me what else it is that I have not expected."

"That woman—the woman in the car— she was not . . ." He trailed off, his face reddening. And then she saw it. She knew.

"She was not simply an employee . . .

someone he didn't know well. . . . He wasn't giving her a ride to her home to be kind. . . ."

The lawyer shook his head. "No . . . She worked in the bar at the hotel where he stayed . . . and she . . . well, she . . ." He was stumbling, trying to make this easier for Cassandra—but he knew he was making it worse.

"What about her?" Cassandra had to ask it.

The man took the plunge. "My dear, sometimes a man wants a woman who isn't of his class, who isn't an equal. . . . Do you understand?"

"Yes," she whispered. In her head a voice was screaming, *I don't deserve this! This isn't fair!*

But then she looked at the lawyer again. "There's more, isn't there?" she said. And the man with the kind expression, who did not want to be the bearer of bad news, nodded painfully, and looked to the floor again. "Tell me," she commanded.

"Your husband had a child. A baby. A girl. Ten months old now."

When he looked up at her, their eyes

met. A picture flashed through her mind—of other eyes meeting and words spoken solemnly: *'Til death do us part.*

"A child?" She couldn't make sense of the word. She couldn't get her brain to take it in. She had wanted to have children, he always said he didn't. "A baby? His?"

"Yes," said the lawyer. "I'm afraid there's no mistake."

In the hall outside the room, there were disembodied voices, too loud and cheerful: "Hello! Good to see you! You're looking great! Some tan you've got there!"

Inside the room there was nothing but the screaming of the voice inside her head.

I've been a good wife, damhit! A loyal wife. Even with all the doubts—and I have had them, God knows. I've known— deep down—for a long time that Bradford did marry me for the business, just the way Father said someone would. The business and the power, and my gracious home—don't forget that—but I told myself he wanted me too. I told myself most marriages are a bargain and ours was no worse than any other. Oh, the lies I've told myself!

"How's your tennis game these days?" asked the cheery voice in the hall. "You should come play at my club sometime. I don't like to brag, but our courts are the best."

I backed him. When there was criticism of his policies at the glassworks, I refused to listen. I told the foremen and the managers and the men who had been with my father for decades that my husband was in charge. I said they must obey his orders. I made them respect him! And this is how he repaid me. The woman in the car was not a casual acquaintance. She was the mother of his child.

Something was burning on her left hand. She looked down and saw her wedding ring. The lawyer was still watching her with his kind sad eyes.

I will not cry or curse him—the man who was my husband. I will not disgrace myself. Not for Bradford. He was what he was. A lot of men are like him. I know that. I never wanted to know it, but now I do. Suddenly the ring had become too hot to stay on her finger, she pulled it off with a trembling hand, and laid it on the desk in front of her.

"I can't . . ." She stumbled. "I don't want it. Not another second. Would you . . . is there some charity you know here in New Orleans?"

"I could sell it for you. I could give the money to the poor box at my church."

"Thank you."

Mr. Robichaud really was a good man.

* * *

Cassandra got up out of the chair and went to look out the window again. But it didn't stop the memories. So she let her mind go back to New Orleans. To the city everyone said was so charming and colorful, but to her it would always be gray and drab.

* * *

She hadn't planned to see the baby— after all, it had nothing to do with her. Someone would have to take care of it, since both of its parents were dead. Who that someone might be was no concern of hers. She didn't want to know what was going to happen to the little girl Bradford had made with his other woman.

But then the lawyer had said, "Your husband's child has no one. None of our local agencies have been able to trace her mother's people . . . and as for your husband . . ."

Bradford had had one sister who lived in California. She prided herself on being a moral and upright Christian woman and would have been appalled at the idea of taking in her brother's love child.

"I'm afraid you are as close to family as this baby has," Mr. Robichaud said.

How did a person walk away from a responsibility like that? And besides, now that the initial shock had worn off, she had to admit that a part of her was curious. In a sad, angry way that she wasn't proud of, she wanted to see the baby her husband—who wouldn't have a baby with her—had had with someone else.

"I have some time tomorrow," she told the lawyer.

"I'll drive you to her home."

*   *   *

She wasn't a pretty child. She was small
for her age, and her features were weak:
a pinched little nose and thin lips. She
hadn't gotten those from Bradford. And
those brown eyes weren't his—the unknown woman was responsible for them
too. But there was no question that she
was her father's daughter. She had his
square jaw, his chin, and most impor-
tantly, that unmistakable red-brown hair.
Cassandra would have known it anywhere. She looked at a little hand with
its tiny seashell nails and for a few minutes she just stood there, gazing.

The child was very still—shouldn't a
ten-month-old baby be crawling around?
Trying to walk? Crying because there
was a stranger in the room?

"Is she always this quiet?" Cassandra
asked the woman who had been hired
to help take care of the baby since she
was born. It seemed that Bradford had
indulged his lady love with household
help.

"She's good as gold," said the woman
looking down at the child who was sit-

ting in her lap. The little girl was afraid, that was clear, but she wasn't cowering. She stared at Cassandra from behind the nursemaid's fleshy arm.

Good for her! The thought flashed through Cassandra's mind. *She doesn't want to show she's afraid. I wouldn't, either. I think we may be a little alike.* Except for the red hair.

"She never cries," the nursemaid said.

Or laughs, I imagine, Cassandra thought, looking at the serious little face. *I wonder what it would take to make her smile. . . .*

"Lotta has been staying here in the house with the baby. She's been paid through to the end of the month," the lawyer said. "The house is rented by the month too. After that . . ." He let the sentence dangle.

The poor little thing has been through so much already. And if someone doesn't do something for her . . . But there is that red hair . . . his red hair . . . Do I want to see it every day of my life? Don't be so petty, Cassie! Father would say I'm better than that. But am I?

"What will happen to her?" Cassandra asked.

"If you don't intervene? The state will take her."

"And they'll find parents for her. A good family. Right?"

"They'll try. But she's ten months old, and most people want to adopt an infant. It's more than likely she'll wind up in the system."

"The system?"

"Foster care." He sighed. "That's a slippery slope. The longer a child is in it, the harder it is to get them out."

So there they were. A man and a woman had had some pleasure and the result was a human being who didn't ask to be born, but she had been anyway. She was small and weak at that moment, but she had a right to grow and find her place in the world. And there was no one to help her except Cassie Wright—who knew if a stray dog had landed on her doorstep that was half as vulnerable and needy as this child, she wouldn't have hesitated to rescue it.

I wanted a child. I wanted one so much. And this would be the right thing to do. I can ignore the red hair. In time I'll get used to it. . . .

Mr. Robichaud said he'd take care of the paperwork for the adoption. The only thing left to do was shut down the little girl's life in New Orleans. But that was a revelation. It seemed that the house in which she lived, the nursemaid who cared for her, and the bank account that had been opened in her name had all been charged to Wright Glassworks. *Clearly, I'll have to call for an audit of the company now that Bradford is gone,* Cassie thought. It was her first inkling of what was to come.

* * *

Cassandra closed her eyes and leaned against the window. Even now after all these years, now when she was safe, she couldn't think about the time that had come next without shivering. And yet, it had been the making of her. What was that saying? That which does not kill you makes you strong? Well, it was true. Although there were times when she thought if she'd known what she would be facing, she might never have boarded the plane for home.

Chapter Eight

Cassandra arrived in Wrightsville with the solemn-eyed baby she had named Gwendolyn after her mother. The child had had another name, one that had been given to her by the mother and father who had died in the automobile crash. The parents Cassandra wanted to forget. *This baby is mine now. Maybe I should have let her keep the name they called her. Perhaps I shouldn't try to erase all traces of them from her life.*

Well, I'm not that big a person. Sorry, Father.

Gwendolyn was installed in her new home with a new nursemaid to take care of her, and her new mother. And if the child was frightened or unhappy she didn't give any indication of it. She ate her food, she took her naps, and she never cried herself to sleep at night. But she didn't smile, either.

Meanwhile Cassandra was facing disaster as one by one the heads of departments at Wright Glassworks came forward to report to her.

"I'm afraid we're very much behind the rest of the industry when it comes to research and development of new products," said one of the top managers. "Mr. Wright—that is, Mr. Greeley—put more of an emphasis on selling than production. . . ."

"We're pretty much shut out of the fiber optic field," said her father's trusted vice president. "I felt we ought to get into it, but Mr. Greeley didn't agree. Now it's too late."

"We're miles behind Corning and the other companies."

"I don't mean to disrespect your husband's memory, but he never really understood the glassworks. . . ."

"He said our high-end glassware was the jewel in our crown, but that is not where our money is made."

And then came the terrifying reports. The reports that sent ice water down the veins.

"I tried to warn your husband that we were overextended. . . ."

"Your husband kept saying you have to spend money to make money . . . but we weren't making it."

"I'm afraid we haven't paid the taxes. . . ."

"There's a discrepancy in the employees' pension fund. . . ."

"We're late with the bank loans. . . ."

"Good God, what a mess," said the outside accountant Cassandra finally brought in to try to make some sense out of the books that seemed to be bleeding with red ink. "How did your people let it get this bad? I know these men; some of them have worked here since your father was alive. Why didn't they say something?"

Because I told them not to. Because I said Bradford was the boss. Because I was being a loyal wife.

"How much time do I have to turn it around?" she asked.

"I don't see how you can. Your best bet is to declare bankruptcy and get out now."

I'm going to be the one who loses Wright Glassworks? My family's company is going to go under on my watch? No! Never!

"I know how hard that sounds," said the accountant sympathetically. "But it is done all the time. . . ."

But not by my family! I come from a long line of survivors. My great-great-grandfather lost his leg in the Civil War, so he went into the business of making artificial limbs and equipment for the disabled. He made a fortune, sold out, and founded the glassworks. My great-grandfather lost his personal fortune in the Great Depression, but he hung on to the glassworks and he and my grandfather worked three jobs each to make enough money to keep it going. I can't let it go under. I won't!

So she started fighting. *Bail out the financial mess first,* she told herself. *Mortgage to the hilt the house you grew up in, and don't think about the fact that you could be living on the streets if you lose it. Liquidate your portfolio, and don't even let yourself wonder how you'll support yourself if you can't revive the glassworks. Sell the jewelry. Start with all those showy pieces Bradford gave you and pray they'll bring enough, because if they don't you'll have to sell your mother's diamond brooch and your grandmother's pearls. Try not to sell the Tang horse your great-aunt Cassandra left you in her will. Try not to sell the Corot your father loved so much. Gamble although you're not a gambler, take risks with things it will break your heart to lose. You'll have to do whatever it takes. And this time you'll do it yourself. You won't try to find a man to do it for you. Because you aren't going to hand over your company, your legacy, your sacred family trust to anyone ever again.*

What she accomplished with her fire sale was that she bought herself time. "Not a lot," the accountant told her, "but it could be enough to get the business moving again. With a little luck." But she didn't believe in luck anymore. She believed in being smart.

So educate yourself, Cassie. You, who majored in Old English in college. You, who wrote your senior thesis paper on the Wife of Bath. Learn to become an expert on the various industrial uses of glass. Go to the local college and pick the brains of the science and engineering professors. Give yourself a crash course in the photonic products that are used in the telecommunications industry. Learn about optic materials used in the semiconductor industry. Find out what the semiconductor industry is. Find out what a ceramic substrate is, and how it's used in the automotive industry. Oh, and in your spare time, learn to be a businesswoman. And do it all yesterday.

*   *   *

She did it. It took her three years. Years when she didn't sleep. Years when she would have killed Bradford with her own hands if he had been alive. And during those years there were times when she was exhausted and frightened and she'd see his child with his red hair playing in her playpen, or sitting in her highchair. And Cassie would have to turn away. She'd feel herself pulling back emotionally from Gwen; she wouldn't want to, but she couldn't help it. All she could do was hope that the little girl didn't sense it. The smart quiet little girl who still wasn't smiling.

But she had turned the business around. Wright Glassworks had become one of the major providers of the specialized polymer products used in biotechnology. They were a top producer of high-performance glass for computers and television screens. On the retail side, their handcrafted, one-of-a-kind glassware was still the jewel in their crown, but a much more durable and reasonably priced line of tableware went on the store shelves. The marketing division was cut back, and Wright Glassworks was once more focused on the excellence of its products. The unprofitable outlet in New Orleans was closed. And Cassandra Wright became the woman she now was. A formidable woman, some said. A woman whose slightest command was followed instantly, whose life was run like a well-oiled clock. A woman who had survived fear and doubt and betrayal. And for a long time she was a woman who thought she was going to spend the rest of her life without a man.

* * *

There was a footstep behind Cassandra, one she knew very well. She started to turn away from the window but was caught by a kiss on the side of her neck. "Hi," she said.

"Good morning," Walter said. Walter, her husband. And oh, how good that word sounded—even after all these years.

They had met at the dentist's office. "Do we know how to pick a romantic spot or what?" Walter said later—after they had established that they were involved in a romance. And they had both laughed. Because they liked to laugh together.

She had gone to the dentist for her

regular teeth cleaning. He was having a cavity filled. He had the first appointment and when she was finished, he was waiting for her. He asked her to go down the street and have a cup of coffee—only he couldn't drink his because the Novocain hadn't worn off. They had laughed about that too. And then somehow he was coming to her home to pick her up and take her out for dinner and the symphony and she was visiting his painting studio to see his work.

And then he was walking up the hill to Gwen's secret hiding place to ask the little girl if he could marry her mother.

"Gwen's gone off to her never-never land?" Walter asked as he moved to the sideboard to pour himself a cup of coffee.

"She ran out there without any breakfast, not even a piece of toast. I do wish . . ." Cassandra stopped short.

Walter laced the coffee liberally with cream and sugar. It was not fair that he never gained an ounce. "That you could organize her." It was said fondly with a smile.

"Don't you think she needs it?" she countered.

"Since I tend to resist that kind of thing myself, I'm probably the wrong one to ask."

"You are very organized when you work."

"But that's my passion. I'm not particularly good at the rest of life. Remember, you're the woman who refuses to share a clothes closet with me because I'm such a slob."

"Oh dear, I am a monster, aren't I?"

"No. Just . . . organized." She tried to smile, but of course he saw through it. "She'll be all right, you know."

"You think so? Look at the choices she's made! She's so smart, she got into Yale on early admission, and instead she's going to a little local college." This was not a new complaint, but she kept on bringing it up because it was one of the few things in her life she could not fix.

"She can always transfer if she wants," Walter said.

"That's just it, she doesn't know what she wants! She doesn't know her own worth. . . . Do you know why she's up in her never-never land, as you call it? Because yesterday that ridiculous Jewel Fairchild came here on an errand and she ran into Gwen in the library. By the time I got there Jewel was swanning around as if she owned the place and Gwen was wilting in front of her. Just because the girl is pretty in a cheap way and she—"

"Excuse me, who is Jewel Fairchild?"

"The receptionist at the glassworks! You met her when you dropped in on the company Christmas party last year. She was the one who started everyone singing the carols."

"Oh, yes. She is very pretty."

"She's breathtaking. And Gwen is worth ten of her. Make that twenty."

"And Gwen will figure that out eventually."

"I'm not so sure."

"Of course you're not; you're her mother. Hovering is a part of the job description."

But that was the problem. Because there had been those times when she hadn't hovered . . . when she had pulled back. And she would always be afraid that she had hurt Gwen during those times. "In the beginning," she said softly, "when I first brought her home, it was a bad time . . . and she looked so much like her father . . . I wasn't always . . ."

"The perfect mother? I wonder how many women are."

"But I knew how much she needed and I . . ."

"Did you love her?"

That was the hard question. The one that could still flash through a troubled dream. But it had to be answered honestly. "I always felt there was something that made me take her. Some reason that I couldn't understand . . ." The next part was the hardest. "I learned to love her. It grew—the love did. I'm not sure it was there at first."

"It would be surprising if it had been, given the circumstances. Don't you think?"

"But Gwen deserved better."

"Yes. So did you."

"But I was the adult. And now I don't know how to . . . well, to fix it." He didn't answer. "Say something."

"I think you know what I want to say," he said.

"I should tell Gwen about her father."

"I think she'd be able to understand a lot of things she can't now. And it is a part of her history—"

"I know." She cut him off. "You've told me all of that. Repeatedly." But then guilt—an emotion she tried to avoid at all costs—overcame her. "Oh, my dear, I'm sorry for snapping." She drew in a deep breath. "The truth is, I've been wrong about that. And you're right."

He put his arms around her. "It's not a contest, you know."

"I'm afraid it can get to be one with me. I hate being wrong."

He grinned. "I've noticed."

"And I hate being told when I'm wrong."

"Fortunately, it doesn't happen very often."

"Flatterer."

"It's working, isn't it? See, you're smiling again."

She was, but then she pulled away from him. "I know I have to tell Gwen— all of it. But it isn't going to be easy."

"No."

"I've decided I'll do it when we're in Paris. It'll just be the two of us—no interruptions or distractions. I thought about waiting until we get back home because she'd be on more familiar ground . . . but that would be procrastinating." She paused. "All those years when I kept it from her—the truth about her father—I was trying to do what was best for her."

"I know."

"As long as she's happy, I really don't care about anything else."

But that wasn't altogether true. There was a picture in Cassandra's mind that was too private even to share with Walter: a picture of Gwen taking her place someday as the owner of the glassworks. She could see Gwen as the mistress of this house, see her standing in a garden behind the red maples, see her following the path that the Wrights had laid out for their own for generations. With her fine mind and her deep appreciation of all that was beautiful in art and in nature, Gwen would be such a worthy heir to follow Father and Grandfather

and all the Wrights who had come before them. If only Gwen could just . . .

"I want Gwen to believe in herself,"
she cried to both Walter and herself. "Is
that wrong?"

"Did you believe in yourself when you
were her age?"

"No. And I paid for that."

*I nearly lost everything—the glass-
works, this house, the gardens, the lawn
edged with my red maples and the hill
where Gwen runs when she needs
peace.*

"And look at you now," he said.

She knew what he was saying, and
there was no arguing with it. Gwen
would have to find her own way, as
everyone does. She would make her
own mistakes, and she would not learn
from Cassandra's—no matter how
much her mother wanted to spare her.
And yet . . . Cassandra looked out the
window up at the hill where her smart,
sensitive, insecure, shy daughter was
hiding. And yet . . .

"Why didn't I ask them to send my
secretary out here with those damn pa-

pers instead of Jewel?" She let out a sigh of frustration.

"Your secretary . . . she's the one who wears the orthopedic oxfords?"

"She's fifty-three years old and her arches have fallen."

"I see."

"That darned Jewel Fairchild."

Chapter Nine

It was funny the way things happened sometimes, Jewel thought. For the three years that she'd worked for Mrs. Wright, she'd never laid eyes on her daughter. Then she'd gone to Mrs. Wright's house to deliver those papers and she'd had that strange little encounter with Gwen in that fabulous library, and now it seemed like every time she turned around, there was Gwen Wright!

First, the girl had dropped by the glassworks to show her mother the new haircut she'd just gotten for their trip to Paris.

"Très chic," Mrs. Wright said as she whisked Gwen through the lobby. "You'll look like a true Parisienne."

Jewel thought the cut was a disaster. Whoever had done it had gone for a tapered bob and Gwen's reddish brown hair was wiry. It would have been better to have layered it. Jewel had taught herself about hair and makeup; she read every fashion magazine she could get her hands on, and there were three makeover shows on television that she watched faithfully. Gwen probably considered herself much too grand to waste her time with things like that, but as Gwen and her mother walked together down the hallway, Jewel remembered her ride into town with old Albert. Gabby old Albert who told stories about family secrets.

But I know you're not all that grand, Gwen, Jewel thought as she watched the two women disappear into the sacred space known as Mrs. Wright's Office. *I know all about you.*

The next time Jewel and Gwen ran into

each other, it was early morning and Jewel had run downstairs to the deli below her apartment to grab a bagel and a cup of coffee on her way to work. Gwen was sitting on a stool at the counter. At first, Jewel thought she'd mistaken her for someone else, because what on earth would Gwen Wright be doing in Berger's Deli? At best, the neighborhood was what real estate people called "marginal." Yet it was definitely Gwen, looking out of place and lost.

Jewel decided to skip the bagel and coffee, but before she could turn and go, Gwen had spotted her. She'd smiled that tentative smile that seemed to be her trademark, and there was no way Jewel could duck out without saying hello.

"I'm waiting for my stepfather," Gwen said after the niceties were out of the way. "I have to pick up my passport and City Hall is around the corner. We wanted to get there early and Walter says this place has the best breakfast in town." She'd shrugged awkwardly. "So here I am."

Then Walter had shown up and invited

Jewel to have breakfast with them, but she couldn't because it was getting late and she had to get to work.

Unlike some people who have the time for a nice leisurely breakfast while they wait for City Hall to open so they can pick up the passport they need for their trip to Paris.

As Jewel waited for her bus to take her to the glassworks, she thought again about old Albert and the secret he'd told her. And then she thought about luck, and how some people have all of it and some have none. By the time she got to work she was in a rotten mood.

That was happening more and more often. Jewel tried to shake the anger behind her bad temper but the vision of the gleaming white house in which Gwen lived, the diamond and gold bracelet on her wrist, together with the knowledge that Gwen didn't deserve any of it, ate away at Jewel. And the chance run-ins with Mrs. Wright's privileged, pampered daughter didn't help. Then as if Fate was playing a really mean joke, there was yet another encounter. It occurred on a Saturday morning in a shopping mall.

*   *   *

The Algonquin Mall was the pride and joy of Wrightstown. All the expensive shops and two of the town's fanciest restaurants could be found there. And it was to the Algonquin Mall that Jewel went every other Saturday to treat herself to a manicure. While her nails were drying she liked to look through a weekly local magazine called the *Wrightstown Gazette*. It listed all the events that were going on in the area, such as new restaurants and stores that had just opened up, and there was also a society page dedicated to the comings and goings of the citizens of the community. Naturally the Wright family dominated this page. This week the society editor had decided that Cassandra Wright's upcoming vacation with her daughter was newsworthy.

As if there's anyone left in this damn town who hasn't heard that Gwen and her mommy are going to Paris, Jewel thought. *We know, okay?*

But she asked the nail tech if she could take the magazine with her, and when she passed the food court she bought herself a cup of coffee and settled down to read.

"I'm looking forward to this adventure with my daughter," Mrs. Wright was quoted as saying. "I went to France for the first time with my father when I was Gwen's age. It was a bonding time for both of us, and it gave us cherished memories to share."

Well, now, that's interesting, because I had a bonding experience with my father when I was about Gwen's age. We watched my mother die together. Of course he took off a few months later so we didn't get to share any cherished memories, and—Jewel threw the magazine down on the table. *That's enough!* she told herself. *You've got to stop thinking about Gwen and Cassandra Wright. Ma always said jealousy was what did in Pop, and if you're not careful you're going to wind up just like him!*

Jewel stood up, tossed the magazine and her Styrofoam coffee cup into a trash barrel, left the food court, and started walking fast. She was headed toward the one place where she knew she could jolt herself out of her funk—a dress shop named Sofia's. This store, owned by a world-weary but incredibly stylish émigrée from Milan, was the most expensive shop in Wrightstown. And it was Jewel's favorite. The clothes Sofia imported from Europe and sold at huge markups were glamorous, sexy, and classy all at the same time. There were nights when Jewel lulled herself to sleep by thinking about them. Of course it was ridiculous for her to even walk in the door because there was nothing in the place she could afford—the smallest silk scarf would have cost two weeks of her salary.

But there was a salesgirl who worked in the store on the weekends who had become a friend. Edie was about the same age as Jewel and she understood what it was like to be broke and pretty and hungry to dress like a movie or TV star. So if there weren't any customers on a Saturday morning—and often there weren't; Sofia's clientele wasn't big, just rich—Edie would let Jewel try on Sofia's most gorgeous selections: the coral silk gown with the fishtail train that hugged the hips, the black satin dress with the neckline that plunged, and the backless halter in a shade of green that only the young and perfect could wear. When Jewel had chosen a garment and put it on, Edie would bring out a pair of glittering sandals with stiletto heels and an equally towering price tag, and open a locked case full of one-of-a-kind beaded evening purses. Then Jewel would slip on the shoes, tuck a purse under her arm, and do her best imitation of a model's catwalk strut up and down the length of Sofia's cream and taupe shop. She'd look at herself in the full-length mirror and all her disappointments would melt away as the fantasy Jewel smiled back at her. An early Saturday morning visit to Sofia's was the best antidote Jewel knew for depression.

But this morning as she walked into the shop, Edie hurried up and whispered, "Not today. Sofia is here. We've got a VIP in the store and she's waiting on her personally."

And somehow Jewel knew even before she looked in the direction where Edie was pointing who the VIP was.

"I think you'll be happy with the blue, Miss Wright, even if the color does seem a little bold to you," Sofia said as she closed a glossy box with the store's logo embossed on the top.

"Thank you for suggesting it; I wouldn't have picked it out myself," Gwen said. But she didn't look very happy about wearing the blue, whatever it was. "I'm afraid I'm not much for shopping," she said apologetically. "But Mother wanted me to have new clothes to wear on our trip." A stack of additional glossy boxes sitting on the counter next to the cash register bore testimony to a big spree.

Jewel looked from the bags and boxes to Gwen's unhappy face and the anger she'd been trying so hard to shake started boiling inside her. *I come into this store to pretend for a few minutes that I can afford more than bargain basements and discount outlets. That's all I ask for, just to pretend. This morning I didn't even get to do that because this spoiled brat was buying out the place. And now she's whining about it.*

She knew she had to get out of the store before she said, or did, something she would regret. She started for the door, and she would have made it, if a soft, slightly snooty voice hadn't called out, "Jewel. Hello." And she had to turn and give Gwen Wright a big, friendly smile.

*   *   *

Gwen hadn't wanted to call out to Jewel; she'd done it because she felt she had to. It seemed to her that every time she turned around these days she was tripping over Jewel Fairchild. And every time Gwen saw her she looked prettier than she had before. Today, for example, she was wearing a red dress that Gwen was sure Cassandra would say was too skimpy for daytime, but you had to admit that Jewel could carry it off. And she would look heavenly in the blue blouse that Gwen had just pur-chased under duress. It was the exact color of Jewel's extraordinary eyes. Sofia had said the blouse was perfect for Gwen, but it would look a lot better on Jewel.

What is she doing in here? Gwen wondered. *There's no way she can afford to shop in a place like this. . . . That was catty of me. And ugly. She has every bit as much right as I do to be here. It's just that buying clothes makes me feel terrible—it always has—and she's standing there looking so pretty in that tacky dress, and—and I just did it again! What a hypocrite I am! I'm always going on about how cruel humans are to each other and how I admire the animals because they don't attack each other for no reason the way we do, and then I want to lord it over a girl I don't even know because she's beautiful.*

But in my own defense, there is something about the way she looks at me. It's as if she's looking down on me, and I . . . No, I'm not going to let myself off the hook that easily. I'm jealous of her, plain and simple. And I should be ashamed of myself.

And that was why she heard herself call out to Jewel, who had started for the door, "Jewel. Hello."

And when Jewel turned and smiled her big wide smile, Gwen didn't give in to the green-eyed monster that was telling her to get the hell away from Jewel. Instead, because she felt guilty, she invited Jewel to have lunch. And Jewel accepted.

Chapter Ten

Years later when she looked back on that Saturday lunch with Gwen, Jewel would think that what had taken place was inevitable. It was as if fate had been throwing Gwen at her for weeks, stoking the flames of her anger until the only thing that could happen did. And she could trace everything else—the good and the bad of her life—back to that meal. It had been a true crossroads for her. Of course she wasn't aware of any of that when she said yes, she would love to have lunch. All she was thinking was, she couldn't say no to her boss's daughter.

*　　*　　*

The Villa Tuscany prided itself on its authentic Northern Italian cuisine and its pricy menu. Gwen had suggested it to Jewel when they left Sofia's. "I've eaten there with Mother," she said. "I'm afraid I don't know any other restaurants in the mall. If there's someplace you usually go . . ."

Try any one of the chain restaurants or the food court, Jewel thought.

"The Villa Tuscany will be great," she said. And the anger inside grew.

"There's a bit of a wait, Ms. Wright," said the hostess at the Villa Tuscany. "But if you'll come with me, I'll walk you to the head of the line."

"Terrific!" Jewel started to say, but then she saw that Gwen was holding back.

"Thank you, we'll wait our turn," Gwen said politely. It was the classy thing to do, Jewel realized. And that made her even angrier.

The final straw came when they were seated. Gwen ordered a salad with an Italian name which Jewel was pretty sure she'd pronounced properly. Jewel had decided on the lobster ravioli, which sounded very exotic. But as she was about to order, she saw the price. "Oh, it's so expensive," she'd blurted out.

"Please, have whatever you want," Gwen said with a wave of her hand. It was that casual, dismissive gesture that did it. Suddenly Jewel knew the pasta that cost thirty dollars a serving was going to choke her. She asked for a salad and then after they'd ordered and Gwen had nothing to say—as usual—she started talking about families. And of course she knew where that topic could lead them—even though she tried to tell herself later that she didn't.

She told a few anecdotes about her own clan. She was a good storyteller and she could make a tale of five children all getting the flu at the same time sound very funny. She didn't mention that she'd been ten at the time it had happened, and she'd been the one who had to change the messy bedsheets. From talking about the whole family it was a natural progression to her father.

"My pop was a hard worker," she said. "Not as successful as your father, of course, but then he never finished college."

Later, she would swear that the fatal words just slipped out, that she hadn't meant to hurt anyone. But no matter what her intentions were, the effect on Gwen was immediate.

"My father?" she repeated. "I don't have a father. Walter is my stepfather."

And this was where all Jewel's later denials would break down. Because at that moment as Gwen was staring at her, all she had to do was laugh a little and say, oh, of course! *Stepfather* was what she'd meant to say, and how silly of her to make such a mistake. Instead she said, "Yes, I know Mr. Amburn is your stepfather. I was talking about your birth father."

The effect on Gwen this time was downright electric. "No one knows who he was. When Mother adopted me, the files were closed. She never wanted to know about either of my birth parents."

There was still time to back off, and to say something soothing and reassuring. What Jewel said was "Oh." One syllable. Loaded with all the cynicism she could muster. And then she added, "Well, I'm sure if that's what your mother told you, it must be true." But she might as well have been saying, "Your mother is a liar."

It did the trick.

"You don't believe that," Gwen said. "You know something."

Now the game was easy. "It's just . . ." Jewel stammered for effect. "Look, I'm sorry I ever said anything. Why don't we change the subject?"

She let Gwen beg, cajole, and demand for another three minutes before she finally—with lots of fake hesitations—laid out the whole sordid story of the womanizing husband and the mistress in New Orleans. Just for good measure she mentioned twice the fact that Bradford Greeley's hair was a distinctive shade of red/brown. And she waited for it to sink in.

Now who's so high and mighty? she gloated to herself. But as she looked across the table at Gwen, she was surprised. Gwen's only signs of distress were a face that had gone very white and eyes that were dark pools. Well then, it hadn't sunk in yet. But it would.

It serves her right.

*   *   *

There was a little look of triumph on Jewel's face; Gwen caught it even as she was trying to absorb the body blow Jewel had just delivered.

She's enjoying this, Gwen thought. *No matter how much she says she's sorry, this wasn't an accident. She wanted to tell me this—that my father was a cheat and my mother . . . that is, my birth mother . . . was—dear God, what was she? And what about Mother . . . Cassandra Wright? I can't let myself think about her. Not now. Not here.*

"Are you all right?" Jewel asked.

"Oh, yes," Gwen said and she smiled brightly. "I'm not going to pretend that what you've just told me isn't a surprise." Did that make sense? It was really important right now to make sense. "Obviously, I hadn't heard it before." There was no way she could say she had, not after the way she had reacted. "But I have always known that I was adopted. So it's not a total shock. And when you think about it, it's an amazing story, isn't it? I think I'm kind of proud of it."

And I'll be damned if I'll let you see me cry. You thought I'd fall apart, and I still may, but not in front of you. I'm still my mother's daughter—in this if nothing else.

"Would you like some dessert?" she asked cheerfully. "The pastry chef here is from New York and he's considered one of the best." She signaled to the waiter and asked for the dessert menu. "Don't be shy," she said to Jewel, imitating Cassandra at her most condescending. "And for heaven's sake don't worry about the price. This is my treat."

Oh, no, she would not cry now. That would come later.

*   *   *

For a second, Jewel was thrown. It was clear that the awful news had finally sunk in, but Gwen seemed calm—even cheerful. *But she can't be,* Jewel thought. *If someone told me what I just told her I'd be going out of my mind. She can't be that different from me. She's not made of stone. Or is she? That's what I hate most about people like Cassandra and Gwen Wright: You can't read them. Still, she must be dying inside. She has to be.*

*   *   *

Gwen would never remember how she got through the rest of her lunch with Jewel, but somehow she'd done it without breaking down. She'd planned to save her tears for her favorite spot on the hill. She waited until she was home, then she raced out to the flat stump under the oak trees, and sat down in the place where she'd come to cry her heart out so many times before. But once she was there, she stayed dry-eyed. It was as if there wasn't a way to cry enough, so something inside her refused to start. Instead thoughts raced through her aching mind. And they always came back to the same person—her mother. The woman she had always called Mother.

What kind of woman adopts her husband's bastard? Why would anyone do that? Because she was cleaning up his mess? That would be like her. But she must have been so angry . . . no wonder I remember her pulling away from me. No wonder I've always felt so alone.

A squirrel, seduced by a nearby nut, had ventured too close to her for its own comfort; now it scrambled away, the prize left behind. Once, many years ago, a tree that was in the back lawn had fallen and the workmen who were clearing it away had discovered a nest of baby squirrels inside it. Poor little creatures, with pink skin naked to the world because they were just born and didn't have fur, and tiny eyes blue under lids that had not yet opened. They were too

young to live, the vet said when Gwen
and Cassandra brought them into his
office. He offered to put them to sleep.
But Gwen couldn't bear it. To let those
helpless creatures go without a fight, to
just end their lives was too heartbreak-
ing. She began to sob. And Cassandra,
who must have known how hopeless it
was, had told the vet they would bring
the little squirrels home and try to save
them. For two days and nights she and
Gwen had tried to feed them with an
eyedropper full of the formula the vet
had prescribed. And when they died,
one by one, it was Cassandra who had
found the perfect place on Gwen's hill to
bury them.

*There were things about me that she
understood that no one else did. And
she indulged me.*

But then after the deaths, Gwen had
made up a story about the squirrels in
which they had survived, and were living
happily—or at least they were living
Gwen's idea of squirrel happiness. And
her mother, who had been so understanding, suddenly wasn't anymore.

"They are dead, Gwen. You must accept it."

But Gwen couldn't. Walter tried to explain them to each other.

"Gwen's just using her imagination to make the world a place she can bear," Walter said to Cassandra. "Artists do that all the time."

"She's not an artist, she's a young child," Cassandra said. "She has to learn not to dwell on things."

"Your mother doesn't mean to be hard on you," Walter said to Gwen. "It's just that sometimes when something hurts her too much all she knows how to do is try to put it behind her. It's how she protects herself."

Now grown-up Gwen wondered, *Was that why she didn't tell me about my father? Because she didn't want to dwell on something that was too painful? I want to ask her that.* But of course she wouldn't ask. *I don't have the courage. Because then I'll have to ask other questions—about what she really felt for me. And I'm afraid of the answers.*

So next week we'll go to Paris together

and I won't say a word. I'll be a good du-
tiful daughter who never questions her
mother.

And she still couldn't cry.

Chapter Eleven

⁓⌣⌣

"We must remember," Cassandra said, "that the fork goes in the left hand." They were sitting in yet another of the cafés that seemed to be in endless supply in Paris. This was one of Cassandra's favorites. There seemed to be an endless supply of those, too, Gwen thought. And her mother was determined to drag Gwen to every one of them—along with everything else she loved about the City of Light.

If I have to hear one more word about

*the first time she was here with her fa-
ther, or all the other trips she's taken to
France, I'm going to scream,* Gwen
thought. But she knew that wasn't the
reason she was so angry at her mother.

Cassandra's eyes were sparkling; she
was enjoying this. "I often wonder," she
said, "how these customs develop. At
home it would be odd to hold your fork
in your left hand, unless you were left-
handed, of course."

"It's just people minding other people's business," Gwen mumbled. "What
difference does it make how you hold
your fork? It's a lot of nonsense, all this
stuff about manners and ceremonies!"

"Well, I guess it can be, but when you
think carefully, you see it's not *all* nonsense. Manners are the element of society. They keep things in order, they oil
the wheels. Haven't I always told you
that?"

*Oh, yes, you have. It's one of the
things you love to preach about. Although, you're not really in a position to
preach to anyone, are you? Not after
what you did to me for seventeen years.*
Gwen slouched low in her chair.

*   *   *

Cassandra watched Gwen slouch down until she looked like she was going to slide on to the floor. Where were the days when her little daughter, eager to please, sat straight and tall at the dinner table as she'd been taught? Clearly, all the childhood training had worn off and now Cassie was facing an irritating rebel. Or whatever role Gwen thought she was playing.

And I'll admit I don't know what that role might be. I'm trying to understand her, but I just can't. Ever since we got to Paris she's been sullen and rude. I hate rudeness. And I hate that passive arms-crossed-over-the-chest stance that teenagers take when they're angry about something. For heaven's sake if you have something to say, say it!

But at that second Gwen looked up and there was something in her eyes, something that was almost like a plea. Cassandra sighed.

Walter would say I should be patient. He'd say there's got to be an explana-tion for the way she's behaving. And of course he'd be right. I don't know what's going on in her mind—at her age it could be anything.

She made herself smile at her daughter, who was now picking at her éclair. "I bought you a little present," she said cheerfully as she reached into the bag she'd been carrying and pulled out a book. "I thought since we're going to be seeing the Petit Trianon at Versailles we should read up on Madame de Pompadour. Most people think of Marie Antoinette when they think of the Petit Trianon, but it was actually de Pompadour who inspired it, when she was the mistress of Louis the Fifteenth. Her favorite architect designed it and—"

"Thanks, I'll pass," Gwen broke in. She had finished decimating the pastry and had gone back to slouching.

"We wouldn't have to read the entire book, just skim it. . . ."

Suddenly the slumping figure across the table sat up, her eyes glaring. "I'm not interested in reading about Louis the Fifteenth's mistress."

"She was a fascinating woman, a courtesan in the grand tradition—"

"I don't want to hear about kept women or great courtesans or any other euphemism you've got for them. I don't want to hear about their illegitimate children. Or—if you want to be vulgar—their bastards. It hits a little too close to home for me. I should think you'd feel the same way."

"What on earth are you—"

"My mother! She was my father's mistress—right? And my father was your husband. And I'm his . . . how should we say it? Love child?"

And there it was. The secret Cassandra had kept at so much cost for so many years. The secret that was hers and hers alone to tell. When she was ready. In her own good time.

"Who told you?" she heard herself ask through the mists of shock and rage. And she knew from the look on Gwen's face that it had been the wrong thing to say.

"What difference does it make? At least someone finally did."

"I was going to tell you. . . ."

"You've been lying to me for my whole life."

It was the disgust in Gwen's voice that got to Cassandra. She wanted to tell her daughter to drop that tone instantly. She wanted to demand an apology. But Gwen was right. Partially right. "I was trying to protect you. . . ."

"From what? The truth? I had a right to know."

Walter said that. But I didn't see it. He was right and I was wrong.

"It was a complicated situation, Gwen, and I—"

"Other people knew about it! Didn't you realize someone would tell me someday? Did you think about what that was going to be like for me? To sit at lunch with my mother's receptionist and have her tell me what I should have known already?"

It was Jewel Fairchild! For some reason Cassandra wasn't surprised.

"She was enjoying pitying me. . . ."

I'm sure she was gleeful. That horrible girl.

"I did what I thought was best—" Cassandra started to say.

"No, you did what was easiest for you. You weren't thinking of me."

Be patient. Walter would tell me to be patient.

"Gwen, if you'll let me explain—"

"I don't want to hear it. I don't want to hear about the great lady who took in her husband's stray. . . ."

Be patient.

"I don't want to hear that you lied to me for my own good. I don't want to hear that you, in your infinite wisdom, decided that this was something I didn't need to know."

Later, when Cassandra was full of regret, she would realize that Gwen had touched all her most vulnerable points: her dislike of being wrong, her pride, and, most of all, her sense of herself as a decent person. No one had ever attacked her like this. No one had ever called her a liar. And when she looked across the table all she could see was that red/brown hair. And that jawline and that chin. Something inside her snapped.

"Perhaps you're right," she said in a frigid voice. "Perhaps I didn't want to remember that I had the bad judgment to choose an adulterer who married me for

my business and my money, then pro-
ceeded to destroy the first and squan-
der the second on a woman he picked
up while he was slumming. Perhaps I
was embarrassed to admit to you just
how arrogant and shallow and ultimately
stupid he was. However, if you'd like all
the squalid details of his life, I'll do my
best to oblige you. As to your birth
mother, all I know about her is that she
was a barmaid. And, apparently, she
had no problem being kept by another
woman's husband."

"You hated him." Gwen shot the accu-
sation across the table.

"Do you blame me?"

That was when Gwen started to sob.
And then she started to run.

*   *   *

Gwen would have done anything not to
cry. And the last thing she wanted to do
was race out of the stupid little café like
a bad child and run through the streets
of Paris like a bad cliché until she
reached their hotel. But she did just
that. Then she ran through the lobby
and into the elevator, just another crazy

American—well, the staff was used to those—and into her room in the suite she shared with her mother. And she kept on crying. Because she was so angry at herself. And at Cassandra. And at life. *I knew I shouldn't have told her I knew about my father. If she just hadn't brought up Madame de Pompadour . . . no, be honest, I was looking for an excuse to throw it in her face.*

Her mother had entered the other room; had she run through the streets? No, Cassandra would have found a taxi. And now she was opening the door that separated the two bedrooms. *Why the hell didn't I think to lock it?*

"Gwen, I shouldn't have said all that." Cassandra was searching for words. "Your father was very charming . . . and he could be witty . . . people liked him. . . ."

"And you hated him."

"I didn't—" Cassandra stopped herself. "Hate is a strong word," she said.

But it was what you felt, Gwen wanted to shout. *You still do. When I did something that reminded you of him—and there must have been times when I did—did you hate me?*

"Gwendolyn, please stop crying," her mother said. "It won't help."

And for Cassandra Wright, descendant of generations of stoic Wrights, probably it wouldn't. But it was helping Gwen to cry—big gulping sobs with her eyes and nose running and her face getting all blotchy and red. It was like being sick; you didn't exactly enjoy the process, but you knew you were going to feel better after you'd finished. Maybe that knowledge was Gwen's legacy from the woman her father had picked up while he was slumming.

"It doesn't matter what your father was," her mother went on. "That has nothing to do with who you are."

But it does, because I am a part of him. And I am a part of the barmaid who may have needed to cry as I do. I had a right to know about them years ago. And you should have been the one to tell me.

And her mother seemed to be thinking the same thing because she said, "This is not the way I wanted you to find out.

I was going to tell you myself, while we were here in Paris."

You were going to tell me at your convenience—when you were in control. And this is one of the few times I've seen you when you haven't been. Maybe I owe Jewel something after all.

"I wanted this to be such a good time for us. I wanted us to . . . Gwen, I'll do whatever you'd like. If you want to cancel the rest of our trip and go home, just say the word. But there's no point in trying to continue if we're going to be angry at each other." There was a pleading note in her mother's voice now. To her surprise, Gwen stopped crying and looked at her. Every hair was in place, of course, and her face wasn't even pale. But the expression in her eyes . . . had she ever looked so vulnerable? So scared? *She's afraid I'll take her up on it,* Gwen realized. *She can't ask me to forgive her, but she's afraid I won't. And that will hurt her . . . she's afraid of how much it will hurt.* And for a moment, Gwen wanted to do it—to hurt Cassandra as much as she'd been hurt herself.

But then she looked again at those frightened, vulnerable eyes.

"No, Mother," she said quietly. "I don't want to cancel the trip."

"This has been so awful, because it happened in the wrong way." Cassandra was trying to regain control now, and Gwen didn't stop her. "I think perhaps we should put it aside for now and talk about it again when we are less . . . heated."

That means we never will, Gwen thought.

But because they were civilized, and because Cassandra was a Wright, and Gwen—in spite of everything—was her daughter, they put it aside. They patched up their . . . what should it be called? The word "quarrel" was too simple; "fight" was too violent. Gwen had a vision of a piece of fragile silk cloth, thin as a membrane, being stretched until it ripped, and then it was darned. The darning thread would always show, there would always be wrinkles where the fabric had been pulled together to mend the tear—but it was patched up.

*   *   *

Gwen and Cassandra began their Paris stay in earnest. They went to Versailles and they saw the Petit Trianon. In the following days, they ate at the sixth-floor tearoom in Au Printemps, at a fabulously expensive restaurant in the Eiffel Tower, and at a little brasserie on the Ile Saint-Louis. They drank café au lait at the Café Marly and looked out the window at the Pyramid entrance to the Louvre. They toured the Louvre, the Musée Rodin, and the Musee d'Orsay; they stood in awe in front of the *Mona Lisa* and *The Thinker*. They explored the tourist attractions because, as Cassandra said, they were tourists and it would be silly not to admit it. Besides, one could not leave Paris without seeing Notre Dame Cathedral and the Ile de la Cité, the Arc de Triomphe, the Place de la Concorde, the Opéra Garnier, the Obélisque, and what seemed to Gwen to be a million fountains. They window-shopped on the Champs-Elysées and, corny as it was, took a ride on the Seine in a *bateau-mouche*. They wandered through the green metal stalls of the *bouquinistes* along the banks of the Seine and watched the fishermen drop their lines on the waterfront of the Ile Saint-Louis. And garden lovers both, they reveled in the beauty of the Jardin des Tuileries, the Jardin du Carrousel, and most of all the Jardin du Luxembourg.

They didn't have time to talk about fathers or birth mothers or secrets kept too long. If you saw them soaking up Paris together you would have thought that whatever differences they had, had been patched up.

On the plane going home, Cassandra said, "I'm going to fire Jewel Fairchild. I just wanted you to know."

Jewel's beautiful face with the ruby red lips and the extraordinary blue eyes floated in front of Gwen, and in those extraordinary blue eyes she saw once again the little gleam of triumph as Jewel told Gwen the devastating news. For a moment Gwen wanted to cheer her mother on. But then she looked at Cassandra sitting next to her, serene in her conviction that punishing Jewel would make everything all right.

"Why do you want to do that?" she demanded. "All Jewel did was tell me the truth."

There was a certain kind of tear that could never be patched up. Not really.

Chapter Twelve

Times Past ("We sell gently used vintage couture," said the ad in the phone book) was located in a small shopping center about a quarter of a mile north of the Algonquin Mall on the highway. The rent in the Plaza Shopping Center wasn't as high as it was in the Algonquin Mall and the address wasn't as prestigious. But it was close enough to attract the overflow from its more elegant neighbor. At least that was what Times Past's owner, Patsy Allen, believed.

"We appeal to the woman who isn't impressed by the trendy clothes at Sofia's," she liked to say. "She leaves the Algonquin Mall unsatisfied and here we are, practically next door, ready to show her the unique classic pieces she's been craving."

If by "unique" and "classic" you meant "old" and "dated," Jewel thought, then Patsy was absolutely right. Although, of course, Jewel would never say that. Patsy was her boss, and Jewel had a new motto when it came to bosses: Never say anything they—or their daughters—don't want to hear.

She could still remember the day, six months ago, when her supervisor at Wright Glassworks had told her she was fired. The order had come from Mrs. Wright personally—it was the first thing she had done when she came back from her vacation in Paris. "I don't know what you did to make her mad, but she didn't even bother to take off her coat before she told me to can you," said the supervisor.

Of course, Jewel knew what she'd done. She'd told Cassandra Wright's dull daughter the truth about her father. Obviously, Gwen had gone crying to Mommy, and Jewel's punishment for those few seconds of satisfaction had been the loss of her weekly paycheck, followed by three months of panic while she tried to find work and her meager savings ran out. Without a college education and only the minimal computer skills she'd been able to pick up in her one course at night school, the pickings had been slim. By the time she'd landed the job as salesgirl at Times Past her landlord was threatening to evict her. So even though the pay was less than she'd made at the glassworks, and she had to spend eight hours a day on her feet in a store that was only air-conditioned in the front section where the customers browsed, she wasn't going to make waves. No, sir.

"Now, this dress is absolutely divine!" Patsy said, as she pulled a white lace garment out of the tissue paper in which it had been lovingly packed. She'd just come back from a buying trip and she liked to show Jewel her "finds."

"Can you imagine?" she'd crow over a

gown. "An original Pucci and they let it go for a song!" Or, "A Donald Brooks! Just locked away in a closet before I rescued it."

And Jewel would ooh and aah because it made Patsy happy. So now, when Patsy held out the lace dress and said, "Look at the workmanship, Jewel; they just don't make things like this anymore," Jewel nodded reverently, and said, "I love the bolero jacket. You're amazing, the way you uncover these treasures."

Privately, she thought, she wouldn't be caught dead in a dress that looked like something someone's grandmother would wear. Although, she'd actually bought a few items from Times Past herself. The clothes were classy—they reminded her of the suits and silk dresses Cassandra Wright brought back from her trips to Paris—and there was no other way Jewel was going to own a cashmere sweater. Even with her generous employee's discount from Patsy, her few purchases had stretched her budget. But the truth was, she really didn't enjoy wearing them. No matter how pretty an

outfit was, or how much it had cost originally, Jewel simply couldn't forget she
was wearing secondhand clothing—
someone else's leavings. Like the secondhand furniture in her apartment.
*Someday I'll be able to go shopping and
buy everything I want—all of it brand-
new! I don't know how, but I'll do it.*

"Whoo, it's warm!" Patsy said and she
fanned herself with an invoice sheet. It
was going to be a scorcher of a day and
they were unpacking the clothes in the
back workroom where the air-conditioning did not penetrate. "Let's go out front
for a minute and sit." She started out of
the workroom. "Don't bring the white
lace out," she said over her shoulder.
"Hang it here in the back. It's delicate
and I don't want people handling it.
We'll show it when we have the right
buyer."

It took Jewel a couple of seconds to
find one of the special padded hangers
they used for the clothes that were
especially fragile, and by the time she
left the workroom, Patsy was already
perched on one of the stools that had
been placed next to the counter in front

of the cash register. She'd been leafing
through the *Wrightstown Gazette*—Jewel
had suggested that they keep a copy for
the customers to look at—and now she
bent a page back and handed it to
Jewel.

"I'd kill to be invited to that party." She
indicated the lead story on the page.
"I'd wear the Armani—you know, the
purple satin from the spring collection in
'82—and I swear, it wouldn't take me
more than twenty minutes to have all
those fancy women dying to come here
to do their shopping. That's the thing
about selling, all you have to do is show
people. . . ."

But Jewel had stopped listening. Because there was a picture accompanying the magazine story and Jewel had
recognized the subject. It was Gwen
Wright, looking as dull as ever. She began skimming the story, which was all
about the party Cassandra Wright was
throwing for her daughter's birthday—
the daughter who had been responsible
for Jewel being fired.

The party was scheduled for that evening, and, according to the newspaper,

it was going to be huge, with tents on the front lawn and a lighting system installed especially for the occasion. The caterer—the best one in the area—had been working on the entrée for three days, and the florist was quoted as saying he hadn't had any sleep for the last two nights. The governor had been invited and he had accepted, as had two state senators—and, Jewel had no doubt, all the eligible young men Cassandra Wright had rounded up to meet her daughter. That was the way the parents of rich girls made sure their daughters stayed rich; by introducing them to the sons of the rich. Jewel's pop had always said wealthy people protected their kids by sending them to expensive colleges where they made friends who gave them six- and seven-figure jobs—networking, he called it. And maybe that was true for boys, but Jewel knew it was different for girls. No matter how many women became lawyers or doctors or heads of companies, the best bet for a girl was still to marry a rich man. But first she had to meet one. That was why Gwen would belong to all the right clubs, and she'd go on vacation to all the right places, and lavish parties with all the right people would be held in her honor. Because sooner or later some rich boy would be attracted to her—the glassworks she'd inherit one day would help—and he would marry her and they would combine their fortunes and have children who were even richer than they had been. The tight little world of the rich would go on for another generation. And no outsider, no matter how pretty or charming she was, was ever going to break into it. That was what was so unfair—there was no way for a girl like Jewel Fairchild to get a chance at the rich boys who would attend a party like this.

Jewel looked down and realized that she was gripping the magazine so hard she had crumpled it. She put it down carefully. "I'm all cooled off," she told Patsy. "I think I'll go back to the workroom and finish unpacking."

"It's got to be a hundred degrees back there!" Patsy protested.

But Jewel needed to be busy so she'd stop thinking.

*Gwen's probably picked out her jewelry already—I'd wear that gold and diamond bracelet if it was me. There will be a hairdresser coming to the house and someone to do her nails and her makeup and—*Jewel stopped herself.

"It's not that bad in the workroom," she told Patsy with a cheery smile. "I'll turn on the fan." And she hurried to the back of the store. Anything, including hundred-degree heat, was better than sitting around imagining how Gwen was preparing for her big night.

*   *   *

According to the thermometer, it was ninety degrees in the shade. Gwen looked out through the kitchen window, where a man was hanging electrified lanterns on the new posts that had just been installed between the house and the hill. Along with the lanterns, there was a large white tent at one end of the back lawn, and round tables covered with white cloths dotting the other end. Huge, flowery umbrellas had come with the tables to shade them from the sun, but the crew that was setting up the party had taken them down. They wouldn't be of any practical use after dark. Cassie—for some reason, now that she knew her father's identity Gwen had started thinking of Cassandra as Cassie—had purchased the umbrellas and the tables because she had assumed Gwen would be entertaining regularly. That was part of the social life that a nice young girl should be enjoying.

But at this particular moment, Gwen was wondering, as she often did wonder, what someone who wasn't a part of her social world, say, someone like the young workman who was stringing up lights, might be thinking about all these elaborate preparations.

He was interesting-looking rather than classically handsome, she decided. His dark hair was a little too long so it kept falling in his eyes and he had to push it aside. His features were strong, and his eyes were brown. As Gwen watched him through the window she thought they looked light, almost hazel. But that could have been a trick of the sunlight. He moved easily—the way people who do physical jobs tend to move—and there was a surety in the way he worked. He knew what he was doing.

Right now, he had stooped to pick up a bottle of water, but apparently finding it empty, had laid it down again on the grass. Gwen scanned the lawn; the workmen who had just finished putting up the tent had taken a break for lunch and the place was deserted. Wouldn't it be nice to give the young man with the unruly hair some of the lemonade that she had just taken out of the refrigerator? She filled a small pitcher, placed it on a tray with a glass, and went outside with it.

"I thought you must be thirsty in this heat," she said.

"Oh, this is so nice of you!" His eyes *were* hazel, it hadn't been the sunshine.

She saw that he was unsure whether he ought to stand up in the blazing sun while he drank, or move under the trees where there were lacy, wrought-iron chairs in the shade. Of course, Cassie would say—and most men would agree—that a man wasn't supposed to sit down while a woman was still standing. So perhaps Gwen ought to go back into the house and let him drink in peace. But how, after a few polite words, does a person simply turn around and walk away? Wouldn't that seem odd? Or rude? The lacy iron chairs were just a few feet away. She walked over to them and so did he. But then after they'd both sat down, neither one of them seemed to know what to say. It occurred to her that perhaps he was waiting for her to speak first, but the only thoughts that came to her mind were the kind of shallow questions people asked at social gatherings when they didn't care about the answers. She didn't want him to think she was like that. On the other hand, it was getting embarrassing sitting and listening to the silence.

"Do you live here in town?" she finally asked.

"Yes, I have for a while now. Originally, I was planning to go to New York to work with a cousin, but I changed my mind."

"But it would've been nice to work with your cousin, wouldn't it?"

Shallow, she thought. *Shallow chit-*

chat. But he looked like he was considering the question seriously.

"Well, that depends. We had a falling-out. He put a big dent on somebody's car on the street, and I told him to leave a note with his name and telephone number, but he wouldn't do it. He has a head for business, you see, and thank goodness, I really have not. At least for that kind of business. What kind of world would it be if we were all like that?"

So the conversation wasn't going to be shallow after all. Because he didn't do that.

"How old is your cousin?" she asked. "If he's still just a kid maybe he doesn't know . . ."

"He's twenty-two. If you don't know whether you're a decent person by then, when will you know?"

"Well, later. It's never too late."

"Yes, it is. Some things are already there when you're born. I knew a kid who could play the violin when he was seven, and he's in an orchestra now. He just had it in him."

She hadn't noticed that there was a

jagged scar on one of his hands. "Goodness, what happened to you?"

"Cut it when I was in school, like a careless idiot."

"Oh, my!"

He had finished his lemonade, so it was time for her to put his glass on her tray and take it back inside. But having begun to talk to the man, she was not sure how to stop without being awfully rude. And shallow.

"What school?"

"Trade school."

"To be an electrician?" Stupid question. He wouldn't be doing this if he'd trained to be a carpenter or a plumber, would he?

"Yup. And what about you?"

"It's vacation time. In the fall, I'll be going to the college here in town to learn how to teach nursery school."

"Didn't I hear somewhere that you were going to a big place, some Ivy League university?"

It just shows how people talk, especially in this town, if it happens to be about the Wright family.

"People say all kinds of things," she

replied. Then because she didn't want
to seem abrupt she added, "I was accepted at Yale."

"You don't want to go there?"

"No, I don't," she said firmly.

"That's unusual. Most people would
give their eyeteeth for a chance like
that."

"Would you?"

"Well, I had a chance, but I didn't take
it. I had a partial scholarship. Not to an
Ivy League university—it was in Chi-
cago."

"So why didn't you take it?"

"Because I like what I'm doing. If it
weren't for electricians—for power—
we'd be stuck in the seventeenth century. We can thank Ben Franklin for what
we've got. Without his tricks with light-
ning, we'd have no cars, no vacuum
cleaners, and the dentist wouldn't be
able to clean your teeth properly." He
laughed. "What am I saying? There
wouldn't be any dentists. You'd go to a
barber who'd pull your tooth out. Without Novocain too."

He had a lively smile. It filled his face
and crinkled around his hazel eyes, eyes

that now were regarding her with frank curiosity.

"I would have imagined you differently, Gwen, if the subject had ever come up."

"How differently? And how do you know my name is Gwen?"

"The newspaper. There was an article about the party tonight, and your name was in it. And about . . . the way I imagined you . . . There was a picture of you too. It was very serious and . . ." He looked down at his empty glass for a second then looked up. "I guess I thought you'd be a young version of Mrs. Wright, sort of a grande dame," he finished, pronouncing the words correctly as they sounded in French.

"My full name is Gwendolyn, and I hate it. And I'm not a grande dame," she said. "And since you know my name, what's yours?"

"Stanley. Stanley Girard. It's French."

"It sounds nice. French was my favorite subject in school."

"My great-great grandfather, or maybe it's three greats, came from there. I've always wanted to see France."

"I've been there. It was only for two weeks, though."

"How was it? As wonderful as they say?"

"It's beautiful. The museums, the gardens, especially at Versailles . . ." But then she stopped. Because the mention of Versailles brought up other images: of Jewel Fairchild's ruby mouth twisted in a little smile of triumph as she told Gwen secrets that she should have already known, and Cassandra's eyes when she had to admit that she had lied for so many years. Gwen pushed the images away. "At Versailles the flowers were all in designs," she said. "They reminded me of embroidery."

He was frowning. "But you didn't like it," he said. He'd picked up on her negative feelings; he was very observant. It would be hard to have secrets with him around. Or lies. What you saw was what you got with him. She didn't know him at all but she knew that much.

"No, Versailles was fantastic. It was just . . . I think there are some things it's better to see on your own." That was partially true, at least.

He was still frowning. He knew she hadn't told him everything, but he was too polite to question her. Suddenly there seemed to be nothing more to say. Each of them waited for the other one to speak first. Locusts were buzzing through the silence, which was once again becoming embarrassing. Finally, this time it was he who broke it.

"I've finished hanging the lanterns," he said. "But I want to replace a couple of the bulbs. I need to get them from my supplier. I'll come back tonight about a half an hour before the party starts and put them in." He handed her his empty glass. "Thank you for the lemonade."

He stood up and started walking. He was going to leave. He was going to gather up his tools and get in his truck and drive away. But then she heard herself call his name. "Stanley," she said. He turned and came back. "You said . . . ," she stumbled; she could feel her face getting red, but she couldn't stop. "You said I wasn't what you imagined." He nodded. She tried to come up with a smile and failed. "So what am I?" she asked. Her face had to be the color of a tomato; a part of her wanted to melt into the ground right here in the hot sun and be done with it. But she'd had to ask. And if he laughed or made a joke, or if he even smiled the wrong way, she really would melt into the ground.

But he had that considering look in his eyes. "Old-fashioned," he said slowly and seriously. "There's something about you that is kind of . . . quaint." Now it was his turn to be red-faced.

"I think I like that," she said after a minute.

He nodded and then he turned and left.

Gwen brought the tray and the lemonade pitcher back into the kitchen. She looked up at the kitchen clock. It was a little after noon. In the driveway a truck from the caterer had arrived. In a few minutes the kitchen and the butler's pantry would be crowded with workers putting trays of canapés and little bits of puff pastry stuffed with creamy fillings into the refrigerator for the evening. The caterer's assistants and the florist's assistants would be bumping into each other as they set the tables and unloaded the centerpieces. And Stanley Girard would be coming back to the house in six hours.

Gwen left the kitchen, and started upstairs for her room. She was under strict orders to relax and be fresh for the night's celebration. "I want you to sparkle," Cassie had said as she drove off to her appointment at the beauty salon. Gwen had refused to allow her mother to make an appointment for her after Cassie's hairdresser said something about giving her gold highlights. Gwen walked into her bedroom, and there hanging on the closet door was the dress she and Cassie had chosen for the party. It was green—Cassie was convinced that was the best color for redheads—and it was the absolute latest style. Nothing about it was old-fashioned or quaint.

Gwen started to run. She ran out of her bedroom, down the stairs, and into the foyer, where she grabbed her car keys—thank heaven she'd finally broken down and gotten her license—and out the front door. She got into her car and she began to drive.

There was a shop she'd seen advertised although she'd never been inside it. It was in a small shopping center just north of the Algonquin Mall. According to the advertisement, the place, which was called Times Past, sold vintage clothes.

Chapter Thirteen

Gwen Wright had come to Times Past to shop! On the day of her big birthday party, no less. Jewel couldn't believe it. Seeing her again was like having one of those bad dreams where you're caught in an incident that keeps on repeating it-self over and over and you can't get out. The only consolation was that Gwen had been as surprised—and dis-mayed—to see Jewel as Jewel was to see her.

"Oh, my . . . Jewel! I didn't expect . . .

that is, I didn't know. . . ." she'd stammered.

"Yes, I work here now," Jewel had
said. "Since your mother fired me."

Princess Gwen didn't have a response
for that. She'd just looked away.

*   *   *

Of all the people to run into, Gwen
thought. Why did it have to be Jewel
Fairchild! It had been six months since
Jewel had thrown Gwen's life up in the
air like some blue-eyed earthquake, and
Gwen was still living with the after-
shocks. Her relationship with Cassie
was strained in ways that it hadn't been
before; and she'd had to face the fact
that the birth parents she'd sometimes
dreamed were beautiful and noble were
actually a couple of lying cheaters.

Then as if that wasn't bad enough,
she'd raced to this store that no one she
knew would ever dream of entering, for
reasons that she didn't even want to admit to herself, and who was standing
there with her perfect face and her gorgeous hair? Who was the salesgirl who

would help Gwen? It was like some kind of sick joke.

I'd rather have root canal without an anesthetic than let her help me! Gwen thought.

I can't wait on her, Jewel thought. *I'd rather die.*

They stood facing each other. Jewel was pretty sure the smile on her face was as sick as the one on Gwen's, and it was clear that neither one of them could figure out how to get out of the situation. That was when, thank you, God, Patsy came in from the back room. She recognized Gwen from the picture in the newspaper and fluttered around for a few seconds, welcoming her into the shop. Then she said, "Now, Miss Wright, how can I help you?"

And if she noticed the sighs of relief from both Gwen and Jewel she didn't give any indication of it.

*   *   *

The white lace dress was exactly what Gwen had been looking for. Patsy Allen had showed it to her, Gwen had tried it on, and now she stood in front of the mirror seeing herself as if for the first time. The bodice had a square neckline that framed her small face, and the delicate lace fell gracefully to her ankles. "You look like a heroine from a Jane Austen novel," Patsy Allen sighed happily. And Gwen knew she was right, the look was perfect—from the neck down.

"But my hair . . . ," Gwen moaned.

"An upsweep," Patsy decreed. "Not too period—you don't want to look like you're going to a costume ball—but your hair must be off your face."

"I don't know how to make it do that. I'm not good with that kind of thing, and I think it's too late to get an appointment at the beauty salon, they were booked weeks ago. . . ."

"I'm sure they'd make a place for you. . . ."

"Oh, I couldn't impose," Gwen murmured sadly.

*   *   *

She needs to be as pretty as she can be tonight, Jewel thought. *It has to be a man. When a girl is like this—and it's the*

*first time I've seen a spark of life in her—
it always is about a man.*

But now Gwen looked as if she was
going to cry. Which served her right, of
course. But it almost made Jewel feel
sorry for her. And it had been . . . well,
kind of exciting to see how the white
lace dress had transformed her. All three
of them, Jewel, Patsy, and Gwen, had
been caught up in the perennial feminine fantasy of the perfect gown turning
an ordinary girl into Cinderella. It would
be a pity if Gwen's frizzy mane spoiled
the look. . . .

What the hell, Jewel thought. "I can do
your hair," she said.

Gwen looked terrified.

"Don't worry," Patsy said, "Jewel is a
genius with that sort of thing."

"If you don't like it, you can always
take it down," Jewel said briskly. And
before Gwen could protest, Jewel was
seating her on a stool in front of the
counter, and Patsy was rushing across
the shopping center to buy hairpins and
hair spray.

Jewel worked fast and with assur-
ance—she might not be up on the nov-

els of Jane Austen, but there wasn't too much she didn't know about fixing hair and applying makeup. Her fingers smoothed, twisted, and pinned Gwen's curly mass into place. Finally she stood back to survey her handiwork. "A white ribbon," she said.

"Absolutely," Patsy agreed, and ran to the back workroom to find one.

A narrow silk ribbon was threaded through the curls at the back of Gwen's head and tied in a tiny bow that perched behind one ear. Only after Jewel was completely satisfied with the final effect was Gwen allowed to stand once again in front of the mirror and see herself.

"Oh," she breathed.

"Just right." Patsy studied her critically. "The hair and the dress are perfect, but it doesn't look as if you're trying too hard. It's the ribbon that does it; it looks as if you just tied your hair up at the last minute."

And I did it, Jewel thought. And then a really pleasant feeling came over her. *I just did Princess Gwen a favor. Now she owes me one. Little old me.*

*   *   *

She did me a favor, Gwen thought. *This is exactly the way I wanted to look and she did it for me.* She turned away from the vision of herself in the mirror and said to Jewel and Patsy, "I don't know how to thank you."

But I can't bear being in her debt. Anyone but her.

Then she had an idea. Cassie would be furious, but that was too bad. "I know it's short notice, and I hope you're not offended," she said. "But would the two of you like to come to my party tonight?" She picked up one of the gift cards on the counter and scribbled something on it. "If you give them this at the front door, they'll know you're my guests."

*   *   *

Patsy fell all over herself thanking Gwen, but Jewel thought, *She couldn't stand it when she had to thank me! Now she's got to even the score by throwing me a crust and inviting me to her big shindig—at the last minute. It's insulting. And she knows it.*

For a second, Jewel thought about turning down the offer and not letting Gwen get the upper hand again. But the party would be a chance at the magical inner circle—the one where a girl could meet the right man and change her life. *Someday I'll be able to say no to the Gwen Wrights of the world,* she told herself. *But I can't afford it now.*

"Thank you," she said. And she took the insulting invitation Gwen had scribbled out.

*   *   *

It was almost dark when Gwen seated herself in a rocker on the front porch of her home to wait until Stanley showed up to finish his work on the lanterns. She had rehearsed a little speech explaining why she was out there. "I just wanted to catch some fresh air before the nightmare begins," she would say. Just to make sure he knew—in case he hadn't already figured it out—that she wasn't an ordinary society girl. The speech had the double advantage of being true. She did hate big parties and she usually did sneak off somewhere to pull herself together before one started.

But so far there was no sign of Stanley's truck coming up the driveway. Behind her, the house was brightly lit, the hired waiters and bartenders rushing around taking care of last minute details. Walter would be checking on the champagne. Cassie would be running over her lists one last time with her housekeeper. And the daughter of the house, for whom all the fuss was being made, was sitting outside, wearing a white lace dress and trying to pretend she hadn't bought it for a man she'd talked to for ten minutes that afternoon. *You're a fool, Gwen Wright,* she told herself. But nothing on earth could have dragged her inside.

Two minutes later, she had her reward, when she heard the sound of gravel crunching under truck tires. The door of the truck opened and Stanley—she could tell it was him, even in the dim light—got out. He was carrying something—was it the box of replacement bulbs? But he must have seen her, because after a second he put it down and came toward her.

*   *   *

Stanley knew right away who it was sitting on the front porch, looking exactly the way he'd imagined she would. The way she was meant to look. He knew that all of it, the hair, and the dress, and the nonchalant pose in the rocking chair, had been done for him. And something in his heart turned over. She was so young! Which wasn't to say that she was soft. On the contrary, he thought in her quiet way she could be quite strong when she wanted something. And she was smart—ten minutes of talking to her had told him that. But there was something so . . . open . . . and vulnerable, and . . . there was no other word for it . . . so young . . . about the way she was sitting there waiting for him. He wasn't sure what to do. If he told her she looked lovely, she might blush with that fiery red spreading over her cheeks. He found it endearing but he knew it embarrassed her. And besides, she wasn't really lovely in the classic sense of the

word. To him, what she had was better
than mere loveliness—she was unique.
Like one of those one-of-a-kind glass
vases that were made by the artisans at
the glassworks. But he wasn't sure how
to convey all of that. Or any of it. Still,
she had gone to all this trouble for him
and he had to say something. . . .

*   *   *

The little speech had flown out of
Gwen's head. She walked to the edge of
the porch as Stanley came up to the rail-
ing. They could have played the balcony
scene from *Romeo and Juliet* if either of
them had been an actor. Instead she
said the only thing she could think of.

"It's cooled down since this afternoon."

At the same moment, he said, "I like
your dress."

And then they were staring at each
other. Through the open window of the
house she heard someone in the foyer
say, "No, no, the champagne flutes go
on the tables."

And someone else was asking, "When
will the band be setting up?"

And that broke the spell. In the darkness, Stanley frowned. "I'd better go see about those lanterns," he said, and he started to move away.

And she was going to cry. After everything she'd been through—the mad dash to Times Past, letting Jewel Fairchild do her hair, inviting the woman to her party—she didn't know what she had expected from Stanley but it was more than just "I like your dress," and walking away. But he was going. Then he stopped. And came back to her.

"There's a little movie house over in Tyler," he said. "Art movies, you know, the kind of foreign pictures with subtitles. They're really great, most of them."

"I saw one there, too, an Italian one," she said, and then before she could stop herself, "Would you like to go again with me?"

When he said yes, he smiled at her, and she was glad she hadn't stopped herself.

Chapter Fourteen

The party was in full swing. And Gwen was floating somewhere above all the chatter and the music from the band and the clinking of dishes and glasses. Nothing could get to her, not even a scolding from Cassie—which had occurred a few minutes earlier when Jewel Fairchild and Patsy Allen had walked in and handed the butler Gwen's handwritten invitation.

"What possessed you?" Cassie had demanded.

"I ran into her and I thought it would be polite," Gwen said lamely.

"She's a horrible person."

And because Cassie was so adamant about it, Gwen heard herself say, "She's not all that bad. She did my hair for tonight."

"She did what? How? Where, for heaven's sake?"

"It's a long story."

"Why on earth did you let her do that when I tried for three weeks to convince you to go to Charles? Sometimes I don't understand you. . . ."

"I know."

"And while we're on the subject, why did you decide to change your dress after we spent so much time picking out the green one?"

"I thought this looked nice."

"I'm not saying it doesn't, but where did you get it? I can tell it's old, and it's not something that's been in our family, so why did you . . . Good lord, is that woman giving out business cards?" And sure enough, Patsy Allen was handing a Times Past card to a woman in a gown with huge puffed sleeves. Cassie drew in a deep breath and Gwen prepared herself for a lecture, but fortunately a woman wearing way too much rouge broke into their private moment to say, "Cassie, dear, there's someone I want you to meet."

"Go ahead, Mother," Gwen said heartily.

Cassie murmured, "Later, Gwendolyn." Then she allowed herself to be led away.

Gwen was free to retreat to the sidelines and watch the crowd in front of her. And to see the effect that Jewel was having on the guests at her birthday party. Because Jewel was getting second—and third—looks everywhere she went. She was spectacular in a strapless charmeuse gown that was the same violet blue as her eyes and clung to her curves in a way that left nothing to the imagination. Her dark hair gleamed in the lantern light, her ruby lips formed a perpetual smile, and everywhere men were sneaking glances at her, or not even bothering to sneak and indulging in long besotted stares. Several had found an excuse to leave the women they'd been talking to and had managed to put themselves in Jewel's path as she strolled across the lawn. For a moment Gwen remembered another birthday party long ago that had been hijacked by a girl who was prettier than she, and old feelings, bitter and resentful, flooded over her. But then she remembered the movie house in Tyler where they showed art films in foreign languages, and the feelings melted away. Let Jewel have all the attention she could get. Tonight, Gwen could afford to be generous.

*   *   *

The party—Jewel's chance to break into the magic circle of the rich—was not turning out to be very magical after all. She kept her wide, friendly smile plastered on her face, but she was getting discouraged. Oh, she was getting plenty of interest—she always did. But she'd been around long enough to know the right kind of interest from the kind that never produced anything more than a minor piece of jewelry. Or a lot of broken promises about leaving the wife and children. Not that she'd ever been dumb enough to fall for that. The problem was, she was still an outsider here, even with Gwen Wright's scribbled invitation in her tiny clutch bag. Rich preppies weren't stupid, at least not when it came to spotting their own, and it only took a minute for them to realize she wasn't one of them. No matter how vague she tried to be about her background, or how much she tried to suggest that she and Gwen had known each other forever, most of the men who had found an excuse to talk to her had melted away— usually with regret—after a few minutes of light but unfortunately revealing conversation. The ones who had lingered in spite of the revealing conversation were interested in the kind of relationship that wasn't going to be any use to her. A girl who looked the way she did developed a sixth sense about that kind of thing. Still, she was here and she might as well make the most of it. She fluffed her hair off her shoulders and smiled at a man who was staring at her; he had to be in his sixties if he was a day.

And that was when she saw the late-comer. His long face was becomingly tanned, and although his features were ordinary there was something about him that made you look twice. He was older than she, but not "old-old." His striped tie was of the sort called "regimental"—although she was not sure what that meant, except that, in a vague way, it was connected with something impor-tant. And at a party where most of the men were wearing light-colored suits or pastel blazers, that tie and his navy blue jacket made him stand out. Like the rest of the men present he called to her mind an advertisement of some long-estab-lished shop for men who carry tennis racquets or are mounted on handsome horses. But while he was definitely up-per-class, in some way Jewel couldn't quite describe, he was different from the others. She watched him as he walked onto the patio and stood scanning the scene in front of him. He wasn't looking for anyone, that was clear; if he had any friends here he wasn't in a hurry to find them. He slid his hands into his pockets and leaned up against the back wall of the house as if he might stay there all night. But for all of his casual pose, there was something coiled and slightly dangerous about him. Even from halfway across the lawn, Jewel could sense it. She was wondering if she wanted to try to work her way over to him, when Walter Amburn came up to greet him and lead him to Cassie and Gwen.

*   *   *

"Gwen, Cassie, this is Jeff Henry." Walter introduced the man who had come more than fashionably late to the party. At least, Gwen knew that was what Cassie would be thinking.

Sure enough, when she held out her hand to shake his, she said, "So glad you could make it, Mr. Henry."

If he picked up on the frost in her tone, it didn't phase him. "So am I, Mrs. Wright," he said cheerfully, and went on to wish Gwen a happy birthday.

There's something about him, Gwen thought as she thanked him. *He's like a pirate. One with sandy blond hair and good taste in clothes, but still there's something a little uncivilized about him.*

"Jeff is interested in buying my painting of the little girl on the rooftop," Walter said.

That was a surprise. Walter had made his reputation with the portraits he did on commission, but he also painted his own works—many of them considered to be of museum quality. The painting he was talking about was a delicate, shadowy piece, a picture of a child sitting on the roof of one of the rundown bungalows near the river, with storm clouds above her and gray water behind her. Gwen couldn't imagine it appealing to the swashbuckler standing in front of her. Clearly, there was more to Mr. Jeff Henry than one saw at first glance. You'd always have to be careful around him, she decided. You'd never be quite sure what was going through his mind. And suddenly, a vision of Stanley popped into her mind. She remembered what she'd thought of him, that there was nothing hidden or secretive about him. She remembered how tired she was of secrets and not knowing where you were with people.

And then she realized that she and her mother and Walter no longer had Jeff Henry's undivided attention. Something had caught his eye. Gwen was pretty sure what it was, but she looked in the direction of his gaze anyway. Jewel was standing under a lantern—one of the lanterns Stanley had strung up earlier that day. Gwen felt herself smiling at the memory of him standing in front of her awkwardly holding his glass of lemonade, trying to decide if he should sit or stand. You could count on a man who was that transparent, she thought. And a few minutes later, when Jeff excused himself, she really wasn't irritated when she saw him making his way toward Jewel.

*   *   *

Jewel looked longingly toward the front of the house where she knew there was an attendant was waiting to retrieve the guests' cars when they wanted to leave the party. Just a few hours earlier she'd been giddy at the thought of being at an event where they had valet parking. Now all she wanted to do was get the hell out. She'd played this night all wrong—she could see that now. What she should have done, or at least tried to do, was make friends with the women. They were the ones who ruled this world; they decided who was going to get the stamp of approval and who wasn't. The men followed them. But you didn't make friends with women by wearing a mantrap dress and the sexiest perfume you could buy. On the other hand, she'd never had much luck making friends with women no matter what she was wearing, so there probably hadn't been any right way for her to play this night. Maybe Pop was right—if you were under it when you started out you were doomed to stay that way for the rest of your life. She didn't care anymore. She just wanted to go home and sleep for a month. Unfortunately she was going to have to wait a while longer because Patsy wasn't ready to go yet.

Patsy was her ride for the night because Jewel's twelve-year-old clunker was back in the shop. Again. Just add it to the list.

Jewel walked to the side of the lawn where there were two lacy iron chairs under some trees, and carefully wiped the seat of one before she sat. Her violet blue dress that had been such a mistake was on loan from Times Past, and Patsy would be upset if she got even a smudge on it. She lowered herself into the chair and closed her eyes with relief—it was the first time she'd allowed herself to sit since she'd arrived. Her feet were killing her.

"Mind if I join you?" asked a masculine voice. She looked up to see the man in the navy blue jacket.

If she hadn't been so tired, she might have tried to flirt. But she'd finished with that for the night. "No, I don't mind," she said. He sat next to her and they looked out at the party in silence.

"Forgive me if I'm presuming," he said finally. "But I don't think you're having a very good time."

"I don't belong here," she said. The words just slipped out and after they did she could have kicked herself. Because now he would have to say something like, "What are you talking about?" or "Why, you're the prettiest girl here." And she would have to find some clever lighthearted way to explain herself.

"I know what you mean," he said. "I don't belong, either."

"Of course you do!" The words slipped out again. "You're one of them."

"No," he said, looking thoughtfully out at the party-goers. "I'm not in this league." Then he added softly as if he'd forgotten she was there, "Not yet, anyway."

There was something about the way he said it that piqued her curiosity. She forgot about her aching feet and her bruised feelings. She forgot how tired she was, and sat up to look at him. "You dress the right way, you speak the right way, I bet you went to one of those schools that are right . . . and you're probably married to the right kind of wife."

"Don't have one," he broke in.

"Okay, but I know I'm correct about the rest of it, so what are you talking about?"

He turned to her with a slightly twisted little smile. "Money. I'm talking about money, of course. What else?"

*   *   *

Why the hell am I telling her this? Jeff wondered to himself. But he knew why. There was something electric about this girl; even now, when she was obviously down about something, he could feel the energy in her. He looked at her lovely oval face, and her attractive mouth with its remarkably white teeth and her open, friendly smile that lit up her extraordinary eyes. So many women held no surprises, but every instinct he had said this one was different. Well, be honest, it wasn't a matter of instinct; she'd already proven she was different with this very unusual conversation.

And then she proved it again. "Are you saying you're poor?" she demanded. "Because I don't believe it."

He laughed at that, and she joined in.
"I guess 'poor' is a relative term," he
said. "If you're talking about the Wright
family, and most of the people here
tonight, I'm barely getting by. If you're
talking about the people I grew up with,
I'm doing fine." He paused, and then he
said in a mock bragging tone, "I can
even afford to buy a Walter Amburn
painting. Of course I have to pay in in-
stallments, but I can do it."

"But you don't want to pay in install-
ments," she said. She was studying him
carefully. The attention was actually
rather pleasant.

"No. I think I'm going to be all right
with it, but then I come to a house like
this and . . ."

"You come to a house like this, and . . .
what?" she prompted him.

What am I doing? he thought. *I don't
talk this way to friends and I don't even
know her.* But she was so pretty. And so
different.

"I want," he confessed. "Want everything. It's embarrassing to admit,
but . . ."

"Why?"

"I make a decent living, I work in a brokerage house. I own my own home, a house on Warren Street. It's a good enough address. . . ."

"I know the neighborhood, and it is good. Unless you're someone who wants more. So what are you going to do about that?"

"Funny you should ask," he said, but then he stopped himself. Because now he really was going too far into private matters with a total stranger. "What about you?" he asked. "Where do you live?"

"In a dump of an apartment over a deli. But don't change the subject. What are you going to do?"

He couldn't, shouldn't tell her. But then she smiled again. "I'm kind of at a crossroads," he said. She leaned in closer; she understood about being in that place, he could tell. "There's a business I've been thinking about getting into."

"Could you make a lot of money doing it?"

"Yes."

"Would you be rich as the Wrights?"

"Easily. But there's risk involved. Nothing I can't handle but still, it's there . . . and it's going to mean dealing with some tough players."

"Can't you be tough too?"

"Yes." And in spite of himself, he added, "But I'm not sure I like that in myself."

"Get over that," she said. Her pretty face was so earnest that he couldn't take offense at the abruptness of the command. "I mean it," she told him. "Because you won't be happy unless you try."

"How do you know that?"

"Because I know about wanting."

Across the lawn a woman was beckoning to her. She stood up. "My ride is waiting for me," she said. She held out her hand. "I expect to see your picture in the paper when you make your first million." She shook his hand and walked away. It wasn't until after she was out of sight that he realized that they hadn't exchanged names.

* * *

As Jewel stood with Patsy waiting for the parking attendant to bring the car to them she thought about the nameless man in the navy blue jacket. *I'm kind of at a crossroads,* he'd said. *That's the exact word for where I am—a crossroads. But I don't have a business waiting for me that could make me as rich as the Wrights.*

"Who was that man you were talking with?" Patsy asked.

"Nobody," Jewel said, then she added, "I think he could be someone. A really big someone. If he doesn't think too much and get in his own way."

"Sounds like you got to know him pretty well in one little chat at a party."

"Not really. I don't even know his name."

* * *

The party was over. From her bedroom window, Gwen looked out at the back lawn where Stanley Girard's lanterns were still twinkling. She'd checked the newspaper before coming upstairs to bed and read that the movie house in Tyler was playing a Czech film. She hoped Stanley wouldn't feel that they needed to wait until there was a French or Italian one playing before they went to see it together.

Roads Diverging

"Jealousy is all the fun
you think they had."
—ERICA JONG

Chapter Fifteen

~~~~~

Uncounted millions of written pages in every possible language have described the discovery of mutual love. What was it, Stan was often to ask himself, that had led him to Gwen and led her to him?

She was not really very beautiful; he'd decided that early on—and had also known that it didn't matter to him. She was too quiet, and as he'd told her— and where had he gotten the nerve?— she was the kind of person who is often called "quaint." She was not easy to know—at least, at first. Yet there was something about her that led him to walk into a florist shop, the day after her grand party, and buy her a little bush filled with miniature pink roses.

He took it home to his apartment—he had recently moved to a new building in the center of Wrightstown—and put it on his kitchen table. The rosebush, he now realized, answered a question that had been worrying him. He and Gwen had agreed to go to a movie together, and he had been wondering if he should call her up and ask her in a formal way to go on a date with him, or if he should show up at her home on some pretext— perhaps he would say he wanted to make sure the lanterns were still working—and casually mention the movie as an afterthought. But if he were to bring her a present, there was nothing casual about that. He looked at the little plant he'd chosen so carefully; four delicate roses had already bloomed and two more were starting to open their pink petals. The truth was, the feelings he had about Gwen weren't casual. He had never been this serious about a girl, and there had been enough of them for him to recognize the difference. So, it was no accident that he had bought the little rosebush for Gwen. Deep down, he'd wanted it to keep him honest.

"That movie house I told you about is playing a Czech film," he said to Gwen on the phone.

"I know," she blurted out. Then she added, stammering slightly, "I . . . just happened to see . . . the advertisement. . . ." Obviously, she hadn't meant to tell him she'd been so eager to go with him that she had checked the newspaper. She wasn't sure she wanted him to know how she felt. She probably didn't know herself. Well, hadn't he been sifting through the same sort of thoughts and questions?

"I'd like to take you to see it tomorrow night," he said. "And then would you let me take you out for a late supper afterward?" Because now he wanted to be as clear as possible. *I am asking you out on a date, Gwen Wright. In the old-fashioned term, I'm courting you. Do you understand?*

She agreed to the movie and the late supper.

*   *   *

"Roses need sun," Stanley said the next evening when he presented himself at the imposing white house with the hill behind it. Gwen had opened the door on the second ring of the bell. She must have been waiting for him, because he was pretty sure that there were servants in this mansion who usually did that kind of thing. But Gwen hadn't played the usual game and let him cool his heels in the foyer until she made her entrance. Possibly she didn't know that was how the game was played.

"You can plant this bush outdoors or keep it near a sunny window in your room," he went on, and to his amazement, he realized he was embarrassed by the words "your room." He almost laughed. Because wasn't it funny in these times, in this fast-moving century, to know that he still had a faintly puritan streak buried somewhere inside him? As he handed her the rosebush, he had a vague vision of her room, adorned with ruffles, all in pink. He had never had such a vision with any other girl!

"I'll put it on the windowsill across from my bed," she told him. "It will be the first thing I see when I wake up in the morning."

She didn't seem even slightly embarrassed to be mentioning such intimate things to him. She really was different from other girls. Or was she just so very young for her age?

*   *   *

Tyler, the town where the movie house was, was a perfect place to take a girl for a night out. Once, it had been just another of the hundreds of small New England towns that were dying because the industries that had sustained them had relocated overseas, leaving the citizens with the choice of starving or moving. But the people of Tyler were fighters. Their little community had been prosperous in its heyday, and therefore it had a remarkable number of lovely public buildings and gracious private homes built on an exceptionally pretty stretch of the river. Tyler's citizens had chosen to trade on these assets and become a tourist attraction. The old homes were refurbished as charming bed-and-breakfasts, the nineteenth-century opera house, the town hall, and the library were all brought up to code and listed with the National Registry for Historic Landmarks, and a newly built river walk became a magnet for dozens of delightful little shops and food stalls.

So it was that after the movie and a very good supper in a little bistro near the docks, Stan and Gwen, having opted not to have dessert, found themselves strolling by the river, eating ice cream in handmade cones—peppermint ice cream because the girl behind the counter said it was their most popular flavor. In the sky above, the clouds framed clusters of stars, and the river spread silent and silver underneath it. Stan knew he would remember for the rest of his life the sharp sweet taste of peppermint and the faraway expression Gwen wore when she was thinking about something that mattered to her. As she was at that moment.

"I liked that movie," she said. "Especially the ending—it must have been a big temptation for the screenwriter to just wrap up all the loose ends in a nice big bow, but he didn't do that."

"You don't like happy endings?" he asked.

"Not when I can tell that they've just been tacked on to a story to sell tickets," she said firmly. The firmness was a surprise; most of the time she was tentative when he asked her opinion about something. She was quick to say that she didn't know about this topic, or that she hadn't read enough about that one. But now she was very sure of herself. "Sometimes, if it's light entertainment— and I do think there's a place for that— it's all right to work the plot around until you have a happy ending, even if it isn't totally believable," she went on eagerly. "But with a movie like the one we saw tonight, where all the characters are so real and the situation is so true, you have to stay honest. Even if your audience feels a little sad at the end. Although I must say I didn't feel sad—it was more like being uplifted because you knew the characters had done the right thing even though it didn't make them blissfully happy."

"Do you always analyze movies like this?" he asked. He loved this new intensity in her.

"Actually, now that I think about it, it's storytelling in general that interests me," she said slowly. "Although I never realized it before this minute. I've always wondered why one book touches your heart and another one with a similar plot leaves you cold. It must be in the way it's written—you know?"

"I'm afraid that's something I haven't thought about very much."

"I guess when you read all the time the way I do you can't help wondering what makes it all come together. Do you like to read?"

"Yes. But not a lot of fiction. Mostly biographies."

"Of people like Benjamin Franklin? I ordered a biography of him the other day after you mentioned him."

He told himself it was ridiculous to be so pleased that she was following up on a name he had dropped.

*   *   *

Over the weeks as he continued his careful courtship, he discovered that she hadn't been exaggerating when she said she read all the time—one book seemed to lead her to another. After finishing the Franklin biography, she moved on to *Poor Richard's Almanac,* and from that to biographies of Washington, Adams, and Jefferson. Then for a change of pace she returned to her beloved Tolstoy to reread *Anna Karenina.*

"You put me to shame," he told her.

"I don't have anything else to do with my days," she said. "I don't work the way you do. I'm the one who should be ashamed."

Finally, after several weeks, he felt the time was right to show her his electrician's shop between the stationer's store and the pizza parlor in Wrightstown's commercial district. The shop was his pride and joy; he'd only been in business for a few months, but he was already turning a profit—a profit that had been big enough to allow him to leave his cramped studio apartment and move into one with two bedrooms and an eat-in kitchen in a shiny new building that had all the amenities.

Still, he had hesitated about letting Gwen see the little place he called Stan's Electronics. A girl who'd grown up around a multimillion-dollar enterprise like the glassworks might not understand what an accomplishment his fledgling business represented. It was not that he was worried about disappointing her, he realized; rather, if she didn't appreciate what he'd been able to achieve, he would be disappointed in her.

But he had to risk it. He brought her to the shop, showed her around, offered her some iced tea from the small refrigerator in his small office, and braced himself for her response.

He need not have worried. "You do everything!" Gwen exclaimed. "You can install a new electrical system for a business complex, and you can maintain it too! And you also create your own advertising and you keep your own books.

At the glassworks, there are separate departments for all of those things."

"With a small operation like this, I have to be a one-man band," he'd protested. But he'd been foolishly, childishly pleased. "I'm not in the same league as the Wright Glassworks. I'm not even close."

"But I think if your company was as big as Mother's, you'd still want to be hands-on. Mother is. She may have all those departments and the vice presidents who run them, but she makes sure she's on top of all of it. She learned her lesson, you see, because she almost lost everything when she didn't do that, when she turned it all over to my—" But she stopped short. Stan knew she'd been about to say something more and it upset him that she had changed her mind. *You can trust me,* he wanted to tell her. *Whatever it was that you were about to say, it will be safe with me.*

*   *   *

Gwen felt her face get red. She'd almost spilled the secret of her birth parents! That was what was so dangerous about

Stan; she felt so comfortable with him that it seemed like the most natural thing in the world to tell him her most intimate secret. The secret that could not be told because that would be disloyal to Cassie. And yet, it was Gwen's secret too. Should it always be off-limits? With everyone? Gwen looked at Stan. He had brought her here to his little shop and he'd had faith that she would understand what it meant to him. His pride was tied up in this business of his, along with his hard work, his talent, and his dreams. And he had shared it with her. Because he wanted her to know him better. Wasn't it time to return the favor?

She sat down on a workbench—he'd told her he'd built it with his own two hands—and motioned to him to sit next to her. She said, "I have something I'd like you to know about me." And she told him about her father and the woman who had been her birth mother. The telling didn't take long, as she really didn't know that much about those two figures in her life, but when it was over she felt as if she'd done something very strenuous, like running a marathon, or climbing a mountain. It took her a second to catch her breath and then she turned to Stan. And she realized that without meaning to, she'd just given him a test. There were so many things he could say that would be wrong. If he said, "Cassandra Wright was a good woman to take you in," that would be the worst. "How lucky you were that she didn't turn away from you," wouldn't be much better. Suddenly she was afraid. She didn't want him to fail the test but she wasn't sure herself what the right response would be.

He looked at her for what seemed like an eternity, and then he said. "I'm sorry your mother didn't tell you the truth years ago. It's something you should have known."

He was perfect! She threw her arms around him and she hugged him. And for a second he hugged her back, but then she felt something in him change and he was pulling her to him as if he couldn't let her go. When he took her face in his hands and brushed her hair aside with his fingertips she knew what was coming and she thought perhaps she should warn him that she'd never been kissed before—not in the way he was about to kiss her. But then something inside her began to change, too, and she didn't have time to think or talk because her body was melting into his as if that was what it was meant to do, and her mouth was joining his and she could taste the iced tea on his tongue, and if he had wanted to, she would have kissed him all night.

*   *   *

Stan pulled back from the kiss. He told himself it was because she was so young and he didn't want to go too fast. But he knew it wasn't just for her that he did it. For weeks she'd been filling his thoughts. Tonight he'd been moved by her in ways he'd never been moved before. This was too serious to rush.

"I'll drive you home," he said softly, and was happier than he'd ever thought he could be when she looked disappointed.

*   *   *

He sought a word for her, and couldn't come up with anything that seemed to do her justice. *I should ask her for a phrase,* he thought wryly as he took her home. He had learned that she was in love with words almost as much as she was in love with stories. He had learned so much about her in such a short time. And she had learned as much about him. It was as if, after her initial reticence had melted away, she and he were in a competition to see who could reveal the most personal history. She told him about being different as a child—an odd duck, she called herself—and about her early fascination with language and strange ideas. He had countered with his own early fascination with gadgets and machinery and his later love of mathematics. He had explained how both interests seemed in his mind to be the same. A column of figures either added up or it didn't; either an appliance could be fixed or it was past repair.

"Of course." She'd nodded her head knowingly. "What you see is what you get. That would appeal to you."

Yes, they had gotten to know each

other's history in a very short time. But in those dueling histories there were differences that concerned him. She was unusually innocent for her age because she had been so sheltered. She was a child of privilege who'd grown up with great wealth, which she took for granted—far more than she knew. She'd been damaged by events that had taken place when she was very young and she was just starting to sort it all out.

He, on the other hand, had been brought up in a working-class home, with a father who had a job at the glassworks, a mother who was the office manager for a law firm, and an older brother. His childhood had been uneventful; there had been no great damage that he was aware of. By his own choice he had been on his own since he was seventeen, and he was neither innocent nor sheltered. Since he had been supporting himself for years, he never took money—or the spending of it—for granted. His relationship with his parents was cordial but distant. They didn't understand why he hadn't gone to college to "make something of himself," but they hadn't tried to push him into it. He enjoyed their company in limited doses. Gwen's relationship with her mother, on the other hand, was the kind he particularly disliked—convoluted, claustrophobic, and driven by love and guilt in equal measure.

For a man like him to get involved with a girl like Gwen—and you really couldn't say she was a woman, not yet anyway—did not make sense. But as he lay awake in bed at night—something he found himself doing more and more—he knew that she was going to be a part of his life. However, it would have to happen in spite of her formidable mother, because Cassandra Wright did not like him. And her influence over her daughter was great, no matter how much Gwen rebelled against her.

Chapter Sixteen

Evening coffee, served in the den with a plate of cookies, was a ritual that Cassie always welcomed. There had been times in Gwen's rebellious adolescence when she had considered it an annoyance—just another opportunity for her mother to hide behind a wall of polite ceremony and meaningless friendly chatter. This night, however, was different. Neither the coffee nor the cookies had been touched, and the atmosphere between mother and daughter was neither friendly nor polite. Unfortunately, Walter, who usually managed to lower the temperature at such times, was in Connecticut doing the initial sketches for a portrait of a client. So the argument between Gwen and Cassie had been going on for over an hour.

"You used to complain because I had no dates," Gwen said. "Now I have somebody who really likes me, and you don't approve of him."

"I never 'complained.' " Cassie corrected in that maddening way she had of picking up on a peripheral detail of what one had said and avoiding the essence. "Sometimes I did worry because I thought you might be a bit lonely. And now you're accusing me of doing something wrong?"

"No! That's not—"

"It certainly sounds that way. Forgive me for taking an interest in your happiness, Gwen. If you would have preferred to be neglected and ignored I wish I'd known."

They'd been going round and round in circles like this one, and it was getting them nowhere. Suddenly a small explosion occurred within Gwen and she cried out to Cassie, "Mother, that's enough! We're not talking about you and me. This is about Stan. You don't approve of him."

"I never said that, not exactly. . . ."

"You didn't have to. You don't approve of him because he has none of what you call 'status'! You think he's nobody."

"That's unfair. I am not a snob. And I'm not so trivial that I would object to a good man just because of his position in life."

"Well, I seem to remember a comment once about a barmaid and your first husband going slumming," Gwen said and then instantly regretted opening the old wound. Now she was the one taking them in circles—and a tired rehash of old grievances.

Cassie sighed deeply. "Again, that isn't fair and you know it. I was angry when I said that and I apologized for it. And since then I've never said a word, good or bad, about your mother . . . or your father."

"We might be better off if you had."

"What would you have me say, Gwen? You know what your father did. As for your mother, I didn't know her. I didn't even know she existed until after she was dead. As far as I'm concerned: Let the dead rest. *De mortuis nisi bonum.* You know what that means; you took Latin in school. Don't say anything about the dead unless it's something good."

She pulled herself up to her full height and looked triumphant, as if somehow quoting an ancient proverb in the original language had won the argument. Gwen hated it when she did things like that.

"And now, I believe we have had more than enough drama for one night," Cassie went on, still in her imperial mode, and she stood up and started for the door.

"Wait!" Gwen called out. "You still haven't said . . . What is it that you have against Stan?"

And why do I care so much what you think? Gwen wondered unhappily. But she did.

Cassie came back and sat down. "Please stop putting words in my mouth. I'm not 'against' the man. I simply feel that you are spending too much time with him."

"I like to be with him."

"You're only nineteen and, since you seem to want me to speak frankly, you're very naïve, even for nineteen. And he's naïve too. He's totally ignorant. A babe in the woods. You both are."

"How can you say that? Stan has his own business, for heaven's sake! And he's making a go of it too."

"And admirable as that is, I'm not talking about his ability to earn a living."

"If you think I'm the first girlfriend he's ever had, think again."

There was a pause. Cassie was choosing her words carefully now. "Gwen, the fact that you could even say something like that shows me how naïve you are. I'd be stunned to hear that Stanley Girard hasn't had many other 'girlfriends' in the course of his career." There was another, even longer pause. "But I would be willing to venture a guess that you are the first one of your—as you put it—status."

"Which means 'class.' "

Cassie shook her head in disbelief. "All right, if you must, yes. It is a question of class, but not in the way that you mean. As I see him, Stanley Girard is a man who is either so smug or so lazy that he refused an opportunity to better himself, and—"

"Because he didn't want to go to college? Who says going to college automatically means you're bettering yourself?"

"Society does."

"We're back to class again."

"We're where we always are when it come to that man. He has nothing to offer you. He wants to install air conditioners and refrigerators for a living, Gwen. There's nothing wrong in that, but you were raised for more. You live in a home of great refinement, you have been surrounded by people who believe in achievement. You are well read, you love the classics; great literature and music and art. You and Stan are not equals. And if there is one thing I've learned in this life it is that the man you choose must be your equal."

But now it was Gwen's turn to shake her head in disbelief. "I can't believe you're saying this. You're supposed to be a good person. That doesn't mean you just give a lot of money to charity, it means you keep an open mind about people. And you don't write them off because they can't quote some dead poet, or they aren't in a profession you find admirable."

"I would never do that, and you know it. I have standards, and I'm proud of it. But they are based on character traits, like discipline, a strong work ethic, and yes, a healthy ambition."

"And you know Stan is lacking in all of that? How? You haven't talked to him for more than twenty minutes."

"There are times when twenty minutes is more than enough."

"But you don't know him!"

"Then let's say, I'm giving you my impression of him. And I'm not such a bad judge of people."

Now it was Gwen's turn to get up and start for the door. But before she opened it she looked back. "I want you to know . . . I'm not going to stop seeing him."

"I haven't asked you to."

"And you can't drive him away. He's much too strong to allow himself to be scared off—even though you can't see that in him."

"I don't intend to meddle, Gwen. It's not my way, and you should know that."

But you don't like him. And I want you to! I wish I didn't but I do, Gwen thought. Frustrated with herself more than Cassie, she opened the door to leave the room.

Cassandra's voice stopped her. "Think about what I've said, for his sake as well as for yours, Gwen. He's in over his head." She closed her eyes as though what she was about to say was going to be difficult for her. "I've often wondered about your father . . . would he have done the things he did if he had married someone . . . at his own level? I had the money and the house and the business—it was all mine, and that was too much for him. Maybe if he hadn't had to prove himself . . . maybe he would have been different."

"Stan would never feel he had to prove anything," Gwen said strongly.

Cassandra opened her eyes and looked directly into Gwen's. "I thought that too—once."

There was no way to answer that, nothing more to be said. Gwen opened the door and walked out. But Cassie's words—her sad, bitter words—followed Gwen into the hallway. *I've often wondered about your father . . . would he have done the things he did if he had married someone . . . at his own level. . . .*

And Gwen was still so very young that she hadn't learned that there was no answer for a thought like that.

*   *   *

After Gwen stormed out of the den, Cassie sat staring with unseeing eyes at the fireplace. Anyone watching her would have said her mind was a blank. They would have been wrong. There was a familiar picture in her mind of Gwen taking her place as the owner of the glassworks, and the mistress of this very house. Now, more than ever, that was Cassie's dream, and to give up on her daughter would be unthinkable. Cassie had hoped they would find a new closeness in Paris, but thanks to Jewel Fairchild they had not. However, it could still come.

If only Gwen hadn't met Stanley Girard! The first thing Cassie had thought of when she met him was her own first marriage and the costly mistakes she had made. Not that Stan had anything in common with the late Bradford Greeley—except a lack of money or the means of ever earning much. But Stan with his earthiness and simplicity could be every bit as seductive as Bradford, especially to a dreamer like Gwen. She probably saw him as a working-class hero; a sort of glorified man of the people. Yes, that would appeal to her with her sense of justice and fair play. She would deliberately blind herself to the very real pitfalls in such a romance. And a romance was what she was embarked on—that much was clear. Cassie shud-

dered. All she wanted to do was protect
Gwen from the same kind of unhappi-
ness she had suffered. Was that so
wrong?

Chapter Seventeen

"The Wright Glass Museum is celebrating its fiftieth anniversary today and there's going to be a big blowout," Gwen told Stan during the phone call which had become a daily occurrence for them. It was now several days after her futile confrontation with Cassie. "The museum was built by Mother's father to showcase the Wright Studio Glass line," she went on. "That's the handmade division; it's considered one of the great producers of glass artwork—collectors buy a lot of their pieces and so do museums. . . ."

And I'm babbling on about all of this because I want to ask Stan something and I'm nervous. Get on with it, Gwen.

"Anyway, there's a luncheon and about a hundred speeches and then an awards ceremony. Mother and Walter will be doing all the rounds, and they'll be gone for hours, so I was wondering . . ." She drew a big breath. "I was wondering if you would like to come out here to the house to have lunch with me today." She waited for his answer and realized she was now holding her breath. She wanted him to say yes so very much. Part of the reason was defiance; she knew that. Cassie was opposed to Stan and not willing to listen to reason so Gwen was determined to bring him into the house behind her back. But she had another reason too. She wanted Stan to see the land she loved so much. The house didn't matter as far as she was concerned, and besides, he had already seen some of it—well, the foyer anyway. And he'd seen the gardens and the lawns bordered by the red maples. But he hadn't seen her magical spot on the hillside; he hadn't seen her forest. She wanted him to experience it. So she had asked him—boldly—to come to her house when her mother wasn't home. And because he was a proud man who would never go where he wasn't wanted, she was afraid he would say no.

"What time would you like me to show up?" he asked.

It was amazing the way he never ever failed her.

*   *   *

"Sometimes I almost don't like Cassie at all," Gwen told Stan. They had just finished lunch—sandwiches which Gwen, not the maid, had made and served. She'd brought them outside to him and they'd sat at one of the round tables with the big flowered umbrellas that Cassie had bought so Gwen could entertain her young friends. Her appropriate young friends. "I know it's wrong of me to feel the way I do about Mother, because she's such a *good* person. But sometimes, I want more . . . well, just more." Gwen faltered. Missy and Hank were sitting at her feet, hoping for scraps, and she reached down to scratch two sets of ears. "As long as life moves smoothly, Mother's satisfied. In my friends' houses you hear people argue. Sometimes you can even hear a plate crashing onto the kitchen floor—you know what I mean. In this house that would be a catastrophe! No, it would be . . . I don't know what it would be, because it's so impossible that I can't imagine it!" She giggled. "When I was in high school, mother decreed that for one evening a week we had to speak French during dinner. Poor Walter doesn't understand a word of it."

"How did he know what was going on?"

"He got very good at reading our body language. He said it was a help in his work—it gave him a new insight into his subjects when he was painting them."

"He sounds like a very . . . adaptable man."

"He has to be. He really loves Mother, and you have to be adaptable to live with her."

"I guess it just goes to show that there is someone for everyone," Stan said. He turned to her and there was something in the way he gazed at her that made her look away. He seemed to realize it, because he looked away himself and said, "But what was the reason for French at the dinner table?"

"Why, it was me, of course. So I could get into intermediate French right away when I went to college." She divided the sandwich crusts on her plate, and fed equal shares to the waiting dogs. "And the thing is, I don't want to go."

"Not even to the local college here? I thought Yale was the problem."

Gwen shook her head. "I just don't want to put off my life for another four years." Stan was looking at her intently now. "I'll always learn what I want to learn, that's the way I'm made. And I'll always find out what I need to know. So what's the point of going to classes I'll never remember because someone says I have to, or reading books I'll forget because someone says I can't pass their class unless I do?"

"There's no point," he said slowly. "But

you need a degree to be a teacher. I thought that was what you wanted to do."

She shrugged. "I had to pick something and I love children; playing with them, listening to them, just watching them discover the world. But taking on the responsibility for teaching them— I'm afraid I won't be much good at that."

"Then what will you do with your life?"

"Sometimes I think I'd like to write something."

"Well, go ahead. Do it."

"The trouble is, I don't know what I'd like to write." She threw down her napkin. "The truth is, I don't know what I want."

Stan laughed. "You can always marry me."

Then he stopped laughing. For a second his words hung in the air. Then one of the dogs, she couldn't have said which, moved and Stan reached down to pet it. When he looked up again there was a funny little smile on his face.

Did you mean that? She wanted to ask. No, she wanted to demand. Because as he sat there smiling in that strange way she couldn't read him. And she always had been able to. With him, what you saw was what you got; that was what she loved so much about him. But now, when it was so important, more important than it had ever been before, she didn't know what was going through his mind. She wanted to scream, *What are you thinking?*

* * *

What am I thinking? Stan thought. *I just asked her to marry me. I heard myself do it. First I laughed like some kind of idiotic teenager, then I said* You can always marry me. *What kind of proposal is that? I'll be lucky if she doesn't throw me out.*

"But if you don't want to marry me, and probably you don't," he heard himself say with that same stupid laugh—and what the hell was wrong with him for doing it again—"maybe we could see that favorite place of yours that you've been telling me about?"

Her face flushed crimson, in the way that he loved and she hated. She gave him a quick, jerky little nod. "I have to put the dogs in the house," she said tersely, and led the protesting canines off.

When she returned, the hottest of the flames in her cheeks had died down, but she didn't offer him her hand. They always held hands when they walked somewhere, but now her arms were crossed over her chest as if the perfectly warm day had suddenly turned cold. "This way." She indicated what looked like a hill—or maybe it was a mountain—behind them, and started marching toward it at a brisk pace. He had to walk fast to catch up with her.

Climbing up the hill, or mountain, whatever one called it, they were soon in the depths of a forest. Over Stanley's head was a canopy of branches. And everything was very still—so still he could hear the sound of his shoes as he walked. The only other sounds were the rustling of small creatures scurrying to get out of their way and the calls of birds in the trees. Stanley wasn't much of an outdoorsman—city apartments and small spaces were what he had known most of his life—but even he could appreciate the beauty of this place.

Gwen, still silent, with her arms wrapped around her, led the way upward, going deeper into the woods until all of a sudden, they were in a small clearing. She stopped abruptly and Stan looked around. In spots where sunlight came through the heavy leafage, the grass lay green and soft as a couch. A stump, aged to silvery gray, sat in the middle of the space and Gwen started to move to it, but he reached out his hand and stopped her. Then—and later on he was never quite sure how it happened—they were lying down together on that soft sweet grass, with the ribbons of sunlight playing over them and the warm breezes ruffling Gwen's hair. It was as if the place and the mellow season and the time were all perfectly prepared just for them.

*   *   *

Gwen had thought she was going to be afraid, but as she gave herself over to the ecstasy of her body and its wants, she knew that she would never again experience a closeness like this, a feeling of being joined so totally and blissfully. And after they had reached the moment of release, Stan folded his body into hers and held her, and she truly thought that there was nothing more she could ever want from life.

Often afterward, she would ask herself how this event had changed her. It had made her feel whole, she decided, after struggling to find the right word. Stan had made her see what she was and what she was not. She was not what Cassie called a "hippie," by which she meant some carefree person who lived a carefree life. Gwen knew that was not her. But she was not serious in the common sense of the word. She was an odd duck. And because of Stan she didn't seem to worry about that the way she had. Because of Stan she was starting to be satisfied with herself.

But all of those revelations were to come later. At that moment as she lay on her couch of grass with a tendril of Stan's hair lying like dark silk on her chest, she knew one thing only.

Stan loves me and I love him. I've never been as happy as I am now.

* * *

As if in a state of shock, Cassie lay back in her chair. She had read Gwen's letter over and over; she had even examined the envelope, postmarked "Paris," as if there could have been some hidden meaning there that she had failed to see. *Foolish, foolish child!* she thought. *Nineteen years old and not having the faintest idea of what she needs or what is right for her, or how to fend for herself! Why couldn't she just have had an affair? If it had been a matter of hormones—something that was probably long overdue in Gwen's case—that resulted in a mad dash for Paris and a romantic interlude, I wouldn't have blamed her. Not really. Heaven knows, I've seen enough of that in my family. I probably would have scolded enough for propriety's sake and let it go. But why on earth did Gwen have to tie herself up with this nobody! Why marry him? Think of the trouble down the line; the lawyers, the court, the bitter anger—all that is now invisible, but it is inevitable and it will come to the surface when this marriage ends. And it will end.*

Cassie's head throbbed. She didn't want to guess how much her blood pressure had soared. From the library, where she was sitting, she looked out at the back lawn and the depressing rain that dripped out of the trees and from the pretty lanterns, which had been installed by the man who had caused this headache. Stanley Girard wasn't worthy of Gwen's little finger; he was certainly not worthy of the sacrifices she was making for him: There would be no college for Gwen now, and no wedding where she would wear a beautiful lace veil. Cassie hadn't realized until that very moment how much she had been looking forward to Gwen's wedding day. She would have had all the bells and whistles for her daughter, she would have watched with such pride, such a sense of a job well done, as Walter walked Gwen down the aisle and gave her hand in marriage to . . . a man who was worthy. A man who would grace the

Wright name. A man who was not Stanley Girard!

"I thought I'd find you in here, after you
disappeared on me," Walter's voice said
behind her. She hadn't heard him come
in. But now he was holding out a cup of
coffee and a plate of her favorite cookies. She shook her head at both and he
put them down. "You're going to wear a
hole in that letter," he said as he sat in
the chair next to hers.

"She's doomed herself. She'll have a
dreary existence with a man who
doesn't know which side is up and she'll
have a house full of children—heaven
only knows how many—whether they
can afford them or not. And don't try to
tell me he won't insist on that because
he's the type that will!"

"Actually, I think Gwen will be the one
who wants the house full of children
whether they can afford them or not.
Stanley strikes me as a very practical
person."

"Well, they had better not turn to me
for help."

"You don't mean that."

Cassie sighed. "Of course I don't. I'd never let Gwen suffer—or her children."

"I think the point is a moot one. My sense of your new son-in-law is he'd rather be boiled in oil than take help from anyone." He paused and took a cookie from the plate. "And you haven't made a secret of your feelings about him."

"You think I'm being awful—don't you? That I'm embarrassed because my daughter married a blue-collar worker."

"Of course not! No one works harder than you do, or values hard work more." He looked at her thoughtfully. "I think your real problem with Stanley Girard is that he's such a worthy opponent."

"I don't like him because he's a half-educated man without strength or ambition."

"He has plenty of ambition in his own way, and more than enough strength to challenge your hold on Gwen. That's what disturbs you so."

"I do not have 'a hold' on Gwen! I want her to be her own woman and to make her own way."

"Someday. But perhaps . . . not just yet?"

She bit her lip. "No. I don't think she's ready."

"Clearly, she does." He got up and came over to stroke her cheek. "Cassie, my darling, you can't undo the marriage. So try to give it a chance. That's all anybody can do. If it's going to fall apart, it will do so without anybody's help."

Chapter Eighteen

Patsy Allen had proved to be a far better businesswoman than Jewel had given her credit for. It had been two years since Gwen Wright's birthday party, when Patsy had embarrassed Jewel by handing out her business cards and turning herself into a walking advertisement for Times Past. Jewel had to admit that the ploy—embarrassing as it had been—had worked. Several of the women Patsy had approached that night had checked out the store and found that Patsy did indeed have a great eye for the kind of classic couture they couldn't find anywhere else. More important, they had mentioned the store to their daughters—at a time when the girls were watching popular movie stars wear vintage gowns on the red carpet at various awards ceremonies. Times Past had become a fad with the well-heeled youngsters who had an endless supply of credit cards, and doting parents who cheerfully paid them off. The shop had done so well that Patsy was ready to expand her operation. "We're going to move to the Algonquin Mall," she told Jewel excitedly. It was early morning, and the store was still empty, so Jewel and Patsy were in the back drinking the coffee Jewel brought in every morning. "We'll be doubling our space, and hiring two more salesgirls," Patsy went on. "And here's the best part: I'll be traveling more on buying trips, so I'm going to promote you. You're my new manager, Jewel! Can you believe how far we've come? And it's only been two years!" If she could have produced a trumpet fanfare to go along with her announcement she would have done it. Instead she stared expectantly at Jewel waiting for squeals of delight—or possibly tears of joy.

Jewel wanted to weep, but not from happiness. She'd never felt so frustrated and trapped in her life. The big promotion Patsy was promising her would mean a raise, but it wouldn't be big enough to get Jewel out of her little apartment over the deli or to buy her a car that actually ran.

Two years, she thought hopelessly. *I thought I'd be on my way by now. I thought something would have happened.* But nothing had. She was still working for Patsy, and she was still barely getting by. Nothing had changed except she had gotten a lot better at selling dusty old clothes to spoiled brats.

Patsy was looking disappointed at her lack of enthusiasm. And even though Patsy always said she and Jewel were friends, the truth was, Patsy was Jewel's boss. And you didn't disappoint the boss. Jewel forced herself to smile and she threw her arms around the woman who wrote out her paycheck. "Oh, Patsy!" she managed to squeal, "This is fabulous! I'm so happy, I don't know how to thank you."

Fortunately, at that moment three customers walked in and she didn't have to keep on pretending to be thrilled. Patsy gulped down the rest of her coffee, whispered "Show time!" and headed for the front of the store, expecting Jewel to follow.

But Jewel knew if she had to wait on a trio of over-indulged rich kids this morning she was going to do something disastrous—like tell the fat one that there wasn't a dress in the store that would hide her stomach. So she said, "You go on. I want to check the invoices." As Patsy hustled out to greet the girls, Jewel took a drink of her coffee and tried to make her mind a blank. But of course the human mind never will cooperate when you ask it to do that. As the warm, bitter liquid eased its way down Jewel's throat, the thought that popped into her head was of Gwen Wright.

Surprising as it might seem, Jewel often thought about Gwen. During the past two years of stagnation and frustration the only thought which had been comforting to Jewel was the reflection that no matter what kind of mess she'd made of her life, Gwen had done worse. Jewel could still remember the morning when she'd opened the *Wrightstown Gazette* and read that Gwendolyn Wright had gotten herself married. Not to an eligible young scion of a wealthy and privileged family, no, dull Gwen had found a plumber. Or he was maybe an electrician, Jewel had been too stunned to pay attention. She just knew that the man was a nobody who worked with his hands, as her pop used to say.

I wish I'd been a fly on the wall when Queen Cassie heard that! Jewel thought now. She closed her eyes, and tried to picture the fit the woman must have thrown. But on this morning, trying to imagine Cassie Wright's reaction to Gwen's terrible marriage didn't make Jewel feel any better. She was too miserable about her own life and her own predicament.

She was in her mid-twenties; before she knew it, she'd be closing in on thirty.

True, she was still beautiful enough to attract the attention of most of the men in a room when she entered it, but that wasn't going to last forever. And her friendly, high-energy warmth that had always been such an asset with the opposite sex was beginning to wear thin. It wasn't as if she hadn't tried to find the right man—she wasn't like Gwen Wright who had thrown herself away on Mr. No One. Jewel had screened her potential suitors carefully—so carefully, in fact, that there had only been two of them in the past two years. But in spite of her best efforts, one turned out to be married and the other was a doctor who was so deeply in debt after his divorce that he might as well have been unemployed. Fortunately, she hadn't made the mistake of going to bed with either of them. She'd never been to bed with any man. She intended to wait until she had a ring on her finger—one with a nice big diamond on it—and a lifestyle to match the gem. But she was no closer to the ring, the lifestyle, or the Prince Charming who would accompany them than she had been on that rainy day so long ago when she'd taken the train to the country and seen Paradise in Cassandra Wright's gleaming white house. The only difference was, now there were a couple of lines on Jewel's forehead that no amount of face cream could erase, and she knew that the clock was ticking. She just didn't know what to do about it.

She put down her coffee cup, and made her way to the front of the shop where Patsy was trying to convince the fat girl that the size six skirt she'd chosen wouldn't fit. The fat girl was the kind of customer who treated a salesgirl like dirt. Where, oh where, was Prince Charming when you needed him?

*   *   *

"Jeff Henry," said Patsy. "Isn't he that man you talked to at Gwen Wright's birthday party?" She and Jewel had taken time off that afternoon so Patsy could sign the paperwork for the loan she needed to build her new store. "Come with me, I need moral support," she'd said to Jewel. "I've never borrowed this much money in my life and

I'm scared to death!" Now they were in the lobby of The Amber, the glitzy new office building that housed all the major businesses in Wrightstown except the glassworks. Patsy had been scanning the directory in the lobby to find the loan offices of the Penobscot National Bank, and she was pointing to an entire column of the directory which indicated that the two top floors of The Amber were occupied by a company called JeffSon. A high-tech logo that looked like the tail of a rocket streaking through space accompanied the company's name. The owner of the company was listed as Jeff Henry. Although Jewel hadn't learned the name of the man in the navy blue blazer when she'd met him, she'd caught an interview he'd given on a Sunday morning television show and she had recognized him.

"Yes," she said. "Jeff Henry is the man I talked to."

"Didn't you tell me he could be a big success someday if he put his mind to it?"

"Actually I said he could be a success if he didn't think too much."

"Well, he must have heard you," Patsy said. "Rents in The Amber don't come cheap and I don't even like to think what the two top floors must be costing him. It's obvious that your Mr. Henry is doing very well for himself."

"He's not my Mr. Henry," Jewel said automatically. But when she thought about it . . . he *had* been attracted to her that night two years ago. And it hadn't been a surface-y flirtation; he'd told her things about himself. Personal things. She had a feeling he didn't do that with everyone. On the other hand, he hadn't bothered to get her name and he certainly hadn't made any attempt to find her since that initial meeting. Still . . . Jewel looked at the sleek logo on the directory. He hadn't been married two years ago. Of course, everything can change in that amount of time—especially for a rich bachelor. But what if it hadn't? What if there still was no Mrs. Jeff Henry? It would be easy to find out if he was in the building today; she'd just run out to the parking garage where she'd noticed that the premium spaces had names on them and see if there was a car in his. What did she have to lose? She opened her purse and started fishing around.

"Oh, no," she moaned. "I can't find my credit card case. Patsy, I've got to go back to the car and see if I left it there. I'll catch up with you."

*   *   *

According to the extremely helpful parking attendant, Jeff Henry did have one of the VIP parking slots, and his car had been there, but he'd driven it out earlier. He often did that on Wednesdays, said the attendant, and he would probably be back in three hours. The attendant was willing to make that prediction because whenever Mr. Henry took off on a Wednesday his car was always back in that amount of time. It was a sports car, one with a foreign name that the attendant couldn't remember. Italian, he thought it might be, and it began with an L. Whatever it was, the car had cost enough to pay for a house for most people. Jewel gave the attendant her most dazzling smile when she thanked him.

It was just as well that Jeff Henry

wasn't in the building, she thought as she hurried off to join the waiting Patsy. Jewel needed time to think through her strategy. She didn't want to make any mistakes with Jeff Henry.

Chapter Nineteen

⁓⁓

Horaceville was only twenty miles north of Wrightstown, and it was built on the banks of the same river, but the two cities couldn't have been more different. For one thing, Horaceville was much smaller, and unlike bustling, busy Wrightstown, it seemed to be preserved in a time gone by. The original streetlights still illuminated Main Street, which ran through the heart of Horaceville. Oak and chestnut trees shaded the town hall. The police and fire departments were brick with white trim, in pseudocolonial style. Not far from them were the movie theater and the shops. At Christmastime, bright lights adorned the streets; on the Fourth of July, flags waved. People lived on the cross streets, which, after a few miles, petered out into roads where the suburbs were spreading.

Jeff pulled his Lamborghini into a driveway next to a modest frame house in an area which had been recently rezoned as both commercial and residential—a big change from the days when Jeff had grown up here. Back then this street—his street—had been lined with the homes of families who considered themselves upper-middle-class. It was the kind of neighborhood where two salaries were not desperately needed and most of the mothers stayed home to take care of the children—at least until they were in school full time.

Now there was a bar and grill in the middle of the block, and a dry cleaner's shop on the corner. Several of the houses had two or more mailboxes on the front porch suggesting that whoever owned them was renting out unused rooms to bring in extra income. To put it simply, the area was going downhill— an argument Jeff was going to try to make. Once again. He turned off the purring automobile that was the latest of his toys, and sat for a few seconds trying to put together his thoughts before he went into the house. He would need to be at his most forceful, he knew.

*　　*　　*

"Jeffie, I don't know how many different ways I have to find to tell you that I don't want to leave my home," said Jeff's father. "Besides, where would you have me go? That 'assisted-living facility' into which you are trying to push me would not allow me to take Sammy. I would be allotted one room with no space for my library!" Sammy was Dad's cat. Dad's "library" consisted of the books that filled the shelves on two walls of the room he called his den. They were in that room right now. Jeff looked around. When the house had been built in 1910, this room had been a second parlor meant to be used by the lady of the house for reading and paying bills. It was the smallest room in the house—which was already quite small—and it faced the street so the windows were usually kept closed against the traffic noise. As a result the air was stale. When Jeff's mother had decorated the home some forty years ago, she'd had the room paneled with a dark wainscoting and it had been painted a dark green. Dad's desk was also dark—and immense. The sofa and wing chairs, now cracked with age, were upholstered in oxblood leather. The effect Mother had been trying to create was that of the study of an English country don. What she'd achieved was a stuffy little space crowded with furniture that was way too big. The rest of the house was furnished in the same way, with dark antiques, some of which were quite valuable, all of which required much larger rooms. Mother and Dad had adored every cramped inch of their home.

"We are simple academics," his father liked to say as he sipped what he referred to as his postprandial brandy. "We don't need the trappings of success, just a few old treasures—our books, our antiques, our prints, and of course our music." And Mother, who was not sipping brandy, because that was a masculine prerogative, and besides, she still had to wash the dishes, would nod and smile. His parents were so proud of their status as intellectuals—a self-proclaimed status, but never mind, it was more than enough to impress the neighbors. Dad was a professor of art history at Wrightstown College. One of his prouder accomplishments was the fact that one of his prize students, a man named Edward Lawrence, had become the curator of the Wright Glass Museum. Edward still held the position after twenty years.

Mother had been a high-school English teacher, and she, too, worked in Wrightstown, although the family lived twenty minutes away in Horaceville. "Wrightstown is not for us," she would say with her kindest—and most condescending—smile. "I'm afraid it's a little too . . . well, commercial. Horaceville is much more charming." What Mother did not say was that there would have been no way for Father to be a big fish in a small pond in Wrightstown—that position was already filled by the Wright family—but to Horaceville he was impressive. So Mother and Dad had lived happily in their ugly little house surrounded by neighbors who were awed by Dad's doctorate, his vocabulary, and his successful student, Edward Lawrence the curator—although few of them could have told you what a museum curator did.

Then four years ago Mother had become ill and Dad had taken early retirement to stay home and care for her until she died two years later. Since that time Dad and Sammy had continued living in the house Dad could no longer maintain, in the neighborhood that was quietly slipping. Dad was quietly slipping too—his meals seemed to consist of potato chips and packaged cookies, and Jeff suspected that his brandy sipping was now starting at noon.

Jeff sniffed the air. There had been a leak in the roof which Dad hadn't gotten around to repairing, and now a faint smell of mold permeated the whole house. Meanwhile the old man turned away from his shelves full of books to glare at Jeff. "Well, son?" he demanded. "Could I take all my treasures with me to that warehouse for the ancient you selected for me?"

"Dad, I've already told you, if you don't like the idea of Shady Manor, you can build a house near me."

"In Wrightstown."

"The outskirts. There's a new development going up outside of town."

"Thank you, I've seen those new developments. Raping the land of trees to put up huge ostentatious mansions that have neither artistic merit nor architectural interest."

At least they're not shabby and pretentious, Jeff thought, but he tried to be patient. "Yours will not be ostentatious. You can work with an architect and design it yourself. It can be an exact replica of this place if that's what you want." He hadn't been able to keep the disdain out of his voice when he'd said that last sentence and his father instantly picked up on it.

"This 'place' as you call it was a good home to you for your formative years, and don't you forget it."

Jeff bit his tongue; these belligerent moods were coming more frequently than they used to. He wondered if the brandy bottle had been in use before noon.

"And how will I pay for this brand-new house that is going to be built to my specifications?" Dad went on. "Tell me that, if you please."

"As I've said, I'll pay for it. God knows I don't expect you to do it!" But then Jeff looked at the man. And Jeff saw how alone, and how frightened he was. "Dad, please," he said more gently. "Let me do this for you. I can afford it and it would make me very happy."

His father sat wearily in one of the crumbling wing chairs. Sammy, who had been waiting for just such a moment, leapt into his lap and Dad began absently petting the old cat. "Tell me again what this business of yours is,

Jeffie," he said. "I never seem to be able to understand it."

Jeff sat across from him. "JeffSon is one of the major distributors of electricity and natural gas in the United States. We're involved in the development, as well as the building and the daily running, of power plants and pipelines."

"And how did my son, the philosophy major, get into such a business?"

"Dad, you know I dropped my philosophy major in my sophomore year and went into business administration."

"Yes. More's the pity."

"I'm very happy with my choice. I'm sorry if you're not."

His father sighed and looked down at the purring cat in his lap. "I would never dream of trying to impose my will on you. Please continue, Jeffie. I would like to know how a man working for a small brokerage house in Wrightstown becomes the owner of a multimillion-dollar corporation that sells natural gas and electricity."

Not for the first time in his life, Jeff realized that he should never underestimate his father. Dad liked to say that he was a man of the mind with no interest in worldly affairs, but the question he'd just asked was astute. And the answer was that there had been a series of mergers, some of which were frankly questionable, followed by takeovers of small companies by larger holding companies that had skated perilously close to violating several FTC regulations, although the deals had not been investigated, thanks to some good friends in high places. And when all the smoke cleared, Jeff had emerged as the CEO of the newly formed and branded company called JeffSon. He had offices in New York and Texas, as well as the glossy two floors he and his company occupied in The Amber. He kept his base in Wrightstown mostly for sentimental reasons. And because being in such an out-of-the-way place, and forcing other businessmen to come to his turf, was a demonstration of his power.

"The ways in which companies acquire assets are very complicated, Dad. I started with a small natural gas company in the Midwest and merged it with a similar one in Texas. We used the collateral from that new entity to leverage the acquisition of other similar assets in the natural gas industry, and eventually we branched out into the area of electricity."

"And what do you know about these commodities you sell?"

"I don't sell them, exactly; I distribute them. And I don't have to know the details about the power plants or the gas companies. I hire people for that."

"Then what do you do?"

"I oversee the financial end, as well as the marketing and the legal issues, and of course I decide where and how we should expand next."

"Expand? Aren't you big enough, Jeffie?"

That was another good question; one that both scared and excited Jeff. Because while it sounded fine to say that he didn't need to know the details of the businesses he was managing, the truth was, when you were flying blind you could make mistakes. But it was Jeff's belief that you had to fly blind at times in order to grow, and you had to grow in order to survive. If you lost your nerve and stopped growing, the sharks in the water around you would smell blood and you would find yourself the target of the same kind of financial attacks that you yourself had launched when you were on your way up. Besides, Jeff wanted his company to grow; he wanted to be the CEO of the biggest and the best. People admired him and he liked it. When you came from a home where the standards for excellence were Plato, Shakespeare, and Mozart it was a heady feeling to find yourself hailed as a wunderkind. So it was worth it to fly blind and risk falling.

"There's no such thing as being too big," he told his father cheerfully. "But I came here to talk about you. Now, since Shady Manor is out, I'm assuming you'll move to Wrightstown. We can probably get rid of this house in a couple of months if we price it right, and you and Sammy can stay with me until I have your new place built."

"You know, son, I think I'd rather stay put" was the infuriating reply.

"Why, for Chrissakes?" Jeff exploded. "Why do you want to live in an old dump with a leaking roof in a lousy neighborhood when you could have the best of everything?" But even as he said the words he knew what his father's mawkish answer would be. *I have the best of everything right here.* And then he'd go on with some kind of garbage about materialism and how it corroded the mind. But his father surprised him.

"I'm afraid I don't trust the business you're in, Jeffie," he said briskly. "I know I'm not an expert in such things, but it all sounds a little too much like an old-fashioned Ponzi scheme for my taste." He looked around his den. "I've paid off the mortgage on this place, and the taxes are low. I can manage here on my pension. I'd rather not take any chances."

And that was that. Jeff argued that his father's lack of faith in him was insulting; he pointed out that JeffSon was being hailed in financial circles as one of the most exciting new companies of the year; and he said that his father was just being stubborn. Nothing moved the old man.

"At least let me pay to get your damn roof fixed!" Jeff finally said. "And I'm going to hire a housekeeper to cook for you and to clean up after you."

His father bowed his head and thanked him. Then he said, "I didn't mean to hurt your feelings, Jeffie. I know you meant well. But I'm too old to gamble."

*　　　*　　　*

His father walked him to his car. When Jeff had bought the Lamborghini he'd debated between red and a neon yellow and finally settled on the yellow, which now looked garish in this drab neighborhood. "Oh, my," said his father when he caught sight of the car. "Is that yours?"

"Yes." Even to his own ears, Jeff sounded like a sulky child.

"It certainly is . . . splashy," said his father. Then instead of his usual handshake, he enveloped his son in an awkward hug. "Beware of Faustian bargains, Jeffie," he said.

*　　　*　　　*

NPR was playing Verdi's Requiem. The stately lament suited Jeff's mood, and as he drove back to Wrightstown alongside the winding river, he turned up the volume on his car radio. The visit with his father had, as such visits often did, brought to the surface thoughts that Jeff usually tried to keep buried. Contrary to what he'd told his father, Jeff had been ambivalent about his choice to drop his beloved philosophy courses and go into business administration when he was in college. And the ambivalence had gotten worse when he'd begun working. The daily routine of buying and selling stocks and bonds, the endless phone calls to clients and prospective clients bored him until he felt he couldn't bear it another second. He lost track of the number of times he'd decided that he was going to quit, get his doctorate, and spend the rest of his life teaching eager young minds about Sophocles and Kant.

But then there would be a phone call from his parents, or worse, he'd go home for a visit, and he would remember once again the stuffy rooms in the dingy little house, and the aged car that—fingers crossed—had to last through one more season. He'd remember the much-dreamed-of trip to Europe that was always postponed for lack of money, the months of scrimping for the annual trek to Boston for one night at the opera or the ballet, and the look of longing on his mother's face—quickly masked—when a neighbor gave his wife a pair of diamond earrings that Dad could never have afforded. And Jeff would go back to the purgatory of his job, determined to become one of those who never had to think twice about buying opera tickets, or airplane tickets, or diamond earrings.

But even with all of that, when the opportunity to get into the risky business that was now his had been presented to him, he'd been hesitant. In fact, he probably would have passed it up if he hadn't met that girl at Gwendolyn Wright's birthday party—the girl whose name he did not know. He thought about her sometimes, the lovely oval face, the ebony hair, and the ruby red mouth, with its remarkably white teeth.

I know what it means to want, she'd said. *Get over your doubts.* And he had.

The result had been JeffSon. What would that girl say now, he wondered, if he were to find her and tell her that she was responsible for the creation of one of the hottest new businesses in the country? What would she do if he were to take her on a tour of his office high in the sky over Wrightstown? Would her extraordinary violet blue eyes shine if he showed her his offices in Texas and New York? Would she gasp with pleasure if he took her for a ride in the purring beast that was his car and showed her the drawings for the home he was going to build? Her energy had been like a life force on that night two years ago, and he could use some of it right now. Maybe she could erase from his mind the look on his father's face and the words he'd said. *Beware of Faustian bargains, Jeffie.*

The Requiem was over, and so was his drive; the river straightened as he reached Wrightstown. He checked the time; it was not quite six. His visit to his father had taken longer than usual. He could go to the hotel where he'd been camping out while he waited for his house to be built, take a shower, order an early room service dinner, and call it a day. Or he could go back to the office and see if that call to Brazil had gone through. He opted for the office and Brazil.

*   *   *

Jewel was ready to give up. The parking lot attendant had said that Jeff Henry would be back in three hours, so she'd claimed to have a headache, and asked Patsy to give her the rest of the day off. After dawdling around the lobby of Jeff's office building for almost two hours, she'd returned to the parking lot with a magazine and sat on one of the concrete benches near the entrance to wait for him to drive in. But after four and a half hours, the man hadn't shown up. She'd lost half a day's pay and her left leg had fallen asleep from sitting so long. She stood up, stamped her foot on the ground to get the circulation going, and was starting toward the lot exit when she heard a roar behind her. She turned and saw a yellow car whipping into the garage. But this was not any car; this was the kind of car you dreamed about, the kind of car you would kill to drive just once. She didn't have words for what she would do to own a car like that.

*   *   *

Jeff parked in his spot and got out of the Lamborghini. His gray mood had darkened to black, and he was beginning to regret his decision to come back to work. Even if he could get through to Brazil, after all his father's doubts and warnings he wasn't in the right frame of mind to conduct delicate negotiations. He really should go to the hotel. But that would be depressing too. He locked the car.

"Hey," a feminine voice called out. He turned and there in front of him, miraculously and unbelievably, were the oval face, the blue-black hair, the spectacular eyes, and the smile that he'd been thinking about on the way back to Wrightstown.

"What the hell is your name?" he demanded.

"Jewel," she said. "So, are you rich yet?"

Chapter Twenty

Jewel made Jeff laugh. She was so pure, so unabashed in her pleasure at the things his money could buy. A gold bangle for her wrist, a dress from Sofia's, a trip to New York in a chartered plane, a night at the Waldorf after seeing the season's biggest Broadway musical—all of these things filled her with a child-like delight that banished his doubts and made his father's warning about bargains with the devil seem like nothing more than the fears of a tired old man. When Jeff was with Jewel he was free to enjoy his custom-made suits and shirts, his expensive offices done by the designer of the moment, and his "splashy" sports car. When he said he wanted a yacht Jewel saw nothing wrong in it; when he voiced the wish for a private plane, she thought he should have a fleet of them.

True, she wasn't interested in the eleventh-century Book of Hours he'd purchased for an enormous sum after weeks of long-distance discussion with a rare book dealer in London, and when they were in Manhattan she preferred to spend her day at a spa instead of accompanying him to the auction where he was bidding on a Matisse. What excited her was knowing that they'd gotten a table at a restaurant where the waiting time was normally six months.

But she was an asset in other ways. Jewel had met most of the men with whom he did business at various dinners and parties and she was a big favorite with them, as well as with their wives and girlfriends. In a couple of cases she was friends with both the wife and the girlfriend, and managed the dual loyalty with a dexterity that was a little unnerving to Jeff, although his male acquaintances saw it differently. "You've found yourself a gal who can be friends with both of those women and not tell all she knows? Marry her tomorrow!" said one.

"Jewel is the right name for her," said another, "because that's what she is. Beautiful and fun and she's willing to do anything to please you."

"She's sexy as hell," said a third.

And that last part certainly was true—but then with that body and that face there was no way she could avoid being sexy. When they went to dinner with the married men and their wives she dressed sedately—she told him once she'd learned the hard way to do that around other women. When she and Jeff went out by themselves, she dressed to attract attention, which he didn't mind since she also made it clear that she only had eyes for him. She was flirtatious with him and so overtly affectionate that it probably would have stunned his friends to know that when he and Jewel stayed at the Waldorf, the separate rooms he booked for them were not just for show. She slept chastely in hers, and he stayed equally chaste in his. Because, irony of irony, jaded and cynical Jeff Henry, who had had women throwing themselves at him since he was in his teens, had fallen for a girl who had announced on their third date that she was saving herself for marriage. It seemed Jeff had been right about her when he'd met her that first night: Jewel Fairchild was full of surprises.

At first he had taken her statement as a challenge, and he had tried to seduce her.

Jewel had wept. "I'm sorry," she'd sobbed—she was one of the few women he knew who became prettier when she cried; the violet eyes became even more luminous and the porcelain cheeks flushed a lovely pink. "It's not that I don't want you, because I do, you must know that."

He did, or at least, he thought he did. She seemed as urgent as he was when they kissed, and he could have sworn that it was as difficult for her to pull away as it was for him. But she had her standards. And her rules. "Even if it means losing you, and you know I'd die if that happened," she'd said. "This is the only way I know how to be."

After the initial surprise, he found it rather charming. For all her seeming worldliness, she had held on to this old-fashioned, romantic notion since childhood. And the truth was, she wasn't altogether wrong. There was something intensely romantic—and exciting—about holding back. Soon, his desire for her was far more intense than any he could remember feeling before. He began resenting the comments of men who found her so attractive. When one of his acquaintances spoke about Jewel as "a nice piece of arm candy" he was furious.

And yet . . . and yet. He couldn't seem to make the next move. The one he knew she was waiting for. He couldn't seem to ask the question that hovered on the tip of his tongue: *Will you marry me, Jewel?*

When he was alone; when she was not

in front of him with her wide smile and her spectacular beauty wiping away all rational thought, he wondered whether he and she really had much in common. He was a reader; she was not. He had graduated from college at the top of his class. She cheerfully said that she'd found it a pain getting through high school. But then he would ask himself how important was it really, to have what is called "learning"? Mere *facts* can be taught if there is need. He wanted her and he wanted her for keeps—wasn't that enough? And yet . . . and yet.

He took her to Horaceville to meet his father. And he knew as soon as they walked in the door that it had been a mistake.

"You wouldn't believe how that Lamborghini drives, Mr. Henry!" Jewel had said as they sat down to have tea in the dark room Jeff's mother had called the "drawing room." "It was better than flying. I'd never flown before Jeff took me to New York. In a private plane no less!" Artless, and unknowing as she was, she didn't seem to sense the chill that had filled the room. She hadn't seen Dad's eyes narrow, hadn't understood that she was being vulgar. "You must be so proud of Jeff," she went on.

"I'm afraid I don't believe in being proud of another man's accomplishments," Dad said stiffly. "Jeff is, after all, an adult. I would hardly wish to bask in his reflected glory. Not that I can see anything particularly glorious in the ownership of an automobile."

"But this isn't just any automobile!" Jewel protested with her most sparkling smile. "This is a Lamborghini! It cost six figures!"

Dad's eyes were now slits. "Ah," he said, "a chariot for the nouveau riche." He turned to Jeff. "Son, the next time you are in Boston you must take in the new exhibit at the Gardner. A former student of mine writes that it is quite extraordinary." He turned to Jewel. "Do you like Renoir, Miss Fairchild? Or are you one of those who say his work looks like it came out of a pastry tube?"

"I don't know anything about it," Jewel said. Then as Jeff tried to think of a way to rescue her, his father launched into a lecture on the Impressionists, only stopping every once in a while to ask Jewel questions which she could not answer. After that he launched into the fields of literature and music, interspersed with more questions. It was an exercise designed to expose Jewel's ignorance, and there was no way to stop it without embarrassing her. Fortunately she didn't seem to notice, as she admitted to not knowing who Schopenhauer, Rachmaninoff, T. S. Eliot, Virginia Woolf, Matisse, and Monet were. She had heard of Jane Austen because of the movies that had been made from Austen's novels, but she confessed that sitting through films made from old books made her sleepy.

When Jeff suggested that it was time for them to be on their way, Dad didn't even bother with the ritual of urging them to stay on. Jewel excused herself to powder her nose—a prissy euphemism which won her more narrowed eyes from Dad—and as soon as she was out of the room, Dad began his diatribe. "Jeffie, you cannot be contemplating anything more serious than a fling with that girl. I'll admit she is beautiful—what we would have called in my day a looker. But I would be amazed to hear that she's ever read a book that wasn't one of those ghastly self-help tomes. And as for her taste in music . . . I'm not sure I've ever met anyone before who didn't like Mozart. What do the two of you find to talk about? But I suppose the point is that you do not talk. Very well, as I said, have your fun, but for God's sake don't tie yourself down. Because someday you will wish to converse with your mate, and for that you will want a woman who is your equal in intellect, education, and breeding. . . ."

Dad was doing nothing more than saying out loud exactly what Jeff had been thinking privately, but hearing his own objections coming out of his father's mouth made Jeff realize how incredibly shallow, mean-spirited, and unimportant they were. He should beg Jewel to marry him—he should do it this very day!

And yet . . . and yet. When he was alone with Jewel in his car, taking her back to Wrightstown, he still didn't do it.

Why is that? he asked himself as they drove alongside the shining river. *She's good for me, this darling creature with the wide, warm smile.* She lightened the burden of guilt he carried. She washed away his doubts. And she was so incredibly beautiful.

And yet . . . and yet. They reached Wrightstown, and he still hadn't spoken. He pulled up in front of the deli where Jewel lived and leaned over for the good-night kiss that would end with them tangled like teenagers in the front seat of his car. Since Jewel had never asked him to come upstairs to her apartment, and she'd always refused to visit his suite in the hotel, they were left with the front seat of his car. But tonight when he leaned in, Jewel did not turn to him. He sat back.

"You've been awfully quiet," he said.

"Obviously, I don't have a lot to say. Not about the things that are important to you, like artists and writers and all of that."

So she *had* realized what Dad was doing. "Hey, don't confuse my old man with me," he said. "I'm the one who bought a Lamborghini."

It wasn't much of a joke but he thought it would at least win him a smile. Instead, she turned to him and said, "Yes, and your father is the one who thinks I'm not good enough for you." Then before he could protest, she asked, "Would you like to come upstairs tonight?"

They both knew what she was really saying, and for a moment the thought ran through his mind: *I won!* But then he looked at her. There was weariness in her eyes, and defeat. And he knew that was not what he wanted. Not at all.

"No," he said gently. "I won't go upstairs with you tonight, Jewel, my darling. But I have a question to ask you." And he took her hands in his. *This is right, what I am about to do,* he told himself. *This is so right!*

"Jewel Fairchild, will you marry me?" he asked.

He thought the neighbors up and down the block could probably hear her shriek of joy.

*   *   *

Jewel Fairchild, now Jewel Henry, was on her honeymoon! She stood on the terrace outside the mansion-sized "cottage" her husband had rented—on a private Caribbean island, if you please— and looked out at the beach of sugary white sand below. She still couldn't believe it had actually happened. After that awful visit to Jeff's father—the mean old goat—she'd been sure she'd lost Jeff for good. Even though Jeff thought he didn't care about his father's opinion, any fool could see that he still did, and every time the old goat had tripped her up with a question about one of those dead people with a name you couldn't pronounce who had painted or written something, she'd been sure it was the end of her. Because the old man's message couldn't have been clearer: *This girl isn't your kind, Jeffie*—his father actually called him that—*get rid of her.*

Even now, with her three-carat yellow diamond ring safely in place on the fourth finger of her left hand, the thought of losing Jeff made her shudder. Not just because he was rich enough to give her the life she'd wanted so desperately— although that was the biggest part of it, she never tried to lie to herself about that. But she would also miss the man. Because in spite of all his success, Jeff needed her. She gave him permission to ignore his father's influence and be ambitious and driven and, yes, to be as greedy as he wanted to be. He needed her for that permission, and no one had needed Jewel since her mother died. She felt important again for the first time in years. She never wanted to lose that feeling.

And she could have lost everything so easily. Jewel shuddered again as she thought of those uncertain months before Jeff had finally popped the question. Refusing to go to bed with him had been a calculated risk; it could have turned him off so easily. But her instincts told her that underneath the hard-nosed businessman was a dreamy boy, and wooing an innocent virgin would stir him far more than another easy conquest. And she was still a virgin, although she was not exactly an innocent one.

Then came that horrible visit to Horaceville, and she'd been afraid it was all over. The drive home had been one of the low points of her life—it had been as bad as the day her mother died. But her instincts had come to the rescue once again—and oh, she would trust them from now on! Without thinking about it or analyzing it, she had asked him to come upstairs to her horrid little apartment. They had both known what she was really doing was offering herself to him. That had touched a chord of chivalry in her dreamy boy, and the rest was—as they used to say—history.

Jeff said she could have the biggest, fanciest wedding she wanted. But he seemed pleased when she said she didn't want a fuss. She didn't bother to tell him that there was no one she wanted to invite. She hadn't kept in touch with her brothers or her sisters since she'd left home, and she didn't even know where Pop was anymore. She didn't have any friends, unless you counted Patsy Allen. On Jeff's side, there was his father, and Jewel certainly didn't want to invite the old goat.

So they were married by a judge Jeff knew, and they flew to their private island the next day. And now Jewel had a chef, a maid, and a butler to wait on her. She woke each morning to watch the sun rise over a turquoise ocean, and flowers she'd never seen before perfumed the air outside her windows.

And at night, she went into a bedroom where the bed was piled high with white linen pillows and the sheets were trimmed with lace and Jeff took her in his arms and undressed her, and she lay down on the big beautiful bed and she . . . pretended. She pretended she loved the things Jeff did, pretended his caresses brought her to ecstasy, pretended to a passion she knew she would never feel. Then he fell asleep with his body wrapped around hers and she stifled the wish that she could have this big beautiful bed all to herself so she could really enjoy it. But that thought only lasted a second. Because Jeff was the reason why she was in this palace, and she certainly owed him a little playacting.

There was a breeze on the terrace, and

the diaphanous robe Jewel had worn over her bathing suit wasn't warm. And, face it, she could only look at sand and water and flowers for so long, before she started going out of her mind with boredom. Unlike Jeff, who was happily walking along the beach right now. She went back inside the cottage.

Jeff said he could stay here forever, but she couldn't wait to get home. That was when her new life would really begin. He had promised that when they were back in Wrightstown, he'd throw away the blueprints for the home he'd wanted to build and let her start planning one to suit her taste with the architect. He was going to buy her a car, whatever make and model she wanted. He was going to spoil her rotten, he said.

There were times in bed at night when Jeff's body was wound around her too tightly for her to go to sleep, when it was only the thought of all the spoiling to come that helped her finally drift off. Then there were other nights, when her last thought would be about Gwen Wright—introverted, timid Gwen, who had complained about being forced to go to Paris. Gwen, who had thrown herself away on a man who worked with his hands. *If Gwen could see me now,* Jewel would think.

Roads Intertwining

"Love sees sharply,
hatred sees even more sharp
but jealousy sees the sharpest
of all for it is love and hate
at the same time."
—ARAB PROVERB

Chapter Twenty-one

~~⌒~~

The air in Stan's apartment was heavy this morning. It was funny how Gwen always thought of it as his apartment in spite of the fact that it had been her home since she'd married him four years ago. She sat up in their bed. It was late; Stan had already left for work, moving quietly so he wouldn't disturb her. But she'd been awake; she'd just pretended to sleep so she wouldn't have to talk. Now she looked around the bedroom which had been hers for four years. Had it really been such a long time? Such a short time? She'd lost track. The doctor said that confusion was normal, it was a part of the grieving process. She must give herself time.

Gwen got out of bed and walked to the bedroom window. If she looked directly below she could see a little piece of the courtyard behind the apartment building. This little patch of anemic grass and concrete was supposed to provide the residents with an outdoor oasis. Their other option for fresh air was the roof, where the management put out deck chairs in the summertime. But you couldn't get much of a tan up on the roof because across the street was a big office building called The Amber, which blocked the sunshine for the greater part of the day. Not that Gwen ever went up to the roof. She hadn't done that even before the tragedy . . . but she wasn't going to think that. She wasn't going to let herself dwell on the loss that had turned her into a woman who pretended to sleep because she didn't want to talk. Not today. Today she was going to get dressed. And she was going out. Even though she was longing to crawl back to her bed and stay there. *Get dressed, Gwen, it's a start.*

She managed to get in and out of the bathroom, but the closet defeated her. Picking out clothes to wear was beyond her. There was a little boudoir chair on her side of the bed. She sat in it and closed her eyes. And, as it so often did now, her mind went back. Back to the wild and happy days she and Stan had spent in Paris. The days when her marriage was fresh and new as a shiny penny.

It had seemed so romantic, to be married in Paris. She was the one who had suggested it, and Stan had loved the idea. There had been a moment when she'd worried, because the only other time she'd seen the city she'd been with her mother and she didn't want to be reminded of Cassandra on her honeymoon. It hadn't happened that way, because Stan had insisted on paying for the trip. He had some money because he'd been saving up to buy the building that housed his shop, but even after they had raided his hard-earned savings they couldn't travel in the style that Cassandra had afforded Gwen.

There had been no first-class airline tickets, no VIP lounges, and no palatial hotel once they reached Paris. Lunch was usually bread and cheese, and maybe a salad purchased in a shop and eaten picnic style. There wasn't any couture shopping. There weren't any expensive sight-seeing trips. Gwen and Stan had the streets and parks of the city, the bread and cheese, and at night, in the bed that was a little lumpy but angled so they could see the Eiffel Tower out of their window, they had each other. They had all the sweetness and the ecstasy that two people who were in love could give each other and it had been enough . . . no, much more than enough . . . to make the heart sing. Then they had come home.

*   *   *

Gwen opened her eyes. The room was getting too warm. There were no cross breezes in the apartment, and the only remedy for the heat was to close all the windows and turn on what Stan referred to as "the AC." Gwen hated air-conditioning; the stagnant artificially chilled air was suffocating to her. Despite all her best efforts, the little rosebush that Stan had given her had died after a few weeks in the apartment, and she'd blamed lack of sunshine and the horrid "AC." Stan didn't mind air conditioning because he'd lived with it all his life, although he'd been trying to use it as little as possible lately for her sake.

But now Gwen had to turn it on or the bedroom would become unbearable. She'd get up and do it in a minute, she told herself. Right now, she was feeling a little tired. She'd rest her eyes for a few minutes first. And let her mind go back.

* * *

Gwen had seen Stan's apartment for the first time when they came back from their honeymoon.

"This is it," he'd said beaming with pride. And he'd showed her the four boxlike rooms with low ceilings that made up his nest.

Please God, don't let him read on my

face how I feel, she'd prayed, and she'd tried to smile. The apartment was so small! The walls were so thin!

You shared a smaller space with him in the hotel in Paris, she told herself sternly. But that had been a temporary situation, like camping out without hot water and electricity. One did that for fun knowing that eventually one was going back home. But these four rooms were to be her home now. And she wasn't sure how to live in them. She wanted to do it, she wanted to be blissfully happy just being with Stan. But she was used to space. And privacy. And while she loved the nearness of her new husband, loved sitting next to him, or across the table from him, she knew there would come a time when she would want to read quietly without hearing through the thin walls the sporting event he was watching on the television.

To make matters worse, as she was trying to smile and nod enthusiastically, there came through the paper-thin walls the sound of their neighbors.

"How dare you, you son of a bitch!" screeched a shrill soprano.

"You don't like it, get the hell out!" responded a furious bass. More curses and obscenities followed while Stan smiled ruefully.

"That's the Hunters. I'm afraid they do that quite a bit," he said. "You'll get used to it. They're not as bad as our upstairs neighbors were when I was growing up. Every Friday Mr. Newton would get his paycheck and he'd have a couple on the way home and then the fight would start. My brother and I had a pool going on how long it would last each time."

He actually thought it was funny! And he was telling her to get used to it!

But come on, Gwen, isn't this exactly the kind of snobbery and elitism you wanted to get away from? You made fun of your mother's home that was so silent and ran like a well-oiled clock. Don't you remember you liked visiting friends whose parents broke the dishes when they had a battle? But visiting was the operative word. She wasn't visiting these small rooms, and she was going to be living with the Hunters' ongoing battle.

Gwen shifted in her chair—the upholstery was getting too warm; she was starting to sweat. Still, she stayed where she was. And remembered.

After they were settled in, there had been the matter of housekeeping. She, who had never vacuumed a floor, or scrubbed a sink, had to try to keep their home clean.

"Let me help you," Stan said. "I'm very good at mopping and dusting. I've been doing it for a lot of years because I've been on my own."

"You're working so hard—and you wouldn't have to put in such long hours if you weren't trying to make back the money you spent on the Paris trip—and I have nothing to do. It's only fair that I do the mopping and the dusting," she said. "Besides, you may be good at housework but I can't believe you like it."

He grinned and took her in his arms. "I'm going to submit you for the Understanding Wife of the Year Award."

But she quickly discovered she had no talent for domesticity, and even less interest. Cooking was a special nightmare, and there was no one nearby she could ask how to go about it. She knew Stan was hoping she'd make friends with some of the young women in the building, but most of them were single and racing out every evening after work to go to the restaurants and bars where they would—hopefully—meet young men. Those who were married were juggling jobs and children. Gwen usually encountered them in the basement laundry room on Saturday mornings where they complained to each other about the high cost of day care and the unreliability of baby-sitters. Gwen tried to think of something to say and usually failed. At such times the loneliness would threaten to overtake her, and when she was back upstairs Stan would find her crying over the sheets she was trying to fold. "If only we could bring Missy or Hank here—just for a few days," she said once. But the building had a rule against pets. All Stan could do was hold her and tell her he understood.

But he didn't understand—especially not about her longing for the outdoors.

Stan had never had acres of woodland to tramp over; he'd never had his own refuge with a special stump to sit on hidden under the trees on the side of a hill.

"There's a public park not ten minutes away from here," he told her when she moved into the apartment. "Everyone says it's a little bit of country right here in the middle of the city." Gwen had tried to go to the park. She'd tried to tell herself that she didn't mind the blaring of other people's music, tried to make herself believe that the overfed pigeons strutting around were a satisfying substitute for the songbirds, chipmunks, and squirrels she'd loved watching. She just couldn't do it.

Once, when she was indulging in a bout of the blues, she'd tried to choose the season in which she missed the land the most. Was it springtime when the hill behind the Wright house was alive with the fresh green of new buds and early grass and the sun that was still warming the winter out of the earth? Or was it summer when the cicadas buzzed lazily in the heat and the roses gave off a heavy perfume as they drooped, waiting for the afternoon rain? Was it the autumn when the red maples burst into flame and the oaks, ashes, and poplars followed with gold and orange and the air was crisp like the inside of an apple? Or was it winter when the snow covered the earth with its magic blanket of softness and embroidered white lace on the trees and bushes? After a day of torturing herself with thoughts like that, she vowed never to give in to them again. But the hunger grew more and more intense. And after a year she began to be afraid that the time would come when her sense of loss would be so bad that even her nights with Stan in their bed could not heal her.

* * *

Then, at the moment when she had started to despair, Cassie had stepped in. When Stan and Gwen came home from France, Cassie was remarkably restrained. There had been no recriminations and no lectures—Gwen was pretty sure she could thank Walter for that—and even after Cassie had toured Gwen's

new home, she had not uttered a disap-
proving word . . . although her pursed
lips and the frown between her eyes
spoke volumes. She had kept her silence for a year. But then she had invited Stan and Gwen out to the house
for Sunday brunch.

"Why don't you go without me?" Stan
said.

"Mother wants both of us to come,"
Gwen replied. "She said she wanted to
talk to us about something."

"She doesn't like me, Gwen, you know
that."

"And you return the favor, dear!" Gwen
had given him a playful kiss on the
cheek, so happy she didn't care that he
was reluctant to go. She was going to
escape the city for a whole long glorious
day! The sun was shining, there were a
dozen different shades of blue in the
sky, from azure to turquoise, and she
was going to see trees, and grass—
acres of it.

*   *   *

Cassie had gotten down to business as
soon as the omelets had been served.

"Stanley, I want to buy a house for you and Gwen," she said. The family was sitting in the dining room where Gwen could see her old refuge through the window, and she'd been drinking it in and thinking that the hillside had never looked more lovely, but when Cassie spoke, she turned in time to see Stan stiffen and she knew what was coming next. So did Cassie.

"Before you say no, hear me out," she went on. "The house I'm proposing to buy is in a new development out here. You probably saw it from the road as you drove by; the construction is eco-logically sound and the prices are rea-sonable."

"It's very kind, but no thank you," Stan said.

But Gwen was remembering the de-velopment. *The houses are small,* she thought, *but they are beautifully de-signed—rustic and simple. And there is land around each of them. Real land!*

"Gwen and I are planning to buy a house when we have enough saved," Stan said.

"And how close are you to being able to do it?" asked Cassie

If the development is the one I think it is, Gwen went on thinking, *and it has to be, because it is the only new one in the area, each of the houses has almost an acre. There are trees that haven't been chopped down at the edge of each property line. If you owned one of those houses you could imagine you were living in a forest.*

"We would have the money for a down payment right now, but the landlord who owns the building where my shop is decided he wanted to sell, and I'm buying it. I have one more installment to go." There was a defensive tone in Stan's voice that Gwen had never heard before. "It was too good a deal to pass up."

"Stanley, please, there's no need to explain any of this to me," Cassie said. "I'm not judging you, I simply want to give you a gift."

"A very expensive gift—no matter how much you say it isn't—and we can't take it."

"I can well afford it, I assure you."

"I know you can."

And if we did let her give it to us, I could plant a garden, with roses that won't die, Gwen thought.

But Stan was talking again. "Gwen and I are not the first couple who will have to wait until we can afford to buy our home on our own," he said. "We're no better than anyone else in our situation."

"But Gwen isn't in your situation, as you call it. She has a family that can do this for her. Why should she wait if she doesn't have to?"

Yes, oh, yes! Why should we wait a minute longer than we have to?

"I didn't marry Gwen's family, I married her. And I will provide for her."

"You married a young woman who is accustomed to a certain lifestyle. You can't think that she's enjoying living in that apartment."

And then Stan turned to her. "What about it, Gwen?" he asked. "Is it so bad living the way we do?"

Oh Stan, I love you. So very much. But we could have trees and fresh, clean air, and I could plant roses. We could have a dog like Missy, who is lying on your feet right now because she knows how much you love animals. The words were on the tip of her tongue, but then she looked at his face. And she saw how important this was to him. "No, it's not that bad," she said.

But on the way back home in the car, she couldn't help herself. "Why couldn't we take Mother's offer?" she demanded. "If she wants to give us a present, what's wrong with that?"

"Your mother wants to keep her hold on you, Gwen. That's what this is about."

"No, it's about you being stubborn as a mule!" She had never said anything like that to him before and they were both surprised.

"Your mother has no respect for me—and she lets me know it every chance she gets. How do you think I'd feel letting her pay for the roof over my head? Gwen, you can't want that!"

She didn't. She didn't want him to lose his dignity or his self-respect. So she tried to make the best of it. She decided to get a job. It would get her out of the hated apartment, there would be people to talk to, and she would earn a little money to add to the down payment fund. She began looking. And quickly discovered how few options there were for someone with neither a college degree nor any skills. That was something she'd never thought about when she had so cavalierly thrown away her chance at a Yale education. She probably could have asked Cassie to find something for her to do at the glassworks, but she was sure Stan would say that was the same thing as letting her mother pay for their house. So Gwen continued her frustrating job search. But in a perverse way that she realized was totally unreasonable, she found herself blaming Stan for it. She was ashamed of herself for feeling that way, and resolved to try even harder to make the best of her plight. In a way, it was that resolution which led—indirectly—to everything else that happened.

Chapter Twenty-two

⁓⁓⁓

As a part of her new positive approach, Gwen began going down to the court-yard behind her apartment building each morning when she looked through the "help wanted" section of the paper. Being outdoors in the fresh air would help her attitude, she told herself. It didn't have the desired effect, but something else did. Gwen soon discovered that several of the baby-sitters working for her neighbors brought their charges down to the dark little courtyard to play, and she quickly fell in love with the children. In her mind she named them; there was a baby boy she dubbed the Adventurer. His little fat feet encased in tiny sneakers, he tottered across the small patch of grass like Columbus discovering the New World. The Thinker was a sweet baby girl, whose little round face was usually topped with a pink headband and bow. She was content to spend a quarter of an hour at a time in her carriage contemplating the universe—and her own tiny fingers.

Watching the children, Gwen would let the "help wanted" section drop to the ground. A second hunger—as strong for the need for the country—was born in her.

"Don't you think it's time we started thinking about having a family?" she asked Stan one night when they were lying next to each other.

"Let's wait until we're in our house first," he'd said.

"That's going to take so long. I don't want to wait."

"Well, I guess there's nothing that says we can't get a head start," he'd said, as he reached for her. After that, all practical considerations were forgotten. And when after a few months Gwen discovered she was pregnant, Stan was as overjoyed as she was. So she prepared to be blissful.

She hadn't counted on feeling so awful. She knew about morning sickness, but her nausea lasted all day. It didn't help that it was summertime and they were in the middle of one of the worst heat waves in Wrightstown history. The air that hung over the city was so thick it was hard to breathe. The heat rose up from the concrete sidewalks, and the traffic was angrier and louder than usual.

"Get exercise," the doctor told Gwen. "Walking is best." So she walked every day to a small shopping center in the heart of town. It was air-conditioned, a necessary evil given the heat, and it wasn't very busy, so Gwen could circle the perimeter without bothering anyone. Round and round she went and tried to not to think about the way it felt to walk on a country road when you could stretch your arms out into open space and sing and no one would hear. She also tried not to think about the phlox and peonies she would have planted in her garden if Stan had been willing to accept the house her mother had wanted to buy for them. Something deep and primitive in her said that her baby needed a garden. It needed space and singing. But she couldn't give it that. So she walked in the shopping center. And she had her reward when the baby moved.

Stan was with her when it happened the first time, and they had looked at each other with the time-honored wonder that only parents can know.

"It's sending us a message," Gwen said. "It's saying 'I'm here.'" And the baby was real to her in a whole new way. She and Stan picked out two names, one for a boy and one for a girl, since they hadn't wanted to know what sex the child was. They selected Michael and Abigail. There was no reason; they were just names that sounded good to both of them.

Then something occurred to Gwen. "Whenever I wonder what the baby will look like, I always think about you and me," she told Stan. "I think, *Will it have Stan's nose and my mouth? His hair or mine?* But what if it looks like . . . someone else?"

"You're talking about your father."

"And my birth mother. Will my baby look like that woman I've never seen? Will it have her eyes? At least I've seen his picture, so I'll know if it takes after him."

Stan had taken her in his arms and whispered, "No matter who it looks like, it will be a part of them. Those two people you never got to know."

Gwen had whispered back, "I'll be giving them a new life. I'll be able to do that for them!"

The nausea stopped after the baby moved. Suddenly Gwen was full of energy; she made over the second bedroom into a nursery, painting it a happy, gender-neutral yellow. Cassie had given Gwen a gift certificate to the most exclusive infants' shop in town, and Stan didn't say a word when expensive, state-of-the-art baby paraphernalia started showing up at the apartment. Their child was more important to him than his pride. Gwen couldn't remember when she'd been happier.

"I thought being with you in Paris was the best time I would ever have in my life, but I'm afraid Little Whosis has beaten you out," she told Stan one night as they were drifting off to sleep.

"That's Little Mike or Little Abby to you, lady," he murmured, and without opening his eyes, he gave her belly a pat.

Then suddenly everything was wrong. Terribly, terribly wrong. There was no more movement inside her and Gwen knew, with a terrifying primitive knowledge that she couldn't explain, that the messages from the baby stopped. Stan rushed her to the obstetrician, where they begged the woman to say that everything was all right, that this was normal, that Gwen was just having some kind of first-time-mother panic attack and that she was imagining things. Tests were run to try to prove that what Gwen felt in her bones and her blood wasn't true, that she was wrong. But she wasn't wrong.

Finally the word was said. "Stillborn." Their baby daughter—she was a little girl—would never see her yellow nursery or the brightly colored mobile that was hanging over her crib. She would never wear a pink hair bow and she would never grow up to play the violin, or be president of the United States, or just be a happy, loving woman. Stillborn. All the dreams and hopes and joy died with that word.

I failed you, Abby, and I failed Stan. I failed myself, Gwen thought when she was told. And then after a long shuddering moment: *And I failed those two people who died too young in a car wreck outside New Orleans. This baby was to have been their legacy and I failed them.*

*   *   *

The room was hot. Gwen opened her eyes and looked at her watch. It was almost noon, she'd been sitting in the chair in her bedroom for over an hour. She had to get dressed.

"Don't try to push yourself too hard," the doctor had said. "Remember you need time to grieve. It's only been two weeks."

Two weeks since they took my baby. My little Abby. I should have given her a garden. I should have seen to it that she had space and fresh air and trees and grass. I knew that was what she needed. And crazy though it was—and Gwen really did know it was crazy—there was a part of her that believed her baby would have lived if she and Stan had had their own house with their own land.

She got up out of the chair and walked to the window to turn on the hated air conditioner. They'd done a Caesarean when they took the baby and she had spent two nights in the hospital. When she came home, Stan had dismantled the nursery. He had painted the walls a soft taupe, and gotten rid of the furniture from the fancy baby shop. Gwen had never asked him what he'd done with it. Their nursery was now a guest bed-room.

She couldn't bear to be with people af-ter she came home. Well-wishers had tried to be comforting. "You and your husband are young, you'll get through this," they said, or, "Just remember, God never sends a bigger burden than we can carry," or worst of all, "You'll have other children."

Mercifully Cassie had known better than to try to help with words, but she had offered to send Gwen and Stan on a vacation cruise. "The ship is beautiful, I've taken it myself," she said. "Get away from everything for a while. You need a change of scenery."

But changing the scenery wouldn't bring Gwen's baby back, and the mere thought of sitting on the deck of a ship with nothing to do but think was intolerable. Gwen said no thank you.

Stan had stayed home with her after she'd come back from the hospital, and he had tried to talk to her about their loss. But her husband had never been one for putting his feelings into words. She was the one who had done that, but now she had nothing to say. The truth was, the crazy part of her mind blamed Stan for not accepting the house her mother had offered. She didn't want to feel that, knew how unfair and wrong it was, but she couldn't help it. Finally, after three days, she told him she was feeling better and he should go back to work. Perhaps it was just her imagination but she thought he'd been relieved.

Then last night he'd said to her, "Get dressed tomorrow and I'll take you to lunch. You need to get out of the house."

And she had screamed at him, "We don't have a house. We have this goddamned apartment."

Stan had looked as if she'd shot him.

*   *   *

Gwen moved to the closet. She knew how much she had hurt Stan. That was why, this morning, even though he hadn't mentioned lunch again, she'd decided to go to his shop at noon and surprise him. She started pulling clothes out of the closet. She had to get dressed sometime.

Chapter Twenty-three

The Amber office building sat on the northwest corner of the busiest intersection in Wrightstown. It fronted on the city's main thoroughfare, unimaginatively named First Street. The cross street was Wright Boulevard. If you walked south on Front Street for about a quarter of a mile, you'd find yourself in the older, less affluent part of Wrightstown. If you started at The Amber and went north, your journey would end in a small park. Wright Boulevard stretched out to the suburbs to the east and if you were to take the number 6 bus going west, you'd eventually wind up at the Wright Glassworks—as did many of the company's employees who lived in this up-and-coming neighborhood.

The intersection of First and Wright was one of the few areas of Wrightstown where people actually walked, and Jeff enjoyed standing at his window in The Amber sixteen floors above the street to watch the pedestrians bustle to and fro. It reminded him of New York, which was probably his favorite city in the States.

He had favorite cities worldwide now, was enough of a regular visitor to London, Buenos Aires, Moscow, Beijing, and Okinawa that there were hotel concierges and headwaiters in all of those places who knew which suite was Mr. Henry's favorite, and which wine he preferred. JeffSon had continued to grow— as it had had to, to hold off the waiting sharks. Now the little business that had started out as a small natural gas company in Omaha, Nebraska, was a conglomerate of gas lines and power plants involved in the transmission and distribution of power around the globe. JeffSon's lawyers dealt with the legal infrastructure and rules in at least a dozen countries. Along the way the business had also acquired, almost by accident, a bundle of communications companies. The opportunity had presented itself out of the blue, and Jeff had had to move quickly. It had been a little too fast for his comfort, and he'd hesitated, almost until it was too late, but at the last second, on the advice of several of the young Turks he'd hired to advise him, he had taken the plunge. Corners had been cut, and research he would normally have insisted was necessary had not been done, but they had been lucky and JeffSon's bottom line had benefited exponentially. Jeff had learned a lesson from that experience: that there are times when you cannot listen to that little voice in your gut that is telling you that what you are about to do is too risky. There are times when you have to listen to the youngsters you've brought on board straight out of business school who know how to gamble better than you do. And then you pray.

He was ignoring that little voice in his gut again these days. Because JeffSon was poised to involve itself in a new area—the water utility market. For this move, which even the gambling young Turks admitted was risky, he had done his homework as much as he could. But at a certain point you just had to go for broke.

Beware of Faustian bargains, Jeffie, his father had said.

Jeff shook his head to clear it. This was no time to think about his father's antiquated notions. He started to turn away from the window, when down on the street below, he saw Gwen Wright . . . only her last name was something else now . . . coming out of her apartment building.

It was his wife, Jewel, who had first told him that the former Miss Wright had married a man who owned some kind of service shop and she now lived in the center of downtown Wrightstown across the street from The Amber. For some reason Jewel always seemed to know what was going on with the Wright family, especially Gwen.

When Jewel had first mentioned Gwen's name, Jeff hadn't been sure who she was talking about. Then he had remembered the party he'd attended at the Wright house and the quiet girl whose birthday it had been. That night—Was it really four years ago?—he'd thought that there was something a little other-worldly about the party's honoree, but it could have been the old-fashioned white lace dress she'd been wearing. He had pegged her as one of those intro-verted young women who were proba-bly interesting if you wanted to spend an enormous amount of time getting to know them, but he didn't. She was not his type and anyway, back in those days he hadn't had much time for anyone but himself.

Then one morning he'd seen Gwen in the neighborhood. She had come out of her apartment building and headed in the direction of the old part of town. He soon realized that this walk was a regular occurrence. Every morning like clockwork, she left the building at the same time. He could have set his watch by her. He found he liked to watch her walk. Even in her condition—she was pregnant—her stride was long and fast and . . . well, joyful was the only word for it. He thought she belonged on a country road or an open field, and he tried to picture her in such a setting. The free, athletic way she moved shouldn't have fit with the demure white dress she'd worn on the night when he'd met her, but it did. There was something re- fined and pure about both. Jeff's father would have said Gwen Wright was a "thoroughbred." It was one of the high- est compliments he could bestow on a woman.

*　　*　　*

Jeff watched Gwen now as she headed down the street, once again in the di- rection of the old part of town. She hadn't been out of her apartment since she'd lost her baby—this bit of gossip had come to him from Jewel, naturally— and he was glad to see Gwen out and about. But she was moving slowly, wearily, without her usual joy. Well, that was probably to be expected after what she'd been through. Still, it made him feel sad, as if he was watching a lovely animal—a deer perhaps, or a wild horse—hobbled by pain.

He watched Gwen until she was out of sight, then turned away from his window and went back to his desk and the packet of papers on it. He was leaving in two days to conclude a deal for the water concession in Buenos Aires and he had reading to do. But the information so carefully distilled and condensed by his young Turks didn't hold his attention. Thinking about Gwen Wright and her birthday party had reminded him of the painting he'd bought from her stepfather Walter Amburn. He looked up; it was on his wall here in the office, the simple little picture of a small girl sitting on a roof watching the river flow by her house at dusk. Until Jeff married Jewel it always had hung in a prominent spot in his home. Even after he moved to the hotel where he and Jewel now lived while they waited for their house to be finished, the painting had hung over the fireplace in his penthouse suite. In the past few years he'd become something of a collector. He now had scouts who called him when a David Hockney went on sale, or when a Utrillo was up for auction. But the little painting by Amburn was still a favorite of his; there was something about the isolation of the child and the endless river which spoke to him.

But when Jewel came to live with him in the hotel suite, she'd asked if it would be all right if they took the picture down and put it in storage.

"It's so gloomy, honey," she'd said in the sweet cooing voice she used when she wanted to convince him of something. "It gives me the creeps." She'd shivered deliciously and laughed. "I'm sure we'll be able to find some place for it when the new house is finished, although the interior decorator says you have paintings that are worth a lot more that we should be showcasing. That dinky little thing was awfully cheap, wasn't it? I mean, you bought it when you couldn't afford anything better."

That was his wife. His Jewel. Jeff closed his eyes for a second, and thought about the changes she'd brought into his life, changes that did not thrill him.

You have only yourself to blame, pal, he thought in a rare burst of honesty. Take the matter of their new home. It was he who had told Jewel to tear up the plans for the sleek modern house he had originally commissioned. The architect had designed it to be light and airy with clean lines, but Jewel had found the stone and glass structure "creepy"— it seemed to be her favorite word—and had lobbied instead for a "McMansion." Jeff had given her carte blanche to do as she pleased, because in the beginning, she had taken possession of him as if he had been a foolish teenager in the throes of a crush. He'd told himself that it didn't matter that his house was a vulgar attempt to recreate . . . he didn't know what. A stately mansion in Great Britain? A French chateau? A Tuscan villa? All of the above? A house was like a suit of clothes, he'd told himself back in those halcyon days of passion; the one you bought to cover yourself, the other for shelter. But the truth was, such things also sent a message. The message told the world your taste, your pocketbook, and in an arrogant, subtle way, your "class." And when he actually found himself faced with the prospect of living in Jewel's mansion/chateau/villa—and it was going to happen soon—he was embarrassed. It was the same kind of embarrassment he felt when Jewel wore all of her gold bangles—heavy bracelets studded with diamonds that she had wanted and he had purchased—at once. He remembered his mother saying that when a lady dressed for the evening the last thing she did was look in the mirror and remove at least one accessory.

But his discontent went deeper than embarrassment. He wished just once his wife would have something interesting to say. It could be about anything—politics, or the weather—as long as it wasn't yet more chatter about the latest celebrity gossip. When he'd married her, he'd known she didn't read, but he wished she'd take up a hobby or a sport—tennis or bridge or quilting—anything to keep her from touring the shops in the Algonquin Mall in her endless search for more clothes, more objects, more loot. . . .

Stop that, Jeff, he told himself sternly. *You have to be patient. She had nothing when she married you, so it's only natural that she would go a little wild now.*

Besides, hadn't he married her in part because she knew how to spend money? He hadn't been embarrassed by her when she encouraged him to buy the yacht he wanted. But the funny thing about that was that after she had encouraged him, he hadn't done it. Somehow watching her shop day after day had soured him on it for himself.

She did try to be a good wife to him. They'd had apricot pie a month ago because he'd said he liked apricots. That had been very thoughtful of her—and he had thanked her. But since then he had had so many apricots, fresh, canned, in pies and other desserts, that he never wanted to see another one.

And in her sweet voice that could at times have a cutting edge on it, she had said, "Don't tell me you're not going to eat it. I thought you'd love apricot bread. I went to so much trouble to find the recipe for the chef." He could recognize that voice even when she was speaking on the phone in the next room. And what was she always talking about? Not about the headlines in *The New York Times,* that was for sure. Hell, she wasn't even talking about taking a walk with the dog. Because they didn't have a dog. It was something he had always wanted; when he was a kid, his parents would only tolerate cats. But first the collie, then the Irish setter, then the small poodle had all been sent back to the various breeders because it was discovered that they were all too dirty to live in the new house. A dog, Jewel had declared, would ruin her décor.

There was something else that she didn't like: his music. He couldn't remember a time when he hadn't listened to music. But the symphonies and operas that he loved, and that were at times the only balm he knew for the soul, left her cold. Before he'd married her, he had thought that none of this would matter to him; now he was finding that it did. It mattered very much.

Be patient, he told himself again. *She*

*never had the time or the money to en-
joy what you think of as the better things
in life.*

Surely there would come a day when
she would have her fill of shopping and
acquiring, when her McMansion was
finished and her jewelry box was full.
Then he would slowly, and gently expose her to Bach, Schubert, and Wagner. There was time for her to discover
the joys of intelligent, informed conversation, of a good book, or a great painting. And in the meantime? Well, she was
still heart-stoppingly, breathtakingly
beautiful. And heads did turn when he
walked into a room with her on his arm.
And, if she never did change? And if that
continued to irk him? Well, the world
was full of women.

Jeff tried once again to focus on the
documents on his desk, but his mind
kept wandering. He stood up and went
back to look out of the window at the
ever-changing parade of humanity beneath him. And he saw Gwen Wright
Whatever-Her-Last-Name-Was walking
back from wherever she'd gone. Her
weariness was even worse now; she

was moving with the trudging step of someone who was sick or elderly. She stopped at the entrance to her apartment building, and seemed to be thinking about something. Then instead of going inside, she shook her head and began to walk in the direction of the little park at the end of the street. That had to be her destination.

But there are children playing in that park, Jeff thought. *That's no place for a woman who is obviously suffering from the loss of her own baby.* Without thinking, Jeff ran out of his office toward the elevator.

* * *

Stan had not been in the shop. Even though Gwen knew it had nothing to do with her, that he had probably gone out on a job, after her outburst the night before she'd felt as if he was avoiding her. For the first time in weeks she found herself thinking about something besides her child and her loss. She'd read an article once in a magazine which quoted a lot of statistics about couples who had been driven apart by a tragedy.

She'd forgotten the exact figures but she did remember how high they were.

Stan and I aren't handling our tragedy well, she thought. *At least, I'm not. When we were first married, I couldn't have imagined that anything could ever come between us. Loving Stan was the easiest thing I'd ever done.*

But now she realized there was a reason for all those thousands of self-help books and dozens of television shows dedicated to helping married couples communicate. And commiserate, and empathize. And forgive.

I will not let our tragedy destroy us, she'd thought as she stood in the middle of Stan's empty shop. *The blaming and the anger and the guilt stop here. I'm done with it.* And with those brave thoughts in her head, she'd turned around and started back to the apartment building.

*   *   *

The trouble with brave thoughts is finding the actions to match them. Particularly when you are younger than your years and naïve enough to believe that good intentions are enough. Gwen had reached her building, walked firmly up to the entrance, and stopped dead in her tracks. *I can't go back in there,* she thought. *Not with Abby's ghost and the ghosts of all my own dreams waiting for me.* She stood in front of the entrance, knowing she was being irrational, and without wanting to, she wondered, *What would Cassie do now?* The answer came back loud and clear: Cassandra Wright would face down her pain. She would look at it squarely and she would wrestle it to the ground. Galvanized, Gwen started for the little park at the end of the street—the one where all the kids played.

At first it seemed to Gwen as if there were hundreds of children—boys and girls—in the park, and the sweet little faces and high, delighted laughter overwhelmed her. She stood at the park's entrance unable to breathe. But she was Cassandra Wright's daughter. She forced air into her lungs until she could see that the actual number of children was closer to ten. Mercifully none of them were infants. But it was still too hard, too painful, to watch them. She was about to turn away when a voice at her side said, "Excuse me, aren't you . . . that is, *weren't* you Gwen Wright?" And standing next to her was a man she recognized from the many stories written about him in the newspapers. He was the owner and CEO of the JeffSon Corporation, but she would always think of him as the pirate who had come to her birthday party.

"I've been to your house . . . your mother's house . . . it was about four years ago. But you probably don't remember."

"But I do. How do you do, Mr. Henry?" she said. She held out her hand for him to shake. "I used to be Gwen Wright. Now my name is Gwen Girard." Then, she added because she couldn't help herself, "Didn't you marry Jewel Fairchild?"

Chapter Twenty-four

Stan looked at the note Gwen had left for him on his workbench. *I stopped by to take you up on that lunch offer,* it said, *but you weren't here. I want a rain check. I love you, Gwen.*

So she was ready to forgive him. His heart leapt. They had never been seriously angry at each other before and he hated the feeling. On the other hand, he wasn't sure that she was the one who should be doing the forgiving. Their loss had been his every bit as much as it had been hers, but she had not tried to comfort him as he had tried to comfort her. Instead she had blamed him—not in so many words, because she knew she was being unfair and unreasonable— but he was not a stupid man. He'd known what she was thinking. Stan sighed and unwrapped the pastrami sandwich he'd purchased at Berger's Deli down the street.

He'd known when he married Gwen that she'd been privileged, and protected, and as a result, she really didn't have any idea how the rest of the world lived. That naiveté had been a part of her charm as far as he was concerned. But living with it wasn't always easy.

A case in point had been his apartment. Gwen had hated the entire building from the moment she'd set foot inside it. He was rather proud of the shiny lobby, the up-to-the-minute exercise room, the courtyard, and the roof garden, and he'd been surprised and more than a little hurt by Gwen's reaction. His four small rooms could not compare with the Wright house, but Gwen had always insisted she didn't want to live in a mansion with artwork on the walls and Aubusson carpets on the floors. But it was clear that she missed certain elements of her old life.

The things she had complained about had seemed rather trivial to him—the lack of privacy and quiet, for instance. You didn't have much of either in an apartment, that was a given, but you learned to adjust to your neighbors' noise, and when you couldn't, you just tuned it out. As for the woodlands and the wild animals Gwen mourned so much, well, he couldn't see that it was worth it to make a fuss over a few trees and squirrels. Of course it was nice to have some land of your own, and he certainly planned to buy a house, but when he could afford it; he was not about to saddle himself with a huge mortgage. In the meantime his present apartment, which was far better than his last one, was a stepping-stone along the way.

When he'd said that to Gwen, he'd realized for the first time just how wide the gap between them actually was. His wife didn't understand about stepping-stones. Not really. Intellectually she knew that when she'd married Stan she'd given up the life of wealth she'd once had, but she'd never had to do without something she considered a necessity because she couldn't afford it. To her, a house was a necessity, and the idea that they had to save up for one was a hardship for which she just wasn't prepared.

So when Cassie had wanted to buy a place for them, Gwen had seen it as a way to escape the living arrangement she hated, and she'd been eager to accept. To Stan, it had been a demeaning offer from a woman who felt he wasn't worthy of her daughter. He'd been hurt and angry that Gwen hadn't understood why he couldn't accept Cassie's offer, and she, he knew, had been equally hurt and angry that he had not jumped at the chance to end a situation that was intolerable to her. Then they'd lost the baby. And Gwen, who had been so protected, did not know how to accept the fact that life is full of random cruelties which are no one's fault. She had needed someone or something to blame, and he and his apartment were available. He had resented it, even though he'd understood why, and he hadn't reached out to her the way he should have.

But today she had come to the shop to have lunch with him.

I love you, she'd written.

He knew that, would have bet his life on it. And he loved her. He thought that perhaps he'd stop at the florist down the street when he went home after work tonight. He wouldn't get pink roses for Gwen, although he thought of them as her flower, because he didn't want to remind her of the little bush she'd fought so hard to keep alive. Maybe some daisies.

* * *

Jeff and Gwen had left the little park together, and he invited her to have some coffee with him. She had accepted and they walked back to his office building, where there was a fancy little café that dispensed lattes and other such trendy variations on the good old-fashioned cup of Joe. As they walked they had established that yes, indeed, he had married Jewel Fairchild, and for a brief moment he had wondered if for some reason Gwen Wright—and why couldn't he remember her new last name?—was keeping tabs on his wife as much as his wife kept tabs on her. But why would she do that? Jewel was jealous of Gwen for all the obvious reasons, but surely Gwen Wright Whatever had no reason to return the favor.

When he and Gwen had reached their destination and they were seated across the table from each other, Jeff found himself momentarily at a loss for something to say. The thoughts in his mind— *There are dark circles under your eyes; are you sleeping enough? And there is a haunted expression in them that I find horribly sad. Is there anything I can do for you?*—wouldn't be appropriate. Finally he settled on, "Do you go to that park often?" And he thought to himself, *Wonderful, Jeff, could you have asked a question that was more of a cliché?*

But she answered seriously. "I haven't been there in a while. I . . . haven't been well. . . ."

I know, he thought of saying but didn't.

She didn't need to be reminded that she was still a Wright, and the loss of her child was the subject of gossip in their city. She didn't need to know that one of the chief gossips was his jealous wife.

"I'm afraid I don't like that park very much," she went on. "It's so small and crowded."

He thought of her athletic stride and the feeling he'd had that she should be walking on country roads and open fields. This was the wrong setting for her, he thought. It was so very wrong. But what had Jewel said about the man she'd married—the one whose name Jeff couldn't remember? Jewel said he was beneath Gwen. A nobody. So probably this was the best they could afford. But still it didn't seem right.

"What does your husband do for a living?" he asked.

"Stan has his own electrician's shop" was the answer. An electrician's shop! Probably a one-man band where he repaired people's toasters. And her family owned one of the biggest glassworks in the country. No, make that the world. Jewel was right, the poor girl had married beneath her. Still, it was an interesting coincidence that the man was an electrician and JeffSon owned power plants.

"I really should be getting home," Gwen Wright—no, it was Gwen Girard, he remembered now—was saying. "Thank you so much for the coffee."

"I'll see you to your building," Jeff said.

"You don't have to do that."

"We're right across the street from each other. We're neighbors."

*   *   *

"I don't know what to do for Gwen. That idiot she married won't let me help them," Cassie said to Walter. They were sitting on the front porch of the Wright house watching the sun set behind the red maples.

"You can't take Gwen's pain away."

"But I want to make it easier for her."

"There is nothing you can do or give, darling. And if there were, you shouldn't do or give it. Don't you see? Gwen has a husband now. He's the one she must lean on."

"Him? You heard what he said when I

tried to buy them a house! All that twaddle about how no one should have special advantages because of their family or their background. Or some such nonsense."

"I believe he actually said that he and Gwen were no different from any other young couple just starting out."

"In the old days, my father would have said he was a Communist!"

"Isn't it nice that we've all evolved since then?"

"I'm serious, Walter."

"So am I. You mustn't interfere, Cassie. Right now, Gwen is still a girl. If she's to grow up, to become a woman—and for her own happiness she must—she has to find her own way in life. And she must do that with Stan. Not you."

*   *   *

In the dark, Gwen could make out the daisies Stan had brought her. They were in a blue vase sitting on her nightstand, where she had insisted on putting them. Stan was asleep, his body wrapped around hers the way it always was after their passion was spent. It was as if they couldn't bear to separate from each other after such closeness, as if they had melded and would have to tear themselves apart. But Gwen's mind could always wander. She closed her eyes. Once when she was a child, she'd spilled boiling water on her arm and burnt it badly. What she remembered about the burn was not the initial searing agony, but the days and weeks that followed as the blistered skin peeled away, leaving the raw, exposed wound. The slightest breeze passing at random over that wound could trigger new pain that was almost as strong as the original. She felt that the pain that was now inside her was like that; it was always there, waiting to hit her when she didn't expect it, and she didn't know when or if it would ever stop. All she could do was wait and see. She wondered if Stan felt the same way. She looked at his arm draped so possessively over her shoulder. The books said it would be better if they could talk about these things—if she could have said, *I was so hurt and angry that I took it out on you, and I'm sorry,* and then he could have said, *I was so hurt that I pushed you away and I'm sorry.* But she was learning that that was not their way. They said "I love you" and "I'm sorry" with daisies and surprise lunches and unspoken compromises. And then they came together in their bed. It might not be what the books suggested, but it lifted the gray mood for a little while and made the pain more bearable.

Gwen turned her head to look out the bedroom window. All she could see was the office building across the street, but somewhere behind it was the moon. Tonight she was able to summon up the imagination to picture it shining down on Stan and her.

* * *

The penthouse suite in the glittery hotel where Jewel and Jeff were camping out consisted of five rooms with views that stretched as far off as the glassworks. Jewel got up out of bed, and walked to one of the massive bedroom's floor-to-ceiling windows. How many times had she done this in her old apartment when she couldn't sleep? Back then, she had looked out onto a dirty street and a tree that was old and bent. Tonight, she could see the whole city spread out at her feet. And soon her view would be even more grand, when she moved into her new house. The house that would make it up to her for all the early years of desperate wanting, for the time of watching Ma die so slowly and painfully, for Pop's abandonment. And the house would do even more than that for her; it would be her ticket into the echelon of Wrightstown society populated by the likes of Cassie Wright and Gwen Girard. Finally, Jewel was going to belong!

She wished she could go into the next room and look once again at the plans for the new swimming pool her land-scape designer had submitted to her earlier that day. Behind the pool there would be an artificial waterfall that could be activated by a switch found on a panel in the foyer of the house. There was another switch which would turn on the amber, pink, and golden lights that would play over the pool. Still another switch would turn on the sound system. If Jeff had been away on one of his business trips she might have driven out to the building site, even though it was the middle of the night, so she could picture her miraculous backyard coming to life in all its glory. But Jeff was home. Jewel turned back to bed where he was sleeping. He used to love watching her pleasure at the toys and gifts he was able to shower on her. But lately she'd sensed a certain disapproval coming from him, as if there was something distasteful about her throwing her arms around him and squealing with joy over her new diamond earrings, or their new Lear Jet. At such moments he looked a little too much like his father. Trying to keep him happy was going to be difficult if he turned into the old goat. She walked quickly to the mirror and stared at her image—even without the lights on, she could see that her talisman beauty was still there. In a couple of years she'd need a nip and a tuck, but her figure was still perfect, as were her violet eyes, and her ebony hair shone in the darkness. There was no way Jeff would walk away from all of that. She went back to bed, and slipped in between the sheets—the sheets with the five-hundred-thread count from Porthault. Her negligee was French silk from Léron. The perfume she dabbed on herself every night after her bath had been specially created for her by Floris.

As she started falling asleep she thought of something Jeff had told her at dinner. He'd seen Gwen Wright that afternoon. He'd been taking a walk around the block to clear his head and he'd bumped into her, and he'd felt that it was only good manners to invite the Dreary One to have a cup of coffee with him.

It had been all Jewel could do not to laugh out loud. She still couldn't believe that Gwen Wright was living in downtown Wrightstown! In a building that was fine—it was actually rather glamorous—if you were trying to make your way as a paralegal or a dental assistant. But if you were Gwen Wright . . . for an instant there rose in Jewel's mind an image of a grand old house with a hill behind it and a row of glorious red maple trees on the front lawn. Now Gwen was reduced to living in an apartment build-

ing with the children of blue-collar workers who were trying to better themselves. And Jewel was the one who was
going to have lawns and trees. Could
anyone have imagined that this was
how things would turn out? That Jewel
Henry, born Jewel Fairchild, would one
day be able to buy and sell Gwen Wright
ten times over if she'd wanted to?

Chapter Twenty-five

Gwen had learned that those who said time heals everything were wrong. There are certain hurts that never go away, like the one she'd sustained when she learned that Cassie had been lying to her about her birth parents. Gwen would never forget the look of triumph on Jewel's face when she "spilled" the secret. Or the look on Cassie's face when she confirmed that it was true. That ache was permanent, as were the questions it raised about the man and woman who gave her life.

But the loss of a baby was different. That pain would never go away, either . . . but you finally did figure out how to absorb it. It became a part of what you were and it changed who you were. At first you were convinced that you'd never be happy again, that the gray fog that enveloped you would always be there, then one morning you woke up and it was autumn, and the trees in the little park at the end of your street were spreading the seasonal gold and orange carpet on the ground. And you noticed in a deeper and more satisfying way the beauty of the fresh flowers your husband now brought home every week. And you found that far from avoiding the little room Stan had redone as a guest room you now enjoyed sitting in there when you read. The soft taupe on the walls was a soothing color, the light was excellent, and it was the one room in the apartment which was airy. That was why you'd chosen to make it the nursery—and when you realized that now you could say that word "nursery" to yourself without tears, you knew that you'd turned a corner. The sorrow for your dream of a child was in your heart, in the very blood that pumped through it, but somehow that released you to get on with your life.

Stan seemed to feel that she was ready to move on too. One night he gave her a box wrapped in pink paper with artificial roses in the bow. Inside was a computer.

He had one at his shop that he used for the business, but they'd never had one for their own use. "You already know how to work one . . . well, you do a little," he said, talking fast in his excitement. "I understand that you don't think of yourself as the technological type, but this is so user friendly it won't take you any time to catch on." Then he smiled his smile that made the skin crinkle at the corners of his eyes. "You always wanted to write, Gwen, why don't you try?"

So she did. She practiced with the computer until she knew she could work it well enough that the mechanics of using it wouldn't interfere with her train of thought. Then she sat in the taupe-colored guest room and tried to write a children's story about a pigeon who lived in a park. But she couldn't make her mind think like a city pigeon who lived by begging for crumbs from strangers. She tried to write a story about a squirrel who lived near a stump on a hill behind a big white house. But she found she'd lost her connection to the squirrels and chipmunks she'd once watched for hours in her refuge. Finally, she put the computer in the living room where she and Stan both could use it, and she went back to reading when she sat in the guest room.

But Stan wouldn't give up. "Writing was your dream when I met you," he said. "You say you don't have any stories to tell, but I know one day you'll do it."

She didn't say that she needed space and sky to spin her stories. That was one of the things they didn't talk about.

But she didn't go back into her shell. She made friends—in a casual way— with a few of the women she met while she was washing her clothes in the basement of the apartment building. She learned about popular television programs and romance novels and trendy shoes from them. They heard about foreign films, the Metropolitan Opera broadcast on Saturday afternoons, and Emily Dickinson from her. And while she never actually bought the uncomfortable shoes, and she doubted seriously that they ever bought a volume of Dickinson's poetry, she found it was nice to have someone to talk to while you folded your towels. A couple of her new friends were taking a cooking course in the evenings and she signed up too. Cassie was particularly impressed by this new venture, because she couldn't boil water.

Once or twice a week, Gwen saw Jeff Henry's long black limousine from her apartment window, as he was whisked away either to some meeting in town or to the airport so he could fly to some exotic place halfway around the world. She could usually tell which it was by the amount of luggage—or lack of it—that was handed so carefully into the trunk of the car.

And once in a while, when she was walking to the market or to the park, she and Jeff would run into each other. And he would ask her if she'd like to have coffee with him and she would say yes because it was fun to talk to a man who shared her taste for Dickens and Tolstoy, and they both enjoyed their ongoing debate over the merits of his favorite opera composer, Wagner, versus her beloved Puccini. She liked the way he matched his swaggering pirate's stride to hers when they walked down the street together. And if there was a childish part of her brain that liked it all a little more than she otherwise might have because he was married to Jewel Fairchild who was now Jewel Henry . . . well, so be it. Jewel had so much these days—the beauty which had always been hers, a handsome exciting husband, and all the money even she could want. Surely, there was no harm in Gwen enjoying the admiration she saw in Jeff's eyes when they shared overpriced coffee and trivialities.

But gradually, as one does with a good friend, she and Jeff started opening up about less trivial, more personal matters. He told her about his teenage years as the nerdy son of two pretentious intellectuals, and Gwen talked about her childhood as an odd duck, the animals she loved and the stories she used to make up about them. And then she found herself opening up even more.

"I'm adopted," she told him. "And I've thought so much about my birth parents. Wondered about them. And then . . ." She paused. She wanted to tell him everything about those two unknown figures who still loomed in her life, but she couldn't. The story of the man who had been married to Cassie Wright and cheated on her with another woman was Cassie's to tell. Jewel had spilled the tale without Cassie's permission and that had been wrong. Gwen was not about to do the same thing. She changed the subject.

"And then when I knew I was going to have a baby I felt like I was . . . not carrying on their legacy, exactly, but . . ." She searched for the right words.

" 'Leaving behind their footprints on

the sands of time.' " Jeff supplied a quote.

"Longfellow," she said.

"Slightly mangled." He smiled.

"Thank you."

"For what?"

She paused again to search for the right words. For he had given her a gift—the one we always receive when we hear or see or read a work of art that has endured the test of time. Because we are reminded then that we are not isolated, that whatever we are thinking or feeling has been felt and thought before, and we are comforted by the connection to the rest of the humanity that has been where we are.

"For putting things in perspective for me," she finally said. And he nodded that he understood. And if that childish part of her brain gloated again because she knew there was no way he could have this exchange with his beautiful charming wife . . . it was such a little victory; it wasn't hurting anyone.

So time passed, and Gwen's gray fog lifted more each day, and before she knew it, a year had passed since she'd lost her baby. For that day the fog threatened to descend again. She hadn't told anyone that she'd hoped that before the sad anniversary came she'd be pregnant again. It wasn't the kind of thing she could say to Stan; he might find something morbid about re-membering the date, and there was no point in saying something that might cause him grief. Still, she wished she could talk to someone. She thought of Jeff, who listened and would find some-thing to say that would help. It would be nice if she were to run into him today, she thought, as she left the apartment and headed to the elevators. She was going out into the neighborhood, to pick up Stan's jacket at the dry cleaners.

*   *   *

Jeff stood at his window and watched Gwen walk out of her building. He thought about rushing down to the street to stage another of his "acciden-tal" run-ins with her, but instead he looked back to his desk where a report waited for him. It had been assembled by his staff at his request some time ago, but he had not read it yet. Because when he did he would have to make a decision that he'd been putting off. It was the worst kind of decision—it mixed his business and his personal lives. It concerned the woman who was now walking down the street in the direction of the shops that serviced the neighborhood. Gwen Girard was probably doing some wifely errand, shopping for some last-minute item at the grocery store, or picking up some shoes that had been repaired. He frowned; he didn't like to think of her involved in such mundane pursuits and yet he knew from a recent conversation with her that she had finally found a kind of peace in them. She still longed for a house of her own, he knew that, but she had told him that Stan didn't want to purchase one until they had enough money put away for a sizable down payment. "Stan's careful," she'd said with a laugh.

Stan's a dolt, Jeff had thought. And he couldn't help contrasting her minimal desire with Jewel's never-ending grasping.

*   *   *

Jeff moved back to his desk and sat. For a while now, he'd been serially and consistently unfaithful to his wife. He was discreet, when one was away from home as much as he was, that was easy. Although he wondered if it would have mattered to Jewel if she had known. Her passion, he had finally come to understand—or perhaps he had always known it, and just hadn't wanted to face it—had nothing to do with him and everything to do with what he could provide. She never ever denied herself to him—of course she wouldn't; she was an ideal wife. But he'd had enough women to know the difference between skillful fakery and the real thing. The only time Jewel was genuinely excited in their bed was when she wanted something. Or when he'd just given her something she'd wanted. At first, when he was still besotted with her, he'd happily handed out the baubles and gifts she craved. But his first wild desire for her had died, as infatuations must, and, as his father had warned, there was no basis for anything more between them.

The realization had come to him slowly, as it dawned on him that his hopes for the day when she would share his tastes and interests were futile. His campaign to introduce her to what he thought of as the finer things in life had failed miserably. Not that she ever refused to go with him to the ballet or a museum. She would sit through a performance of *Die Zauberflöte* or *Die Meistersinger,* but it was clear that she was just waiting for the outing to be over so she could go back to her celebrity magazines, her gossip, and her shopping. His fantasies of opening her mind to fine books and great art once she had the leisure and the money to enjoy them, were just that—dreams. It wasn't her fault that this annoyed him now; he was the one who had changed. And he did understand her desire for expensive things, because he shared it with her. But he wanted more. She did not.

The final blow had come when they had finally moved into the nightmare of a house she had designed and loved so much—the house that humiliated him. Because it reminded him of what a fool he'd been. That was when he started noticing how irritating she was. And how noisy. It wasn't just her incessant, mindless chatter; it was the bracelets clanking on her arms, her high-heeled shoes that clicked and clacked down the hallways of her large vulgar home, the sweet voice that now grated on his ears, and her laugh, which had once seemed so warm and free to him, now sounded like a strident bid for attention. It was no wonder that Gwen Wright, who was so quiet, and so intelligent, attracted him.

Jeff picked up the neatly typed report on his desk and began to read—but then he put it down. The stapled sheaf of papers was the result of the research he'd asked his staff to do on Stanley Girard. The business decision he had to make concerned the husband of the woman he wanted. But in what way did he want her?

He knew Gwen enjoyed his company, and he was pretty sure that he could push their relationship further. After all, could Stanley Girard really give him a run for his money? He didn't think so. Gwen's husband was probably one of those inarticulate, salt-of-the-earth men who bought his wife a blender for her birthday and took her on vacation every year to a place where he could kill small animals and fish.

So why hadn't Jeff pushed the relationship? Because Gwen Wright wasn't the kind of woman who would have a little fling with a man. She would have to be desperately, passionately in love— and he knew with every fiber of his being that she was capable of it—before she would betray her salt-of-the-earth husband. And then she would probably insist on ending her marriage. Cheating, lying, and sexual encounters on the sly would not do for her. And while Jeff would have loved to be the one to ignite that desperate passionate love he was sure was in her, he wasn't sure he was ready to throw over everything for it.

The trouble was, when you looked at it logically, there were elements of his arrangement with Jewel that worked. She still looked fabulous on his arm, and as long as the conversation was light social chatter, she could be charming. She had never expressed any interest in having the children he very much didn't want, and as he'd already noted, she was not likely to curtail his freedom in the matter of other women as long as he continued to pay the bills. But if he were to try to divorce her there would be hell to pay. Jewel might not be in love with him, but she wasn't going to give up being Mrs. Jeff Henry without a battle. And at the moment there were reasons—serious business reasons—why he could not afford that.

Jeff rubbed his temples where a headache seemed to be starting. The deal for the water utility concession in Brazil had gone through about a year ago and at first it had seemed like another one of his golden-boy moves, but lately there had been some disturbing rumblings coming out of São Paulo. The sharp young man Jeff had hired as his second in command—his name was Mark Scotto, and Jeff had stolen him at huge expense from a German conglomerate—had brought on a new accounting firm from New York to help handle the growing concerns. The pencil pushers at D. E. Alexander had assured Jeff that the solution was to create a separate corporation for the water concession. "To leverage the investment," they said. That was a polite way of saying they were trying to spread the risk around. The new corporation would then be part-floated on the New York Stock Exchange. Of course some creative accounting would be required to pump up the value of the stock for the market, but this was not an unusual practice. They would be skating fairly close to the edge with a few FTC regulations but what the hell, Jeff had done that before. Perhaps, Mark and the accountants suggested, as a way of boosting the company's standing on the stock exchange, Jeff should invest more of his own money in JeffSon. The unspoken understanding was that should the worst happen—and it wouldn't, everyone agreed on that— but just in case it did, Jeff would have plenty of time to pull his funds out. It all sounded logical and there was nothing about it that everyone else wasn't doing, so there was no reason in the world for Jeff to suddenly remember his father saying *Beware of Faustean bargains, Jeffie.* At the same time he didn't want Jewel's divorce lawyers going through his books right now, as they would be sure to do if he were stupid enough to rock the boat.

But still, there was Gwen and the way he felt when he listened to her talk. Sometimes she'd tell him funny stories about her cooking classes, which were not going well, or the sweater she had tried to knit and abandoned in disgust. And every once in a while she would talk about her old home and the hill behind the house where she used to sit and watch the squirrels and the chipmunks. Her voice was so soft, and her intelligent eyes were so full of curiosity and excitement.

Jeff looked down at his desk and the report on Stan Girard. He already knew what was in it; the young Turk who had investigated Gwen's husband had given him a verbal summary and said that Stanley Girard was a talented guy who was parlaying his little shop into an operation that specialized in the installation, maintenance, and repair of some very sophisticated electrical systems for major corporate clients. He was not a wheeler-dealer, but he was growing his business steadily and surely. He was a good candidate for what Jeff had in mind.

Jeff walked back to the window and looked down at the street where Gwen had stood a few minutes earlier waiting for the light to change. She had looked unhappy today. He thought for a moment—wasn't it about this time last year that he had heard she'd lost her baby? Yes, he was sure it was. Suddenly, he wanted to give her something, something that would make the sad look go away.

The report on Stanley Girard was on his desk. If he were to make his offer to the man, Gwen could have her house. And—be honest, now—Gwen would be indebted to him; she would feel the full power of Jeff Henry, the man behind JeffSon. Power was an aphrodisiac. For that matter, gratitude—of a certain kind—could be too. And while there might be repercussions—what the hell, Jeff was a gambler, wasn't he? That was how he lived his life. He picked up the phone on his desk and buzzed his secretary. "Set up a meeting for me with Stanley Girard," he said.

Chapter Twenty-six

꧁ ꧂

"You want to buy Stan's Electronics?" Stan looked at the man sitting across the desk from him in disbelief. He'd seen pictures of Jeff Henry in the newspaper and in the kind of magazines that ran articles about people who were celebrities in the worlds of business and philanthropy, and he'd caught sight of him at a distance because his offices were across the street from Stan's apartment building. But they'd never actually been face to face. Now he was sitting in a huge office that was decorated in shades of gray with lots of glass and chrome, and Jeff Henry had just offered to buy him out.

"What could you possibly want with my operation?" Stan asked. "I'm strictly small potatoes."

"Good question," Jeff Henry said. "You must know the JeffSon Corporation has been expanding all over the country. We purchased that twenty-five-hundred-megawatt plant in upstate New York last year, and connected it to the local grid; and we're looking at buying several other plants in the area, which we will connect in a similar way. We'll need centrally located stations from which to install, operate, and maintain these new plants. Your shop is in an ideal location because it's in the center of Wrightstown."

Things were starting to make a little sense. "And I own the building and the land under it."

Jeff Henry nodded. His attitude seemed rather brusque, Stan thought. The man was supposed to be such a great negotiator, and so loaded with charm. But it

was almost as if he was deliberately being rude.

*   *   *

Jeff was a little thrown. Stan Girard was
not the fool he'd thought—no, all right,
admit it—Stan was not the fool Jeff had
hoped he'd be. Jeff assessed the man
in front of him with the shrewdness for
which he was famous. Stanley Girard
had the kind of looks that could definitely be attractive to women, with his
shock of untamed black hair that fell
into his eyes, and his craggy features.
He had a straightforward way of speaking that a woman might find appealing,
and there were lines around his eyes
that said he laughed often, so presum-
ably he had a sense of humor. But Jeff
couldn't imagine him ever following
the intricacies of a mind like Gwen's.
The whimsy of which she was capable
would escape him completely. *I'm staring at him,* Jeff realized and turned
away.

*   *   *

Stan was aware of being scrutinized as he had seldom been before. And he didn't like it much. "So what you want, essentially, is to buy my real estate," he said.

"Not only that," came the answer. "When we purchase a small business, like yours, it isn't a total cash transaction. A piece of your compensation will be in JeffSon stock." The brusque voice now took on a condescending tone. "You'll be a shareholder in one of the biggest and most important new companies in the world. And—"

"If I wanted to do that, I could just go to my local broker and buy your stock," Stan broke in. He was being rude himself now, but the guy was really annoying him. "I wouldn't have to sell my business."

Jeff Henry finally seemed to realize that he'd been handling this badly. He smiled for the first time. And it was true, when he smiled he was charming. "I was about to say that the stock in the company is just a start. You will also have the same kind of deal on stock options that every other JeffSon exec does."

"A JeffSon exec? But I'm not—"

This time it was Jeff Henry's turn to interrupt. "We would want you to work for us. Overseeing the crews and managing the installation and maintenance of our various operations in this part of the country." He shrugged and smiled. "It's an executive position, although of course what we're buying is your expertise in the field."

"And you are sure I have this expertise?"

The smile got even wider and more charming. "We do our research. We know you're the best around here."

"That's very flattering." *But why do I feel that there's something you're not telling me?*

* * *

Why the hell isn't he jumping at this? Jeff thought angrily. *Doesn't he realize what I'm offering him? Poor Gwen, she really did marry an idiot.* But there was nothing idiotic about Stanley Girard's eyes. Or the thoughtful way he was studying Jeff.

"Look, Stan . . . may I call you Stan?" There was a nod of assent on the other side of his desk. "I think you know the situation as well as I do. JeffSon is going to be taking over more and more small companies all over the state. And to say it plainly, those we don't buy, we'll put out of business. As the whole field of energy distribution consolidates, your customers will start coming to us for the same kind of service you now provide because with all our resources, we can bundle it into a much more efficient and economical package.

"Your choice is to continue with a small business that will eventually be obsolete, or to sign on now with us and be a part of a growing and expanding organization that will be around for the rest of your working life. Your salary will be commensurate with that of all our top management, and I think you'll find, when you add in your benefits, your JeffSon stock, and stock options, that you'll be doing much better than you could ever hope to do on your own."

"I see." For whatever his reasons Stanley Girard was handing him the classic noncommittal response.

You should be on your knees thanking me for this, you jerk!

"Well, that's our offer in a nutshell," Jeff said. "Think it over and let us know. I have to go out of town for a few days, so you'll be dealing with Jon Kaiser. He handles hiring on the management level. I must admit that normally I don't involve myself with that, but since you are a local businessman and I live here in the area, I wanted to talk to you myself."

And the other reason you're getting such preferential treatment is, I have coffee with your wife.

"Thank you. I'll be in touch," said Stan.

*   *   *

When Stan left The Amber and was back out on First Street, he knew he should have been thanking his lucky stars. The offer from Jeff Henry was an amazing opportunity. But for some reason, the uneasy feeling Stan had had in the man's office was even stronger. More than anything he wanted to talk to

Gwen about it. This was her decision as much as it was his. And that wasn't just paying lip service. Stan knew that he and Gwen saw certain things very differently and he'd learned the hard way that he shouldn't take her reactions for granted. He had made mistakes in the past when he'd assumed that she would feel as he did about things, and she'd been hurt and angry. This time he meant to be guided by her.

*   *   *

"How did you hear about the offer Jeff-Son made to Stan?" Gwen demanded.

She and her mother were sitting in the food court at the Algonquin Mall. It was not a usual haunt for Cassie, but when she'd called Gwen and issued what was almost a royal summons, she'd claimed she wanted some of the admittedly terrific pizza sold in the mall pizza stall. Since Cassie never ate junk food, Gwen had found this sudden desire a little suspicious, and she'd been right. What Cassie had wanted was anonymity, a place where no one would see Cassandra Wright and her daughter sitting and talking together in the middle of a work-day. Normally Cassie took her forty-five minute lunch in the executive dining room at the glassworks, but there were too many opportunities for the curious to eavesdrop there.

They had purchased their slices of pizza and taken them to a secluded part of the food court next to the coffee stand. Then Cassandra had delivered her bombshell.

"You must keep Stanley from accepting Jeff Henry's offer," she'd said.

The offer had only been made three days ago, and Gwen herself had known about it for less than seventy-two hours, so she repeated her question, "Mother, how did you know about this?"

"There is very little that goes on in the business community in this town that I don't know. Besides, this was predictable. JeffSon's gobbling up small companies like Stanley's all over the place. Add to that the fact that Stanley owns his building free and clear, and it's in a great location on a busy avenue that's going to be even busier in a few more years. Stanley probably doesn't even realize how much that real estate is worth."

"Oh, he does, believe me. Stan knows to the penny. But it's not just the shop they want. They want Stan to work for them too. In a management position. Or didn't your spies tell you that?"

Instead of looking chastened, Cassandra sighed. "No, I didn't know that. It's even worse than I thought."

"Worse? What do you mean? I think this is a great opportunity for Stan. That a man like Jeff Henry sees his worth and . . ."

"Gwen, listen to me," Cassie broke in urgently. "Stanley is doing well with his shop, and I'm very happy for you. He works hard and he deserves as much success as he can handle. But for him to get himself involved with a company like JeffSon . . ."

"What's wrong with JeffSon?"

"Maybe nothing. But there are things that bother me. They're buying and selling way too much for my taste, creating offshore corporations that are hard to monitor, and just a couple of months ago, they hired a new accounting firm that has a reputation for skating very close to the line. . . ."

"Somehow I think Jeff Henry knows what he's doing."

"Jeff Henry is a Johnny-come-lately who appeared out of nowhere and has made an enormous amount of money very quickly. One has to wonder about that, Gwen. One has to wonder."

"Why?"

"I just explained."

"No, you didn't. You said that it was impossible for someone like Jeff Henry who came out of nowhere to outearn a member of the almighty Wright family. Maybe he's just brilliant. Maybe he's a genius."

"Good Lord, why are you defending the man?"

It was a good question. Too damn good. The answer was, Gwen had been pleased that Jeff had offered her husband a big job because it meant that she and Jewel were closer to being equals. Because, childish as it was, when she thought about Jewel, it bothered her that Stan hadn't set the world on fire, and accumulated a pile of money.

But that's crazy. I don't give a hoot about any of that. Stan and I are getting along just fine. He's the dearest man in the world to me. And the kindest. Oh God, how long am I going to carry this old baggage around with me?

But she couldn't seem to stop defending Jeff. "None of what you're saying means that Jeff Henry is doing anything wrong."

"Not necessarily, but it can be a red flag." Cassie drew in a deep breath and then she said, "The truth is, the people at JeffSon are big-stakes players—high-fliers, if you will. And with all due respect to your husband, I don't think he's . . . well, sophisticated enough for that kind of environment."

Gwen tried to fight the anger that was rising inside her. "Do you have any idea how insulting you're being?" she cried. "You're talking as if Stan were an idiot."

"I never said anything like that. But I do know something about the Jeff Henrys of the world, more than you or Stanley do, and I'm giving you some advice I think you need. Tell Stanley to stay with his honest business and a decent profit."

And then it burst out. It was the last thing Gwen wanted to say, but she couldn't stop herself. "You're just saying all of this because Jeff is Jewel's husband!"

"What?"

"You've never forgiven her. We're supposed to forgive and forget; you brought me up that way, remember?"

"I was not—"

"But you haven't forgiven Jewel, and you don't like Jeff Henry because he's married to her, and—"

"For heaven's sake, it's not that way at all. It would be sick to harp on that old stuff, and I don't think I'm *sick,* Gwen. The thought never crossed my mind, although obviously, it did cross yours, and I must say . . ."

But whatever it was that she must say didn't get said because they were interrupted by an enthusiastic voice. "Gwen! Cassandra!" it called out. And there was Jewel, loaded down with packages and waving at them. She was several yards away—at least at that distance she hadn't overheard them talking about her—and now she hurried over.

"How wonderful to see both of you!" she said as she approached their table. "I can't believe you're here in the food court of all places! I drop by that little coffee stand over there for old time's sake whenever I come to the mall!" She laughed. "Back when I was a kid, one cup of coffee with no sugar or cream was my big treat. I used to get it here before I had my nails done—my other big treat!" She rolled her eyes with a droll little smile, to make it clear that those days were gone forever. *In case you've been living under a rock for the past five years, and didn't know she's married to one of the wealthiest men in the country,* Gwen thought uncharitably. She looked at Jewel, who was now standing close to the table, waiting to be asked to sit down. *Jewel's as beautiful as ever,* she thought. *Maybe even more beautiful than she used to be. She has the kind of looks that are enhanced by money—but then, maybe everyone's looks are. Her hair is fabulous with that new cut, and she always did know how to put on makeup, and that dress . . . well, it's a little fancy for noon on a Wednesday, but it does flatter her so.*

I wonder what she's thinking. She's been smiling and staring at Mother and me as hard as we've been staring at her.

*   *   *

Cassandra looks the way she always has, Jewel thought, *and dear dull Gwen is still a mess! That dress must be at least two years old! And she never has figured out what to do with her hair. I bet it never has looked as good as it did when I fixed it for her. She probably doesn't even remember that.*

But as she gazed at the mother and daughter sitting side by side, Jewel felt something like a lump in her throat which totally surprised her. Gwen and Cassie looked so . . . together. And sure of themselves. They knew who they were and where they belonged. *I wonder if I'll ever feel like that,* Jewel thought. *I wonder if Gwen will ever realize how unbelievably lucky she is. And I wonder what Cassandra is thinking right this second. Whatever it is, it has something to do with me, I know, because she's looking right at me.*

*   *   *

It isn't fair that Jewel never ages or puts on weight or looks anything other than gorgeous! Cassie thought indignantly. *She has the kind of bone structure that will look marveous when she's in her nineties. She's standing there in that dress that is completely inappropriate, but it had to cost a fortune—from the looks of those packages, she's probably spent another fortune today—and in another minute I know she's going to start trying to lord it over Gwen because she has more money now than Gwen does. She'll find a sneaky way to do it; it'll come out of nowhere, and then Gwen will start cringing. There are times when I hate women. Give me a man's world any day. But I'm not in a man's world. I'm here with two other women and we're all staring at each other and the silence is getting ridiculous.*

"Hello, Jewel," Cassie said, hoping her voice didn't sound as chilly to everyone else as it did to her.

Gwen followed her lead with a polite, "How are you, Jewel?"

"Fine, couldn't be better," Jewel said heartily. She looked down at their paper plates. "Oh, my! You're having pizza! I don't dare eat it, goes straight to you know where!" She smoothed one hand over a slim hip. "May I sit with you?" She drew out a chair at the table. "I'm simply exhausted. I must've walked ten miles in this mall today."

There was nothing to do but ask her to join them before she did so without being invited. "I've finished my errands for the day," she went on. "I just stopped at the jeweler's to have my bracelets cleaned. They do it so much more thoroughly than anyone else does."

It is an automatic reflex to look at an article, be it a hat, a book, or anything, that someone has just mentioned. Cassie and Gwen both did so. It is also automatic to make some comment about that article and Cassie was the one who did the honors.

"Very pretty, Jewel," she said, as she was expected to say.

"Jeff gave them to me for our anniversary."

"Lovely." Gwen spoke this time.

"Jeff spoils me rotten. And of course he's doing so well, I just can't believe it. He's into so many different businesses. Why, just the other day I heard him talking to someone on the phone about water rights in Brazil—can you imagine?"

Something cold prickled down Cassie's back. She glanced at Gwen to see if she had picked up on Jewel's remark, but Gwen hadn't. Gwen didn't understand business, so there were no tiny alarm bells going off for her. And it was more than possible that there was no reason for them to be going off for Cassie—or so she tried to tell herself. Still, she couldn't help trying to get a little more information.

"I certainly appreciate the need for any company to diversify," she said to Jewel. "But it was my understanding that JeffSon is in the business of distributing energy. What could that possibly have to do with water rights?"

Out of the corner of her eye she saw Gwen stiffen. Clearly, her daughter thought she was being too much of a stickler. Cassie wondered once again why Gwen had taken on the role of Jeff Henry's defender.

And Jewel is looking at me as if she'd like to tell me to go to hell, Cassie thought.

Instead, Jewel gave her a little chuckle and dismissive wave of her hand. "I'm really not worried about what's going on at JeffSon. That's my husband's department and believe me, he can take care of himself." Then she turned to Gwen and changed the subject. "Do you still go back behind your house and sit on that stump the way you used to? I'll never forget when that old gardener told me you did that—Oh, but wait, you live in the city now, don't you? That must be very hard on you, the way you used to love all those rabbits and things. Not a lot of those on First Street."

And there it is, the sneak attack, thought Cassandra. But for once, Gwen wasn't cringing.

"The apartment is what Stan and I can afford right now," she said. "We're saving up for a house."

For a second Jewel looked defeated. Then her face brightened. "I have an idea," she said. "Jeff is out of town, and I'm at loose ends; why don't you come out to my place? You can follow me in my car and I'll show you around. We've just finished the house and I'd love for you to see it. I've never forgotten the first time I saw your home, Cassandra."

"I'm afraid that's not possible—" Cassie started to say, but then, inexplicably, Gwen interrupted.

"It sounds like fun, Mother!" she cried. "We have the time, don't we?"

"I do work," Cassandra said frostily.

"Yes, but didn't you tell me they weren't expecting you back in the office until late this afternoon?"

"It'll only take an hour, I promise," Jewel chimed in.

There really wasn't a graceful way for Cassie to back out.

Chapter Twenty-seven

Gwen waited for her mother's protest to begin. Sure enough, it came as soon as they were in Gwen's car.

"What were you thinking?" Cassie demanded.

That I won't let Jewel intimidate me, Gwen thought. *And besides, I want to see this mansion she's built. According to Jeff she's been at it for the better part of a year.*

"There is absolutely no reason for you to be traipsing off on this fool's errand,"

Cassie went on protesting. "And still less reason for me to go with you."

Gwen flicked on the turn signal as, ahead of them, Jewel—predictably behind the wheel of a car that was new and looked very expensive—turned left. "Do you know if that's a BMW?" she asked her mother. "The car Jewel's driving?"

"It's a Jaguar," came the testy reply. "Why do you care?"

"I don't. Not really." She looked at her mother. "Oh, come on, Jewel just wants to show off her house. Let's give her the satisfaction."

"I do not want to give Jewel Fairchild . . . Jewel Henry . . . satisfaction for anything."

"You see? I knew it. You are still angry at her after all these years!"

"Are you trying to annoy me, Gwendolyn?"

Gwen took a beat. "No," she said thoughtfully. "I guess I'm just trying to put an old ghost to rest." She looked at the scenery that was passing by them. "It is a lovely ride, isn't it?"

"Charming," Cassie admitted grudgingly. "It's old America out here, all these colonial houses—" Then she stopped short. "And some new ones," she added grimly as Jewel's car led them through the wrought-iron front gate of an enormous house that sprawled at the head of a long, sloping driveway. Architecturally speaking, the thing was a hodgepodge of styles and periods. A few of them seemed to work together; most did not.

"Is that a pond?" Cassie asked.

"Where?"

"There, at the top of the driveway."

"You mean where that fountain is spurting? Yes, I think it is a pond. Or possibly a moat."

"Ah."

They ascended the drive. Above them, Jewel got out of her car and waved them onward. Meanwhile Cassie sat forward in her seat. She seemed to be scanning the house.

"Are you looking for something?" Gwen asked.

"Hold on just a minute, I know there has to be one . . . yes, there it is!" she said triumphantly. "It was hidden under that little balcony."

"What was?"

"The Palladian window. In a house like this there had to be at least one fake Palladian window."

They got out of the car and Jewel bustled up to them. *Jeff must be crazy about her to put up with living in a place like this,* Gwen thought. *It's like those showy bracelets he gave her. I know there's no way he'd ever have bought them if he wasn't trying to please her.*

"I can't wait to give you the tour," Jewel burbled as she ushered them through the massive front door of her home.

The inside of the house wasn't any better than the outside. From the great circle of the entrance hall, there radiated corridors—the floor of each had been done in a different kind of exotic wood, Jewel proudly pointed out—and they all led to the varied luxuries of the house— the card room, the billiard room, the bowling alley, the media theater, and the spa with a connected gym. There was no library, but in a rather grand chamber that Jewel announced was Jeff's study, there were books bound in handsome, wine-colored leather that matched the leather chairs and sofas. Gwen tried to imagine the man she knew sitting in there and comfortably reading one of those color-coordinated, pristine tomes while sliding around on the slick over-stuffed furniture.

The tour wound up in the foyer, where the windows looked out upon the lawns, the guest cottage, and the pool, which was backed by what looked like a slab of some kind of rock. A touch of a but-ton on a huge electrical panel on the foyer wall turned the slab into a violently rushing waterfall worthy of Niagara. Jewel frantically adjusted levers and switches until the flood was under con-trol. "I'm still not used to working this thing," she said with her wide smile. The nearby tennis courts were soaked. Gwen didn't dare look at her mother for fear that they would both start laughing.

"The designer kept trying to convince me to put a fire pit behind the pool, but I said, no, no, I wanted a water feature," Jewel said.

"Well, you certainly got one," said Cassandra and Gwen had to look away some more.

*   *   *

They're laughing at me, Jewel thought. They think I don't know it, but I'm not dumb. What kind of good manners is that? And what have they got to laugh about anyway? My house is bigger than that musty old place that Cassie owns— I used to think it was so grand but I've learned a whole lot since then—and as for Gwen, living in her little city apartment, she doesn't have the right to turn up her nose at me or anyone else.

But even as she was thinking these things, Jewel was remembering the way Jeff had reacted when the house was finally finished. At first he'd seemed stunned, which hadn't bothered Jewel at all because she and the architect had been trying for what the architect referred to as the Pow! factor. But then that funny little look that was halfway between pity and disgust had come into her husband's eyes—it was the same look she was seeing now with Gwen and Cassie—and he had muttered under his breath, "Thank God, Dad doesn't drive much anymore."

She had pretended she hadn't heard him—she was always very careful not to get into a quarrel with him—and she had dismissed the incident from her mind. But it had seemed to her that since they'd moved into her dream home, Jeff had spent even more time at work than he had when they were living in the hotel. And when he was home he seemed distracted. He told her he didn't like her perfume, but when she changed it, he didn't notice. He was irritable, too, and sometimes it felt as if he was always correcting her. "We have a *cook,* Jewel," he said one night. "The woman is not a chef and it's pretentious to call her that." And another time when they were about to go out for an evening, he'd looked at her and shaken his head. "Do you have to wear all of your jewelry at once?" he'd demanded. Once when they were dining with friends she'd overheard him say to his end of the table, "Of course, when it comes to a news item, if it doesn't show up in a gossip magazine, my wife will never read it."

For a while she had put the unkindness down to business pressures. She knew that he was under a lot of stress, even though, as she'd told Cassie, she never tried to find out what was happening at JeffSon. But lately she'd begun to wonder what else might be going on. To be blunt, he had cooled toward her in the bedroom. When they were first married and he couldn't get enough of her, she would have welcomed the nights when he moved to his side of the bed to read a book. But now she was finding it bothered her. Jewel wasn't naïve; she'd always accepted the idea that men being men, he would have a fling or two. But she hadn't thought it would happen so early in their marriage while she was still so beautiful. And she wondered if there was a bevy of women, or just one. There was safety in numbers. If there was only one woman . . . But she wasn't going to think about that. Not with Cassie and Gwen standing there, watching her.

"That husband of mine is so generous," she said loudly—maybe a little too loudly? "He's a Santa Claus! He gives me anything I want, even if it costs a fortune!"

Now Cassie and Gwen didn't look like they wanted to laugh. Now they looked embarrassed for her, as if she'd done something awful like eat with her mouth open or scratch herself when she thought no one was looking! People like Gwen Girard and Cassie Wright felt superior to the rest of the human race because they had money, but when someone like Jewel brought the subject up, she was crass and crude. It wasn't fair!

For the first time in years, Jewel wanted to cry. Because in one of those flashes in which we see ourselves with total clarity, she realized that she hadn't just brought Gwen and Cassie to her house to make them jealous or show them that the worm had turned; she'd wanted them to . . . accept her. She'd wanted them to say that she had overcome the sawdust Pop brought home on his clothes every night, and the little house packed with too many kids that had finally killed her mother. She had wanted Cassie and Gwen to admit that, at long last, Jewel Fairchild belonged to the exclusive club they'd been members of forever. But now they were letting her know that she'd never belong. No matter what she did she would always be the outsider at Gwen's birthday party who'd been given an invitation as an afterthought, and came wearing a borrowed gown. *How I hate them,* she thought as she blinked back tears.

*   *   *

Is Jewel going to cry? Gwen wondered. *What does she have to cry about?* Her home was a travesty, of course, but if you looked past the pool and the ridiculous water feature and the silly Tyrolean guest cottage, you could see beautiful land with trees and wildflowers that Jewel and her landscape designer had not managed to destroy.

More important than that, Jewel's husband, who was brilliant and funny and far too good for her, had given all of it to her. Even if it was not his taste, he loved her enough to want to make her happy, to "spoil her rotten." Gwen's husband loved her too, but he expected her to be patient and wait for the house she needed and wanted so desperately. Suddenly, Gwen wanted to get away from Jewel and her mansion, and the vision of Jeff Henry living in it for Jewel's sake. It was obvious that Cassie wanted to leave, too, because she was looking at her watch. "I think . . ." she was starting to say, when a man's voice in the hallway startled all of them.

"I'll take my bags up to my room, George," said the voice.

And George, whoever he was, answered, "Of course, Mr. Henry. Mrs. Henry is in the living room with guests, sir."

Before the three women could take a breath, Jeff was entering the room with his swaggering stride. He seemed a little put out that his wife was entertaining visitors, but Gwen thought she saw his eyes light up when he spotted her. But there was every possibility that she had imagined it. The moment passed in an instant, and Jeff was greeting Cassandra, and then giving Jewel a kiss on the cheek and explaining that he'd come home early because one of the guys from Texas had fallen and broken his arm and the whole bunch would be flying up the next day in somebody's private jet. And Jewel flashed a gloating look at Gwen because her husband and the men with whom he did business all had their own airplanes.

*   *   *

Jewel couldn't help shooting a glance at Gwen, then she slipped her hand possessively through Jeff's arm. For a second when he'd first walked in the door she'd thought she'd seen something in the look he gave Gwen—a warmth and a tenderness that he never displayed— and Jewel had wanted to demand an explanation on the spot. But then she realized it had been her imagination. That was what happened when you let people like Gwen and Cassie make you feel inferior. If you didn't watch it, you found yourself imagining that dull, shy Gwen could actually be attractive to your husband. Jeff went for women who were beautiful and charming—well, look at the one he'd married for Pete's sake. It was ridiculous to think that Gwen Girard could ever compete with Jewel Fairchild Henry.

Chapter Twenty-eight

"A penny for your thoughts," Gwen said to her uncharacteristically silent mother as they drove back to Wrightstown. The visit to Jewel's house had ended quickly after Jeff's entrance. He'd tried to start a little idle chitchat with Cassandra. "My father taught art history at Wrightstown College," he'd told her. "One of his students, Edward Laurence, is the curator at the Wright Glass Museum. He was brought on board by your first husband."

Of course Jeff had no way of knowing that any mention of Bradford Greeley was enough to send Cassandra out of a room. Instead of picking up on the opening he'd given her, she had murmured that she must look up the man sometime and hustled herself and Gwen out the door.

"You look angry," Gwen now said as they drove. "Are you?"

"No. I'm just . . . thinking."

"You're not going to start that stuff about JeffSon again, are you? Because anyone can see from looking at that house that Jeff Henry is in fine shape."

"I'm sure he's making money hand over fist; his type usually does—for a while."

"His 'type'? What is that exactly?"

"It's not important." Her mother frowned; she really was disturbed. Finally she said, "There's something else."

"Now what?"

"I—" her mother stopped then started again. "If you want my opinion—and I don't suppose you do, but I'm going to give it to you anyway—I didn't like the way Jeff Henry looked at you when he walked in the room. You're a married woman. He's a married man."

"I cannot begin to imagine what you're talking about!" But Gwen could feel her face getting red.

"Oh, Gwen! Yes, you can. He looked like . . . well, it was worse than just a man undressing a woman with his eyes. That happens. This was more like a smitten boy seeing his prom date for the first time. You can't tell me you weren't aware of it; women are."

"Well, I wasn't!" Gwen said. "Because there was nothing to be aware of!" But of course there had been. Now Cassie was confirming it, which was making Gwen feel guilty. And since guilt is one of the least comfortable emotions we can experience, she got angry at Cassie. "And you are wrong about Stan and the JeffSon offer," she said defiantly. "I liked the idea, but I wasn't sure what to say to Stan. You helped me make up my mind. I'm going to tell him to take it!"

*   *   *

Stan hadn't expected Gwen to be so strongly in favor of the JeffSon deal. Nor had he expected his own reaction to her enthusiasm. He was proud of the small business he'd built from nothing and it hurt to see how easily his wife could contemplate selling it. It had been a dream of his that one day he might hand it down to his son, or—why not?—his daughter. The dream was one he hadn't shared with Gwen—the subject of children was still a raw and painful one between them—but he had hoped it might occur to her. After all, if anyone should understand about family businesses and legacies it should be Gwen. On the other hand, he knew that she was being sensible. Jeff Henry's offer was an excellent one and most people in his position would have grabbed it.

Still, in his heart he wanted to turn it down.

Then the letter came. It was addressed to him at his shop. He recognized Cassandra's correct handwriting at once.

Dear Stanley, she'd written. *I find myself in a difficult position. I am your mother-in-law and it is well known that for the sake of family peace, in-laws should not meddle with young people's lives. So I have had a few misgivings about bringing up a subject that really is none of my business. But I've decided to go ahead anyway and risk your displeasure. And in the interests of total candor, allow me to tell you that it is my intention to discuss my views on this issue with Gwen as well as writing this letter to you. She and I may have spoken by the time you receive this.*

To put the matter plainly, I understand that you have received an offer to sell your business to the JeffSon company and, in exchange for various financial considerations, to join them. The more I think about this, the more I feel that it is not a good idea. You are doing well where you are, and I do not trust some of the things I hear about JeffSon or the people connected with it. You are a man who works hard and you are to be commended for that. Let the highfliers at JeffSon do their wheeling and dealing; you stick to what you know.

Stan took the letter home and showed it to Gwen. "Did Cassie talk to you about this?" he asked.

"Yes," she said.

"It's clear she doesn't think I'm up to the challenge of a big company."

Gwen took the letter out of his hand and tore it in half. "And I told her that you could hold your own with the people at JeffSon or anywhere else," she said proudly.

And with Gwen looking at him with that mixture of love and defiance and perfect faith in his abilities, there was only one thing he could do. "I guess you're looking at a new JeffSon employee," he said. And when she hugged and kissed him and told him how happy she was, he told himself that he was doing the right thing.

But that night after dinner, he went outside to walk around the block. And as he rounded the corner, he looked up at The Amber where Jeff Henry had his offices. And a nagging little voice in the back of his brain was saying that Cassie Wright was a smart woman, whether he liked her or not. She knew a lot more about high finance than he did, and if she had doubts about JeffSon, wouldn't he be a fool to ignore her?

But it isn't JeffSon Cassie doubts, it's

you, he reminded himself. *She thinks you're not good enough and smart enough to protect yourself in a company like that if something does go wrong.*

So tomorrow he was going to call this Jon Kaiser and accept the offer and prove his mother-in-law was wrong! But still the nagging little voice persisted. Instead of going inside, he walked around the block again.

By the time he had circled the block twice more he had made up his mind: He would not accept any JeffSon stock for his building and his land. Jeff Henry would have to pay him in cash or there would be no deal. He would work for JeffSon, but he would keep his money safely tucked away. Satisfied with his decision, he walked into the lobby of his building and went up in the elevator to his waiting wife.

*   *   *

Jewel sat on the satin-covered chaise in the bedroom that Jeff had once said was the size of a football field and watched him unpack. One of the maids certainly could have done it, but since they'd moved into the house for some reason he'd insisted on doing little tasks like that for himself. She watched as he took the monogrammed leather case in which he kept his watches and cufflinks from the suitcase and returned the contents to the bigger case in his walk-in closet. His unused shirts, custom-made of the finest two-fold poplin, were re-hung on the wooden hangers that had been specially made for the purpose. He looked down on Jewel for her extravagances but when it came to his own, nothing but the best would do for Jeff Henry! He was like all the rest of the hypocrites who thought they were too good for people like Jewel—hypocrites like Cassandra Wright and dear, dull Gwen.

"She's not the princess you think she is," Jewel told him as she watched him push the cedar shoe trees into his hand-made Italian loafers.

"Who?" He was too busy with the shoes to look at her.

"Your dear friend Gwen Wright Girard. I know a nasty secret about her."

That got his attention. He came over to

stand in front of her. "What are you talking about?" he demanded. And so she
leaned back on the satin chaise and for
the second time in her life she told the
story of Gwen Wright's birth parents.

After she had finished she waited. Jeff
didn't say anything for a minute, then he
asked, "You did say the mother was
from New Orleans—right?"

"Yes. Some barmaid who . . ." But
Jewel never got to finish the sentence
because Jeff had rushed out of the
room.

*   *   *

Stan held out for his own terms in the
negotiations with JeffSon and he finally
got what he wanted. When the deal was
set, Gwen called her mother to tell her
the news. Cassandra's voice on the
phone was icy. "Yes, I know Stan didn't
take my advice, Gwen, I've known that
for several days."

"We thought this was the best thing for
us," Gwen said.

"I'm sure you did," said her mother
and hung up.

*   *   *

A week later Jeff called Gwen at home—the first time he'd ever done that—and asked her to meet him at the Wright Glass Museum the next day. That was all he would say; she couldn't get anything else out of him.

Chapter Twenty-nine

The Wright Glass Museum had won several architectural awards when it was built in the sixties, and most experts still considered it a gem. The building was a beige cube constructed of site-cast concrete with many skylights and mammoth windows, giving the interior an airy, otherworldly feel which was a perfect setting for the delicate displays of the glassblower's artistry. The collection itself predated the building and had been started by the Wright family in the late twenties. All of the work exhibited had come from the Wright Glassworks Studio, where skilled artisans from all over the world had been creating one-of-a-kind figurines, sculptures, vases, tureens, bowls, loving cups, lampshades, chandeliers, sconces, and other decorative works for over a century.

Gwen hadn't been to the museum in years, although she had always loved it as a child. She was standing in the atrium under a skylight promising herself that she would not let so much time pass again before coming back, when a beaming Jeff came toward her.

"There's something I want to show you," he said excitedly. "But first, I believe I told you about my father's student who is the curator at this museum? His name is Edward Lawrence." Jeff paused. "He worked here when your father was running the Glassworks."

It took her a moment to digest what he'd said—that he knew about Bradford Greeley being her father.

"Who told you . . ." she started to ask, then stopped. "Jewel," she said.

He nodded. "Yes, but that doesn't matter now." Gwen was about to protest that it did matter very much, but he went on, "I thought I remembered hearing Edward talking once about an entire series of figurines your father asked the Glassworks Studio to create. He called it the New Orleans Group."

Gwen had never actually believed that the hairs could stand up on the back of one's neck. Now she knew it was possible. "Oh," she whispered.

"Bradford died before he could tell anyone what he wanted done with the figures. And Cassandra didn't . . ." He trailed off uncertainly.

"And Mother didn't want to have anything to do with them," Gwen finished the thought for him.

Jeff nodded. "They were packed away. But I contacted Edward a couple of days ago and asked if I could take a look at them. Would you like to see them?"

"Yes," Gwen breathed.

"They're in the back storage area."

*　　　*　　　*

Gwen followed Jeff through a door marked Employees Only and he introduced her to Edward Lawrence, who led them up a flight of stairs to the second floor of the storage space where a table had been placed directly under a skylight so that a shaft of sunshine shone down on it.

"This is it, Mrs. Girard!" Edward cried. "I have set up the grouping for you as it might have looked if it had been displayed in the museum. Jeffrey has already viewed it." He stepped back so Gwen could see.

Gwen gasped with sheer pleasure. In front of her, in exquisite miniature, was a forest scene full of sparkling woodland creatures. The trees were actual branches that had been cut to scale, but the animals were all painstakingly and lovingly made out of glass. Two raccoons foraged for food under the watchful eye of a frog, while squirrels with threads of glass whiskers ate acorns and two delicate little chipmunks stuffed their cheeks. A rabbit looked up to a tree branch on which sat an array of different songbirds, each feather etched in careful, minute detail. The sunshine from the skylight played on the little creatures, so that they twinkled and glistened and reflected back an ever-changing rainbow of colors: blues, pinks, and ambers.

"Oh," Gwen said. "Oh, it's so beautiful!"

"Yes," Edward said reverently. "I've worked at the museum for over thirty years and I think this collection one of our greatest masterpieces. I always hoped . . ." But then he looked at Gwen, who was, after all, the daughter of Cassandra, and he stopped himself.

"I wish they could be displayed too," she said. "Thank you for letting me see them." She turned to Jeff. "And thank you," she said. "You're welcome," he said softly.

Jeff didn't say anything more until he and Gwen had left the storage room and were back in the museum with the soaring ceilings and shimmering glass displays.

"I wanted you to see that he wasn't all bad," Jeff said.

"Bradford, you mean."

"When Jewel told me that you were his

daughter and the story about your birth mother . . . I could imagine what you must have thought about him."

"I didn't let myself think much about him, to be honest with you. He was not a subject my mother wanted to discuss, for obvious reasons. But I wanted . . . I always wanted to think well of them both."

"Of course," he said. "Children always do."

He stood there staring at her. At the other side of the museum a group of schoolchildren gathered around their teacher.

"Don't touch that vase, Josh!" the woman's alarmed voice echoed throughout the museum. "Lucy, move away from the display case!"

"I really don't know how to thank you," Gwen said.

He was very still as if he was debating with himself about something. Suddenly, Cassie's words echoed in Gwen's head. *I don't like the way he looks at you,* her mother had said. And Gwen knew that in that moment Jeff was on the brink of saying—or doing—some-

thing that would end their friendship forever, and she didn't want that to happen. "I should be getting back home,"
she said. "I still have to shop for dinner."
Then she added, "For Stan."

He came out of his trance. "And I have
a pile of paperwork back at the office."
They walked to the entrance of the museum together. He did not offer to drive
her back to her apartment building. She
took the bus.

*   *   *

"Fool!" Jeff berated himself as the Lamborghini idled noisily in the noon traffic.
He'd driven himself to the museum instead of using his limo because he'd
meant to ask Gwen to drive back with
him. And if, while they were driving, he
managed to take their . . . call it a flirtation, to another level . . . well, why not?
He had seen her face when she looked
at the collection of animal figures her father had commissioned. And he'd remembered her telling him about the
spot on the hill behind the Wright house
where she used to sit and watch the
squirrels and chipmunks. And he knew

she was grateful to him and the time was right. But then as he stood there in the museum, he couldn't do it. Even though she was a grown woman who had known both pain and pleasure, he knew that in some ways she still didn't know her own mind. And he didn't want to take advantage of that. "You're getting in way too deep," he told himself. "This is the last thing you need." Or perhaps it was exactly what he needed. But not yet. Not while things were so unsettled at JeffSon.

He frowned and shifted gears, and the car maneuvered its way through the traffic. His business was in trouble; he was finally admitting that to himself. And while it was just a temporary cash-flow thing, and his accountants were already making moves to take care of it, this was not the time to make waves with Jewel—or with Gwen's husband. Stan Girard was a lot savvier and tougher than Jeff had expected him to be. Well, look at the way the man had refused to take JeffSon stock for his land and building and had insisted on cash only. He'd stuck to his guns, too; in fact, it had been downright insulting. If he hadn't been Gwen's husband Jeff would have dumped the deal just to teach him a lesson. But he *was* Gwen's husband. And Gwen was still in love with him. She could be persuaded out of that, Jeff was sure. But not as quickly as he'd once thought. Stan Girard was more than a worthy opponent. *So take care of business first, Jeff. And then . . . and then you'll have your chance at Gwen. Once you've cleaned up the mess, she will be your reward.*

*　　*　　*

Gwen didn't mention the museum visit or Jeff's surprise to Stan. In a couple of weeks her husband, who had always been his own boss, would be working for Jeff, and she didn't want the two men to start off on the wrong foot. Of course, there was nothing wrong with what Jeff had done—but it might sound funny to Stan. Right now, he didn't need that.

But at night when she lay in bed next to Stan, listening to the sound of his breathing, her mind went back to the little enchanted forest that had been the vision of Bradford Greeley, whose DNA she carried, and she wondered, "Which one of my parents loved the woods and the creatures in it the way I do? Was it my father? Did my father have those figures made for himself? Or was it my mother? Was she the one who sat as still as a stone and watched them and wondered what went on in their minds and if they thought the way she did? From the little I've heard about Bradford, it doesn't sound as if he was the odd duck. So did he order those sparkling figures for her because he loved her so much? Was she that important to him? I'll never know, but I want to think he did it for her. I want to think they loved each other that much."

And at her side, Stan murmured without opening his eyes, "Whatever it is, it can wait until tomorrow, sweetheart." Even when he was three quarters asleep himself, Stan could sense when she was awake. She moved closer to the warmth of him.

I want to think my mother had what I

have. I want to think my father loved her as much as Stan loves me.

The next morning when Gwen woke up, she went into the taupe-colored guest room and opened the laptop computer Stan had given her. She took out a yellow legal pad and a pile of pencils and set them near the computer so she could make notes on ideas as they came to her. She didn't know how she knew this was going to be useful; she just did. In the kitchen she heard Stan padding around making himself coffee, getting ready to start his day, but she didn't join him.

Finally, when everything was exactly the way she wanted it, she sat in front of the computer. She closed her eyes and let her mind drift back, back to her tree stump on the hill. Then she opened her eyes and began to type: *Abby the Squirrel was the odd duck of the forest.*

When the words appeared on the monitor screen, a voice behind her said gently, "You're finally doing it." And she turned to see Stan leaning over to read the screen. "And you're calling her

Abby," he added. Then Stan, her husband of few words, who never showed emotion, leaned over to kiss her, and he was smiling with tears in his eyes.

Collision

~~~~~

"O! beware, my lord, of
jealousy; it is the green-eyed
monster which doth mock
the meat it feeds on . . ."
—WILLIAM SHAKESPEARE

Chapter Thirty

Sometimes Stan couldn't believe it had been two years since he'd become a member of the JeffSon family—one of Jeff Henry's phonier expressions in Stan's opinion—because the months and days had gone by so quickly. But there were other times, like today, when it felt as if he'd been working at the company forever, and the walls of his office started to close in on him. This usually happened when he'd had to stay behind his desk for too long. Or when he had to go to meetings. It seemed to Stan that three quarters of his job consisted of going to meetings. And the business discussed at those meetings was always the same: how to make JeffSon a more attractive company to potential shareholders.

Stan far preferred being out in the field trouble-shooting technical and mechanical problems. He'd done quite a bit of that when he'd first started in his new position; back then there had been big plans for upgrading the existing power plants and buying new ones. But suddenly, all of those plans were put on hold. For a couple of days Stan had heard a rumor about a cash-flow problem, but that gossip had quickly subsided, and soon JeffSon was showing huge profits. Today the all-important JeffSon stock was trading higher than ever on the Exchange, and Jeff Henry was running around the country winning awards as Entrepreneur of the Year and making speeches about the endless possibilities for the business he had created. So if a little voice in the back of Stan's head kept nagging that he was spending more and more time pushing paper—and going to the ubiquitous meetings—instead of producing anything tangible, that voice had to be wrong. Obviously he didn't understand the way a really big business was run. Or maybe it was just that he didn't like big business all that much. But there wasn't much he could do about that now that he was working for one of the biggest. Stan stood up and walked around his office—anything to get the blood flowing again.

He stopped in front of a small shelf, which was empty except for a thin book with a painting of a squirrel on the cover. It was the advance copy of the children's book Gwen had written. She'd named it *Abby,* after the little squirrel who was the lead character, and it would be in the bookstores at the end of the month. Gwen already had several book signings scheduled in nearby towns and she would be going on a book tour after that. His Gwen on a book tour! Stan still couldn't believe it. And her publisher had just signed on for three more books about Abby and her forest friends.

"I'm going to fill my shelves with books by Gwen Girard," he'd told her after they'd received their advance copy of *Abby*. "Someday I'll have an entire wall full of them!" He was so proud of her.

And he was a little proud of himself, too, because he had had a hand in her success. He took the book back to his desk, leaned back in his chair, and remembered how it had all come about.

Gwen had finished her book a few months after he had started working at JeffSon. He'd already sold his business to the company and he was well aware that Cassie was angry because he and Gwen had not taken her advice.

Gwen was angry at her mother as well. "We're adults, for heaven's sake!" she'd said. "Mother has to learn to respect us."

Lots of luck with that, Stan had thought. And he had done his best to steer clear of his formidable—and now very annoyed—mother-in-law.

But then he'd read the manuscript for Gwen's book. And he'd known right away that it was special. It wasn't just the story about a little squirrel who was different and shy and learned to accept herself that fascinated him. It was the way Gwen seemed to get inside the heads of the characters she'd created. Her little creatures didn't think like humans, although they had thoughts and feelings that Stan could recognize as human. Somehow Gwen had managed to find a way for them to express themselves that was their own. Stan couldn't have said how she'd done it, but when he read her book he could see the squirrels and chipmunks and birds so clearly. And Gwen had written with such love for the outdoors—the trees and the sky were like additional characters in the story. Stan finally understood what a loss it had been to his wife when they had moved to the city.

"What are you going to do with this?" he'd asked her after he'd finished the pages she'd printed out for him.

"I hadn't thought about that. I was just glad to finish it."

"Someone should publish it."

"Stan, you don't just write a book and

get it published. People take years to do that."

"But this is good."

"You think that. But you have to. You love me."

So every Saturday for a month he'd gone to the library and read his way through dozens of children's books. When he finished, he went back to Gwen. "I'm telling you, your book is good enough to be published," he said to her. "And by now I'm an expert on the subject."

"I wouldn't know how to start," she said. But of course that wasn't the only reason she was so hesitant. She'd put so much of herself into the story—and particularly into the leading character—and she was afraid. Because in some misty way that had to do with being a writer, if people didn't like Abby the squirrel then Gwen his wife would be the odd duck again. Stan understood this, but he couldn't let the matter rest. He went online and found a list of publishers and sent them copies of the manuscript. And then sat by helplessly as the letters of rejection came in.

"See?" Gwen said crossly. "I told you it wasn't any good."

But it was good; he knew it was. And it seemed to him that most of the publishers hadn't said that the book was bad but just that it wasn't right for them. He knew that could just be a polite way of giving someone a brush-off. But still, he had faith in his instincts. He needed to talk to someone who knew more about this kind of thing than he did. He sought out Gwen's stepfather.

Walter read the book and saw immediately what Stan had seen. "The person you need to speak to is Cassie," he told Stan. "She serves on so many charitable boards and committees, including several that are based in New York, and she knows quite a few bigwigs in publishing."

"My mother-in-law isn't very fond of me right now," Stan said ruefully.

"That's putting it mildly." Walter grinned. "She doesn't like to give advice and not have it taken."

"And I don't like to be told what to do."

"I know. But what you and Cassie have in common is that you both appreciate a job well done—and this book is very good." He paused. "And of course you both love Gwen."

"I'm not sure I'm the one who should talk to Mrs. Wright."

"One more thing about Cassie you should know: She respects anyone who has the guts to take her on."

So, armed with a copy of Gwen's manuscript, Stan drove out to the Wright house to take on his mother-in-law. Cassie was working in her garden and she didn't stop when he parked his car in the driveway, got out, and walked over to her. But she did look up. "Is Gwen with you?" she asked. She was wearing a big straw hat so he couldn't see her face very well but he thought her voice sounded eager.

"I came here alone," he said. "I need your help."

She turned back to her roses. "I'd say it's a little late in the day for that. From what I've heard you've already sold your business. So if you're realizing now what a fool you've made of yourself, there really isn't anything I can do to—"

"This isn't about me," he broke in, determined to keep his temper. "This is about Gwen." Her head snapped up again. "She's not sick or anything like that," he assured her hurriedly. "She's done something that's . . . well, she's written a book."

"A book? Gwen?"

"It's called *Abby*. It's a children's book and it's really fine, at least I think it is, and . . ." He stopped and eyed the woman who had always thought he was a borderline idiot. "Look at it this way," he said. "You think I'm going to do nothing but drag her down. Well, if this book of hers is as good as I think it is, then she'll have her own money and a career and she won't have to depend on me. Wouldn't you like that? Wouldn't that make it worth your while to stop pruning those roses and read the thing?"

She finished the bush she was working on, then she removed her gardening gloves and held out her hand for the manuscript. While Stan stood in front of her she read it. When she looked up, there was a strange expression on her face; it was equal parts sadness, tenderness, and pride. It only lasted for a second. "I'll keep this, if I may," she said, "and I'll make a few calls."

"Thank you," Stan said, and he turned to go.

"Stan," she called out to him. He turned back. "We all make mistakes," she said. "If something were to happen . . . if you and Gwen are ever in trouble . . . please let me know."

He nodded and left. And six weeks later she called to say that Gwen had a publisher for *Abby*.

*   *   *

Stan picked up the copy of Gwen's book and looked at her picture on the back. She was facing the camera head-on, but her thoughtful gaze was fixed somewhere far off. The photographer hired by the publisher's publicity department had tried in vain to get her to look directly into the camera's lens but she couldn't make herself do it. She had also refused the services of the makeup artist and the hairdresser who had been hired for what the PR woman referred to as "the shoot." The PR woman had not been happy with Gwen that day, but

Stan thought his wife had been right to insist on doing things her way. She wouldn't have been Gwen with a lot of goop on her face or with her hair slicked back in some elegant but impossible style. Her intelligence shone through her big brown eyes and her dreamy, far-off look was typical of her. He studied the picture for a moment longer; this was the Gwen he knew and loved, and as far as he was concerned, she'd gotten prettier with the passing years. Not that she would ever be a beauty like, for instance, Jewel Henry. But he'd take Gwen over that woman any day. He frowned a little at that thought—because he was sure Jewel's husband shared it.

Stan leaned back in his chair again and more memories flooded into his mind. These were not as welcome as the others had been. He was not by nature a jealous man, but he knew he wasn't paranoid either, and his suspicions about Jeff Henry had at least some basis in truth. The whole thing had begun when Stan and Gwen had attended their first JeffSon party. When

Stan had received his invitation via an office memo, his initial inclination had been to turn it down.

"Don't even think about it," advised one of his colleagues. "Four times a year we are invited to Mr. Henry's home to dine with the Great Man and his wife and make no mistake, this is a command performance."

So Gwen and Stan had gotten all dolled up and presented themselves at the door of Jeff and Jewel's house, which was way too lavish for Stan's taste. A maid had ushered them in and Jewel had bustled up to them, looking stunning, ordered them to mingle—a word Stan particularly disliked—and left them to their own devices.

Soon Stan had gotten stuck in a conversation about business and Gwen had wandered off. By the time he was able to extricate himself she had joined a group of eager listeners that had surrounded Jeff Henry in the cavernous living room. Stan's boss was holding forth on history, and Gwen seemed to be impressed.

"The world wars came because the

German-speaking people were dissatisfied with their lack of prestige, vis-à-vis France and England with their colonies," Jeff said. "This difference came suddenly in 1914, and by 1939, it had become explosive. It's interesting that European royalty were all cousins, isn't it? Queen Victoria's grandsons were the King of England and the Emperor of Germany!" He'd turned to Gwen and smiled at her. That was all it was, just a smile. But something in it set off a warning signal for Stan.

At dinner that evening they sat at small round tables in the dining room, and Gwen had been placed at Jeff's. And Stan's warning signal grew stronger. It wasn't that Jeff was flirting with Gwen—he certainly didn't cross the line in any way—but he admired her. That was clear. And Gwen, who had thought herself unappealing and odd for so many years, was flattered. That was clear too. But was that all it was? She was enjoying herself, and she didn't usually enjoy big social gatherings like this—but as far as Stan could see that was it. There's a certain sexual tension when a man and woman are attracted to each other—a certain electricity, if you will—and Stan didn't get any sense of that. At least not on his wife's part. She was laughing, a blithe and carefree laugh, and Gwen would not have been capable of that kind of lightheartedness if she'd been in the throes of a secret passion for a man other than the one she'd married. A woman like Jewel Henry might be able to carry that off, but not his wife. *She is an innocent, my Gwen. Very intelligent, but an innocent.*

And so on that night Stan had talked himself out of a desire to punch Jeff Henry in the nose right there in his own overdecorated dining room. But over the next two years, whenever he and Gwen were in Jeff's company, Stan was on his guard. And he became more and more convinced that while Gwen might be an innocent, Jeff Henry had feelings for her that he had no right to have. But there was nothing Stan could do about it. Confronting the man when he hadn't acted on those feelings would be stupid. And it would be an insult to Gwen.

Stan picked up the child's book and

took it back to the shelf. He'd learned
to live with his suspicions about Jeff
Henry—mostly because he trusted his
wife's integrity so much. But he had
never really settled in and become gung
ho about working at JeffSon. He hadn't
joined the company baseball team, and
he didn't go to the morning motivational
meetings. He was probably the only person working at the place who had not
taken advantage of his stock option
plan. The money he'd been paid for his
business had been socked away in a
money market account. He hadn't spent
any of it, because in spite of everything
he still couldn't forget Cassandra's
warning. For two years he'd been waiting for something dire to happen at Jeff-
Son. At the very least, he worried that
he'd be fired and he and Gwen would
need his money until he was back on his
feet.

But in the last couple of weeks he'd
decided he was being ridiculous. Jeff-
Son had just been named one of the top
ten companies in the country in *Fortune*
magazine for the second year in a row.
All around him his colleagues who had

invested in the company were making out like bandits and his money was earning peanuts. It was time to accept the fact that he was a member of the damn JeffSon family—no matter how phony that sounded to him—and he wasn't going anywhere. It was time to stop hoarding his money, and buy Jeff-Son stock. And it was time to buy a house for Gwen. He'd told her to start looking, and she'd already found a place she liked. In fact, she was going to meet him today for lunch and show him some brochures from the real estate agency that handled the property. He checked his watch; he had two hours before he was supposed to meet her downstairs in the lobby.

On his desk was a preliminary draft for one of the newsletters JeffSon released to keep its shareholders—and potential shareholders—informed about the company. Usually Stan skipped reading these things because he considered them nothing more than puff pieces, but this day he was too restless to deal with the paperwork that cluttered his desk. Besides, if he was planning to buy JeffSon stock, he told himself he probably should read up on the company.

Twenty minutes later, deeply troubled, he put the newsletter down and turned on his computer. There were some numbers he wanted to check.

Chapter Thirty-one

As the small jet circled the airport and prepared to land, Jeff looked out the window at the city below him. He'd always considered Wrightstown his good luck charm, the place where great things happened to him. So how had everything gone so desperately wrong? He turned his gaze to the interior of his private plane. This was his third, but he could still remember when he'd bought his first. He'd been coveting one . . . no, *lusting* for one . . . but he hadn't been able to overcome his puritanical background enough to actually make the purchase. Jewel had convinced him to do it. Now he couldn't imagine flying commercial again. But that day could come. Worse than that could come. He closed his eyes and asked himself, again, how he had gotten to this place. How had his company, his brainchild, stopped being a vibrant, growing business with limitless potential and become one that was hemorrhaging red ink? What had started it all? The water contracts in São Paulo? The energy crisis in California? The new Internet start-up that had been sucking up seed money without a penny of profit to show for it? Whatever it was, it didn't matter now. JeffSon was millions of dollars in debt. The New York accounting firm had done all it could to hide the losses, but unless a miracle happened, it was only a question of time before the whole thing imploded. So Jeff had begun a risky game. He continued to make speeches touting his dying company while privately unloading his own stock in Jeff-Son. Mark Scotto and several other top level guys at the company were quietly doing the same. And just in case, Jeff was putting as much of his assets as he could in Jewel's name.

Jeff rubbed his aching head—he seemed to have a headache all the time now. He'd debated long and hard about turning over so much to Jewel. Fortunately she was too stupid—or disinterested—to understand what he was doing. But for some reason he hadn't transferred the house to her yet. It wasn't because he had any attachment to it; he hated the damn place and always had. There was just something about handing her the roof over his head that made him feel vulnerable. But face it, he *was* vulnerable. You couldn't be more vulnerable than he was. And he had to do what vulnerable people did, salvage whatever he could. He pulled out his cell phone, called his lawyer, and told him to prepare the paperwork for the transfer.

"I'll be landing in Wrightstown in half an hour," he said. "Be in my office. I want to get this done."

If it were done . . . then 'twere well it

were done quickly. That was a quote from somewhere; he couldn't remember the source. His head was throbbing now. Putting the house in Jewel's name would tie them together for a far longer time than he'd wanted. For a while now, he'd known he wanted to leave Jewel. Because of Gwen. He wanted Gwen now as much as he had once wanted his private jet and the Lamborghini. As much as he had once wanted Jewel. He had dreamed of being a free man for Gwen so he could ask her to free herself too. But that dream was over. It belonged to a time when he could still make choices.

He closed his burning eyes. He hadn't wanted to make Gwen his mistress, but there was no other way. He had to have her, even if he couldn't free himself for her. She was the one bright spot in the world. And with everything he was going through he deserved something bright and hopeful in his life.

As the jet was landing, there was a call on his cell phone. His lawyer needed a copy of the deed to the house.

*   *   *

Jewel had spent the morning working out in her home gym. When she was finished, she headed for the bedroom to shower and change. The master suite was in the opposite wing of the house and as she walked down the halls they echoed with her footsteps. Except for the servants, the place always seemed to be empty now. It was meant to be a party house, crammed with admiring guests and the sounds of drinks being poured and laughter. When it was silent, there was something chilling about it. At night, when Jeff was gone—and that was most of the time these days—Jewel would lie in her bed listening to the silence, and think about her home when she was growing up. And in her memory now it wasn't as ugly as she'd thought it was back then, and all the noise and confusion didn't seem as bad to her as it once had. At least it had been alive. And there had been times when they had laughed—even Pop. Jewel would turn over on her down pillow and she'd realize that the five-hundred-thread-count pillowcase was wet—and she'd feel the tears on her cheeks.

There were times when she thought she'd die of loneliness. She'd even gotten so desperate that she'd gone back to Times Past—ostensibly to shop, but really to sit in the un-air-conditioned, unheated back room with Patsy Allen and talk.

Jewel picked up her pace; sometimes it seemed as if it took forever to get from one part of her home to the other. Once she had loved that, but now she had changed. So much had changed since she'd built this house.

Jeff was coming home from a business trip this morning and there had been a time when she would have rushed out to the airport to meet him. He would have been so eager to see her that he wouldn't have been able to keep his hands off her. There had been a couple of times in the early days when he hadn't, and only the tinted glass partition prevented the limo driver from having a great show.

But Jeff had been tired of her for a long time now. He thought she was so thick she didn't realize it, but of course she did. She'd known for years that he had girls, and there had always been the danger that he'd fall in love with one of them. Now she was afraid that it had happened. She knew how Jeff acted when he was in love—she'd been around the last time it had happened—and the signs were all there. And Jeff being Jeff, if he really was infatuated with some woman, he'd want to throw over everything like one of the heroes in those stupid operas he loved so much. He would want a divorce.

Jewel had finally reached the bedroom. She stripped off her workout clothes and headed for the bathroom.

She didn't want a divorce. And she would fight against one with everything she had. But if she was honest about it, being Mrs. Jeff Henry hadn't been all that great. Her husband's money hadn't bought her a place among the blue-blood women who ran the charitable events for the museum, the hospital, and the symphony. They'd take her donations, and they'd even ask her to sit on the board, but she couldn't keep up with their talk about books and politics and art and music. And Cassandra Wright was on many of those boards, letting everyone see her animosity toward Jewel. So Jewel never was invited to the homes of the women she wanted to cultivate; she never went to the intimate dinner parties or the casual cookouts where they and their families bonded.

Jewel and Jeff belonged to the most exclusive country club in town, but she didn't play tennis or bridge and Jeff only used the place for JeffSon entertaining, so she'd never made any friends there, either. The wives of the men who worked in the upper echelons of JeffSon were polite to Jewel, but they kept their distance—and she could understand why. Being a friend of the boss's wife was too tricky. What if you had a falling-out with her?

The women Jewel enjoyed the most were those JeffSon employees who would be thought of as "girls" well into their fifties—women's lib be damned— the secretaries and receptionists. Jeff's faithful "office wife"/secretary, Rosetta, and Barbara who answered the phone at the front desk, were Jewel's kind of people. She knew either of them would be thrilled to be invited for a long pool-side lunch featuring margaritas and gossip, but she couldn't ask them. She was Mrs. Henry and she couldn't fraternize with secretaries and receptionists.

Jewel went into the shower stall—four thousand dollars for the steam system alone—and let the hot water soothe her muscles that were aching from her recent workout. She wished the hot water could take away the aches that went deeper. Because it hurt to know that your husband didn't want you anymore—even if you had never been deeply in love with him. And it really hurt to know that he didn't care enough about you to try to pretend otherwise. But she had made her bed and it was a cushy one and she wanted to go on lying in it. She'd be damned if she'd let anyone kick her out of it.

The phone began to ring. There was an extension in the bathroom. As she was drying off, she picked it up. It was Jeff.

"I need you to bring a copy of the deed to the house to my office this afternoon," he said tersely. "Go into my study. Open the left-hand bottom drawer of my desk, and—"

"Why do you want that?" Jewel blurted out. She felt herself go cold in spite of her steamy shower. What the hell was he up to? Was this the phone call she'd been dreading? Was there really another woman as she'd suspected?

"I need it, Jewel. Now, you'll find it . . ."

"What do you want with the deed?" Panic made her shrill.

"Oh, for God's sake, I'm planning to put the house in your name! I'll explain when you get here. Now will you listen while I tell you where the deed is?"

She listened. And she was happier than she had been in months. Because if the house was going in her name, that meant things between them couldn't be as bad as she'd thought they were. If Jeff was giving her the house, then he wasn't going anywhere.

* * *

Gwen tried to concentrate on the cranberry bread she was supposed to be making, but it was a lost cause. She simply couldn't focus on measuring baking soda and sugar when she wanted to dance around the apartment from sheer happiness. In three days she'd be giving her first reading of her book. The event was to take place in a library in Langham, a town that was about forty-five minutes north of Wrightstown. Her publicist wanted her to have this experience as a way of getting her feet wet before her actual book tour, which began at the end of the month. Stan was planning to drive up with her so he could cheer her on, and then they would spend the night in a charming old inn in the town—just to add a little romance to her triumph, he said. He was so excited for her. In fact, Stan and her mother seemed to have started competing for the title of Loved One Who Is Most Proud of Gwen. When Stan had turned to Cassie for help, that had softened her mother toward him. "He's got a good heart," she now told Gwen. "And he does care about you." She hadn't said he was smart or competent—but still, it had been high praise coming from Cassandra Wright.

And then just when it seemed that things couldn't get any better, Stan had decided it was time to buy a house. Gwen had been thrilled, but she felt she had to make something clear.

"I'd love to move, you know that," she told Stan. "But you should also know that I've changed. I know I can be happy anywhere as long as I'm with the right person."

"Got anyone special in mind?" he'd asked.

"There's this guy . . . he's a little stubborn and he always needs a haircut and he never has learned to put his socks in the laundry, but I'm kind of partial to him. . . ."

"How partial?" he'd whispered.

She'd nodded toward the bedroom. "I'll be glad to show you any old time. . . ."

Then of course all thoughts of houses and home ownership were forgotten. But the next day Stan had asked her to make an appointment with a real estate agent and she'd started looking.

Gwen picked up the flyer on the house she'd seen that she wanted to show Stan. Every time she thought about it, she was pleased with herself all over again. Because she hadn't chosen an ancient farmhouse in the middle of nowhere—as she knew Stan would expect her to. Instead she had found a place in a well-established, though decidedly unfashionable, suburb called Brookside. It was far enough out of the city for her to see trees and birds, but it was close enough for Stan to have a little hustle and bustle if that was what he wanted. Brookside was perfect. And so was her life.

*   *   *

"This is Stan Girard again, and I really need to speak to Mark Scotto," Stan said to the assistant who had answered Scotto's phone. "This is the second time I've called."

"I'm well aware of that, Mr. Girard," came the supercilious reply. "But as I

said, he's been on the phone all afternoon with Tokyo and I can't disturb
him."

"Okay, when he takes a break, give
him this message. I think I've discovered something that could be very serious. There's an error in the figures in the
JeffSon newsletter we're sending out
this month. We're reporting profits on
two of our electrical plants that can't be
true. I work with both plants and I know
that for a fact. I'm not sure where the
faulty figures are coming from; I've been
trying to track down the source, and
quite frankly I'm not getting anywhere."

"I'll relay your message to Mr. Scotto"—
the voice on the phone sounded a little
rattled now—"and I'm sure he'll get back
to you as soon as possible."

It seemed that Mark Scotto's important business with Tokyo could be interrupted after all, because five minutes
later Stan's phone rang.

"Thank you for bringing this to my attention, Stan," said Scotto after Stan
had explained the problem again. "I'll
follow up on it personally and I'll be in

touch to let you know what I've found out." The man's tone was smooth and reassuring. Maybe a little too reassuring. Stan would remember that later.

Chapter Thirty-two

For two days Stan waited to hear the results of Mark Scotto's investigation into the inflated figures in the JeffSon newsletter. There was nothing from the man. Not even an e-mail. When Stan tried to call his office he was told that Mr. Scotto was in yet another meeting—which was interesting, because Stan himself wasn't going to any meetings. They were still being held every day—he could hear his colleagues walking down the halls to the conference room—but he was not asked to join them. Instead, he was informed by various secretaries and assistants that those meetings he had been scheduled to attend had been cancelled. They said he would be told when they were rescheduled, but that never seemed to happen. And there were no more deliveries of the reams of paperwork that usually appeared in his office. None of this would have bothered him—certainly he didn't miss the busywork or the useless meetings—but there was no other work for him to do.

On the fourth day he was summoned to Jeff Henry's gray and chrome office. His boss looked weary. And angry. He got straight to the point.

"Stan, I understand from Mark that you've been poking around in some areas of the company that—to be perfectly frank—are way off your turf."

"I just noticed that there was a problem with the newsletter—"

"Get this through your head, Stan, okay? There is no problem. Mark vets that newsletter personally and so do I. Now, thanks to you, he wasted hours of his valuable time going through the whole thing again. Only to discover that there's nothing wrong."

"But the figures—"

"Stan, we have one of the best accounting firms in the country. These guys are tops—we're talking MBAs from Harvard and Yale with years of experience at Fortune 500 companies. With all due respect, do you really think that you with your high school diploma and a couple of night courses at a trade school could catch a mistake that slipped by them?"

Stan didn't. Not really. But he didn't like the sneer on Jeff Henry's face. Or the contempt in his voice. "I know what I saw," he said stubbornly. "I know that the profits we're claiming are bogus and—"

"Oh, that's a great technical term, Stan." The voice was dripping with sarcasm now. " 'Bogus profits.' I'll be sure to remember that. In the meantime, let me explain a few facts of financial life to you. A company the size of JeffSon— which is not to be confused with a little penny-ante electrical shop that rewires Aunt Millie's old lamp—depends on its good image. We have worked hard—way too hard—to build the reputation of JeffSon to . . . ," he paused, "to allow our reputation to be damaged by a disgruntled employee."

"I never said I was—"

"I've cut you a lot of slack, pal. I paid you in cash when you didn't want to take JeffSon stock for your business—and given what it's worth today, what a brilliant move that was. You have never been a team player and I looked the other way. But when it comes to spreading rumors . . ."

"I asked a question!"

"You didn't know what the hell you were talking about! And now you're too damn stubborn and arrogant to admit that you were wrong!"

And that was when Stan quit.

*　　　*　　　*

"You quit your job?" Gwen cried. "Why, Stan?" She tried to keep the disappointment out of her voice but she couldn't control it. She'd been so happy, and now this. And Stan was getting that stubborn look on his face that meant he wasn't going to explain. He was just going to expect her to accept one more time that he was right. "You didn't think you should talk it over with me?"

"It wasn't something I planned. It just happened."

"That kind of thing doesn't 'just happen.' You did it. You quit."

"But it was almost as if I didn't have any choice."

"What are you talking about?"

"I've been thinking about it, Gwen, and I think Henry was trying to make me quit."

"Oh, come on!"

"I've seen him in action, and when he wants something to work, he's smooth. But he was insulting me—treating me like something he'd scrape off the bottom of his shoe. He had to know I wouldn't put up with it."

She couldn't believe that. Not of Jeff Henry. "You're not making any sense. Why would he want you to quit?"

"Because I started asking too many questions, and he wanted me gone. Now, if I should try to tell anyone what I know, I'll just be a former employee who couldn't cut it and left."

Stan had already told her his suspicions—that there was something going on at JeffSon that was, to use his word, dicey. She definitely couldn't believe that. Not about a huge, prestigious company that was lauded in all the media. Obviously Stan was in over his head. He'd seen something that he didn't understand, and he'd gotten all worked up about it. *I don't think Stanley is sophisticated enough to be involved with a group of smart people who are on a fast track,* Cassie had said. And Gwen had been so proud of Stan for proving she was wrong. Now he was proving that Cassie was right. And what about Jewel Fairchild Henry? She was going to be thrilled to think that Gwen's husband couldn't make it at JeffSon.

"Isn't this all a little far-fetched?" Gwen demanded. "A little like all those conspiracy theories about the grassy knoll?"

"I know what I saw, Gwen."

"I'm sure there's some logical explanation for it."

"I asked for one and no one would

tell me anything. They're cooking the books!"

"I just don't believe a man like Jeff Henry would do something like that!"

"But you do believe your own husband is too stupid to understand basic math!"

"I didn't say that!" But of course it was what she'd been thinking. Close anyway.

"I just meant that Jeff is a great businessman—a genius—he doesn't have to do things like cook the books, or—"

But now Stan was angry. "Oh, yes, I know how you feel about Jeff Henry!"

"What is that supposed to mean?'

"You have a crush on the man."

"That is not fair!" But maybe the reason it stung so much was that it was just a little bit true? "And it's a lousy thing for you to say."

"Okay, maybe you don't have one on him, but he sure has a thing for you. His tongue hangs out when he looks at you. And what's more, you enjoy it."

"What!?"

"You know how he feels, Gwen, and you like it. He's Jewel's husband and you've always been jealous of her."

"Jeff Henry is my friend—all right? I do like him. And what's more I owe him."

"Because he gave your stupid husband a job? The kind of job people like you understand?"

" 'People like me'?" She'd never been so furious. But she'd never seen Stan so furious, either. Obviously he'd been thinking this for a long time. "What the hell are you talking about?"

"Snobs like you and your mother!"

"I am not a snob and I am not anything like my mother."

"You could have fooled me."

She wanted to slap him.

"The first time you saw this apartment," he went on scornfully, "I thought you were going to pass out. You thought if Jeff Henry gave me a job at JeffSon—and by the way, could anyone be more egocentric? Naming his damn company after himself?—you'd get back the lifestyle you deserve. That's why he's your dear good friend."

"He is my friend because he helped *me*! Not everything in my life revolves around you, speaking of being egocentric." And then she told Stan, biting off the words in her anger, about the collection of glass animal figures Jeff had unearthed for her to see. "I wouldn't have started writing if it hadn't been for Jeff," she finished breathlessly. And then she looked at Stan's face. And if she could have, she would have taken it all back. Because Stan, who knew her so well, understood better than anyone what seeing those glass figures had meant to her. He knew what Jeff had done for her. Her husband, who had been so proud of her writing career, and so proud of his part in it, was deeply wounded. "Stan, I didn't mean it like that."

"Yes, you did," he said quietly.

"You called me a snob and you said I was jealous of Jewel. You said I was like my mother so I got angry . . ." She trailed off. Then she tried again. "You were the one who got the book published and—"

But he didn't let her finish. "Look, I don't think I'll go with you to Langham tomorrow night." And he turned and walked away.

She wanted to call after him, but she was starting to get angry again. This reading at the library was one of the most important things she'd ever do, and she had been counting on his support. Now he was abandoning her when she needed him because of a dumb fight. Suddenly she felt like a little girl again, knowing that if she did one thing wrong, made just one mistake, her mother wouldn't want her. But she hadn't done anything wrong—the fight hadn't been her fault. He had started it. "Fine," she called after him. "It probably would be better if you didn't come tomorrow."

Chapter Thirty-three

Jeff's head was pounding; it had been ever since the little scene he'd staged yesterday when he'd pushed Stan Girard to quit. If the man hadn't taken the bait, Jeff would have been forced to fire him, which would have looked far worse later on if Stan was in court testifying against the officers of JeffSon . . . and its owner. Not that there was going to be a court case. There weren't going to be any investigations, either, and no one was going to be testifying against the officers of JeffSon, or Jeff Henry. None of that was going to happen. There was still a chance that JeffSon wouldn't collapse, that a bailout would come from somewhere—Tokyo, or London, or Dubai. And if there wasn't one, by the time all the smoke had settled, it would be too late for anyone to piece together what had gone on. As long as Jeff and Mark and the accountants had had enough time to take care of all the loose ends. That was what they needed now—time.

Jeff closed his eyes. They were being careful; they were playing it exactly right. But of course there was always a paper trail. And if anyone were to start asking the wrong questions like Stan Girard had . . . but Stan Girard was out of the company, and out of the loop. The discrepancy in the figures that he'd discovered had been hidden again. And if he were to say anything to anyone, he had no credibility now. Still, Jeff remembered the day he'd hired the guy; he'd thought then that Gwen's husband was savvier and tougher than he looked.

And I never would have hired him, if it

hadn't been for Gwen. That was the irony of it.

Jeff looked over his desk. Back in the days when he was proud of his business and his work, the glossy surface had always been cleared off before he went home at night. No matter how late he had to stay, he finished every last piece of business. Now, there was a small mountain of paper sitting in front of him, and just the thought of going through it made him tired. He stood up—the aching in his head seemed to have abated a little—grabbed the papers, and without reading them sent them through his shredder. That was one way to take care of the potential paper trail.

Tonight he was going to play hooky. He had called the publicity department at Gwen's publishing house and learned that this evening she would be giving her first reading at the library in Langham. He was going to be there. The hope of being with Gwen was the only thing he had to look forward to. She had to be made to realize that she was the only bright spot, that she made it all worthwhile. His headache was gone now. He'd already called Jewel earlier to tell her that he wouldn't be coming home tonight because he had to go out of town. As he'd expected, she hadn't bothered to ask where he was going or what he was doing, and he'd hung up with a sigh of relief. It could be a real plus to have a wife who didn't care enough about you to know your whereabouts.

*　　*　　*

Jewel was packing her overnight bag. She'd called Jeff's secretary and learned that his mysterious business trip would be taking him to Langham, and she'd decided to drive over there, show up at his hotel—there was only one in the town, an old inn, which sounded romantic—and surprise him. A week ago she wouldn't have thought about doing such a thing. It had been years since an infatuated Jeff had taken her on his trips so he could show her off, years since he'd wanted to have sexy little interludes with her sandwiched in between his business meetings.

But three days ago, he'd put the house

in her name. And he'd told her that there were other assets that had already been transferred to her. She wasn't dumb enough to think that these were gifts; she knew there had to be some business reason for the transfers. But still, Jeff wouldn't have done it if he didn't trust her. And more important, he wouldn't have done it if the divorce she often dreaded was looming. So why not drive up to Langham with her prettiest negligee and her brand-new perfume? Why not try to rekindle a few of those sparks that had once burned so brightly? Maybe the marriage wasn't dead after all. She finished packing her suitcase and went downstairs to put it in the car.

* * *

Stan had waited all day for Gwen to say she wanted him to come to Langham after all. He had looked forward to seeing her stand in front of a spellbound audience to read from her book, and he'd been looking forward to the night that would follow. A dozen times he thought of telling her he was sorry for their fight.

But he wasn't. He couldn't forget the vision he'd had of her standing next to Jeff Henry in the glassworks museum looking at the gift Jeff had given her. Because finding those figurines for her had been a gift. The kind a man gave when he was trying to please a woman—to win her. Jeff Henry didn't want to be Gwen's friend; he wanted a hell of a lot more.

And what about Gwen? Stan had accused her of having a crush on Jeff Henry, one that was fueled by her jealousy of Jewel. But was it something more? She had refused to believe Stan when he'd told her that there was something wrong at JeffSon. She'd been adamant in her defense of Jeff Henry. That had shaken Stan more than he cared to admit. He'd been so sure of what he'd seen, so convinced that numbers never lie. But what if Jeff was right? What if Stan had discovered nothing more than a method of bookkeeping that he didn't understand? And what if—and here was the big *if*—Stan had been looking for something to be wrong because *he* was the jealous one? When

he was fighting with Gwen, Stan had realized that he'd been envying Henry for
months, maybe even for the past two
years. *So look at yourself, Stan; what if
you've made all this trouble for nothing?*

Gwen was walking to the front door of
the apartment, carrying her suitcase
and the copy of her book that she had
annotated for the reading. Stan started
toward the door. *I'll drive you,* he was
going to say. *I want to come.*

It seemed to him that her face brightened as if she knew what he was going
to do. But then the words wouldn't
come. Instead there rose once again in
his mind the vision of Gwen seeing her
father's glass figurines for the first time.
And he couldn't forget that she had
never told him about it.

"Drive safely," he said.

Her face fell. She nodded and walked
out the door.

Chapter Thirty-four

The reading at the Langham library had been a success. The children and their parents had listened to Gwen with a hushed attention that was incredibly flattering. They had stayed after the reading to ask questions, nibble on the refreshments provided by the library, and line up so that Gwen could sign their copies of *Abby*. Everyone seemed to having such a good time, Gwen thought they might have stayed for hours if there hadn't been several claps of thunder indicating that a storm was on its way. It was only after that, that people began bundling up their kids and rushing out to their cars before the rain started.

"Didn't you tell me you were staying overnight at the Langham Inn?" the librarian asked, as she walked Gwen to the front door. "It's just around the corner in the historic district. If you'd like someone to show you the way, I can ask one of our volunteers."

"Thank you, but I think I can find it," Gwen said. What she wanted wasn't a volunteer to show her how to get to the inn; she wanted Stan there in Langham making a fuss over her.

The reading at the library had taken a little more than two hours, and since it had started at five to accommodate the kids, Gwen now had the evening ahead of her. A very long evening which she would be spending alone in a hotel room in a town where she knew no one. It had sounded like fun when she'd booked her room at the Langham Inn, but she'd done that when she'd thought Stan was going to be with her. When

she'd thought they would celebrate together with a dinner and maybe a glass
or two of champagne. She wanted some
champagne right now. She'd done well
and there was no one to share the moment with her.

Up to the last minute she'd hoped that
Stan would show up, that she'd look out
into the crowd at the library—and she'd
drawn quite a big one, according to the
librarian—and he'd be sitting there with
that tender, proud grin waiting for her to
start, waiting to applaud when she finished. But he hadn't come. And she
knew it was because she'd really hurt
him. She hated herself for telling him
about those glass figurines. It had been
stupid and mean. But he had said things
that hurt her, too . . . and then he had
abandoned her.

Gwen headed toward her car, which
was parked in front of the library. Suddenly she felt weary—a letdown after
the high of the night's successful event.
Maybe she should cancel her room at
the Langham Inn and just drive home.

"Gwen!" said a voice behind her. She

turned to see Jeff coming toward her with an eager smile.

Oh, God, she thought and didn't know whether to be pleased or dismayed.

"Brava! You were wonderful!" he said.

"Jeff? What are you doing here?"

*   *   *

Jeff had planned to tell Gwen he'd come to Langham on business. He had planned to pretend that meeting her there was a delightful surprise. "This is my lucky day," he'd say. "I can't believe I'm running into you like this." But when he saw Gwen he knew he had to be honest. The time had come for her to understand that she was the only bright spot, that now she was what made living worthwhile.

"I came to see you do your reading," he said. "Did you think I'd miss it?"

"I never expected . . . I didn't see you."

"I stood in the alcove on the side. I was afraid I'd distract you." He looked around. "You're alone?" But he knew she was. He'd checked her audience from his safe alcove and he'd seen that her husband hadn't bothered to come. The guy might be smarter than Jeff had orig-inally thought, but he was still a dolt when it came to women. Well, good. Let Gwen see who had cared enough to show up for her.

"Yes, I'm alone," she said.

"Well, we can't have that on your big night!" he sang out brightly. "Let me take you to dinner."

"I was thinking of going home . . . ," she said tentatively. At that moment, the rain that had been threatening fell from the sky in a downpour.

"You can't drive back to Wrightstown in this," he shouted over a peal of thun-der. "You're staying at the Langham Inn, aren't you? I'll meet you over there."

She hesitated, but only for a second because she was getting soaked. "Okay," she said, and she dashed for her car. Jeff ran to the Lamborghini.

*   *   *

Jewel pulled into the parking lot in front of the Langham Inn. She'd meant to ar-rive earlier in the day so she could sneak into Jeff's room and surprise him, but she'd taken a wrong turn and gotten lost. Now she scanned the parking lot, looking for Jeff's car. The Lamborghini was nowhere to be seen. Good, he wasn't checked in yet either. There was still time to surprise him. She parked her car and sat waiting for the storm to let up. She hadn't thought to bring an umbrella, and when you were trying to seduce your husband you didn't want to look like a drowned rat.

A few minutes later, she'd decided the rain would never stop and she was going to make a run for it, when she heard the familiar roar of a finely tuned Italian sports car and she saw Jeff pull the Lamborghini up to the front of the hotel. Now there was nothing to do but forget about surprising him, and let him know she was there. She watched her husband get out of his car. She was about to call out to him, but then she saw that he wasn't rushing into the hotel. He was standing next to his car as the rain fell on him and it was clear that he was waiting for someone. Sure enough, a second car drove into the lot and he waved, indicating that it should park next to his. The driver pulled into the spot next to Jeff's. And in the light from the windows of the inn, Jewel watched as the car door opened and a woman whose hair frizzed around her in a rusty red cloud stepped out. Jewel watched her husband move to the woman, take off the jacket of his five-thousand-dollar custom-made suit, and hold it over her head as a makeshift protection from the rain. They ran into the hotel together.

For a second, Jewel froze. Then her stomach began churning. There were two large bay windows at the front of the Langham Inn; through them, one could see everything that was going on in the lobby. Jewel got out of her car, ran to the inn, and fought her way through the boxwood hedge that surrounded the windows. There, in spite of all the demeaning clichéd scenes she'd watched in a hundred bad movies about jealous women and cheating men, she stood in the mud and spied on her husband.

*   *   *

Gwen's mind was whirling. It was sweet of Jeff to have come to hear her read her book. But why did she feel so uncomfortable? He had led her into the hotel lobby to get her out of the rain, which was nothing more than any gentleman would do. And he wanted to take her to dinner. That was all.

"This looks good!" he said, as he looked over the menu that was posted outside the inn's dining room. He smiled enthusiastically. Maybe too enthusiastically? Maybe a little desperately? Or was she just imagining things because Stan had accused the man of having feelings for her? *His tongue hangs out when he looks at you,* Stan had said. And he'd said that Gwen knew it and she enjoyed it. And that was terribly, horribly unfair. Jeff had never done anything to suggest that he wanted to be more than friends. All he wanted to do now was celebrate her success—a success, mind you, that her husband hadn't bothered to witness. It was all perfectly harmless. Or was it? Did a busy man drop everything and drive to another town to celebrate a woman's success because he wanted to be her friend?

"Jeff," she said, "I'm very grateful to you for having come all the way up here, but given what happened between you and Stan, I'm afraid I feel a little awkward. . . ."

For an answer he grabbed her hands. "Oh, don't," he pleaded. "The fight with Stan was really for the best. I don't think he ever really wanted to work for Jeff-Son—it was always a bad fit. But you mustn't let that get in the way of us."

He held her hands up to his mouth and he kissed each of them. And then he looked at her. And that was when she saw it in his eyes—there was no mistaking it now—she knew. Stan had been right about Jeff. Her mother had been right all those years ago. And she, Gwen, had been an idiot. She'd been flattered by Jeff's attention. And yes, like some careless competitive teenager she'd loved it that she was besting beautiful, charming Jewel. She'd been irresponsible and childish and unbearably insensitive. She tried, ever so gently, to pull her hands away, but Jeff held on to them.

"What we have is something special,

Gwen. I've never felt this . . . kind of friendship . . . with any other woman." Then he paused. "Don't let Stan come between us." She couldn't help shivering. "You're cold," he said softly.

"It's because of the rain. . . ." She stumbled. "I got wet . . . I should probably go upstairs and change."

"That's a good idea. We both should."

And he let go of her hands to push the button for the elevator. "You're on the sixth floor," he said as the elevator doors opened. "So am I."

* * *

Jewel's face was scratched from the boxwood branches, her shoes were sinking into the muddy mulch that surrounded the hedge. For once in her life, she didn't give a damn what she looked like. She had watched her husband take Gwen's hands and kiss them. Had he ever looked at Jewel with that kind of tenderness? Even when they were first together, had he ever held her hands as if she was something breakable and oh so incredibly precious? He had gotten into the elevator with Gwen. The indicator arrow above the elevator registered that they were going to the same floor. You didn't have to be a genius to know what was going on between Jewel's husband and Gwen Wright. Gwen was the woman Jewel had been fearing all these months—the woman Jeff loved, for whom he would uproot his life and get a divorce. Gwen who had had everything handed to her on a silver platter and deserved none of it! Gwen who was the daughter of Cassie Wright's womanizing husband and his whore . . . Jewel wanted to smash Gwen's face into a wall; she wanted to tear at Gwen's skin with her perfectly manicured nails until the blood ran; she wanted to hit and maim and hurt. . . . She scrambled away from the window of the inn and through the boxwood hedge and ran for her car.

* * *

The elevator had reached the sixth floor. During the ride, Jeff had gone on about Gwen's reading.

"I watched your audience tonight," he said. "The kids were enthralled. I predict that Abby will take her place someday next to Winnie the Pooh, and all those creatures written by Dr. Seuss."

"She's just a little squirrel trying to fig-ure out who she is, and what she wants." Gwen had tried to shrug away the gushing compliment.

"Aren't we all?" He had turned to her. His eyes were fixed on her face as if he was searching for something.

Mercifully, at that moment, the eleva-tor doors had opened.

"I don't think I want anything to eat tonight," Gwen said as she moved into the hallway. "I think I'll skip dinner." She held out her hand for Jeff to shake. He ignored it. He was smiling that desper-ate smile again. "Thank you for coming all this way," she faltered.

"It was my pleasure." He didn't move. But when she turned and headed for her room, he started following her. They reached her door. She opened her handbag and fished around for her room key. "Thank you again for coming. It was so nice of you. . . ."

*　　　*　　　*

Jeff watched Gwen fumble with her handbag. She was nervous—and he knew why. She didn't want to sit through a long meal knowing what was coming after. That was why she'd said she didn't want to have dinner. She'd finally understood what was happening between them—surely her remark about the little squirrel proved that—and now she didn't want to wait for him any more than he wanted to wait for her. Their time had come! He wanted to laugh out loud. There could be something good in his life!

He watched as she found the key, but it slipped through her fingers and fell to the carpet next to her feet. Before she could bend down, Jeff had scooped it up. He put the key in the lock, opened the door, and was moving into her room.

*   *   *

Later, when Gwen thought about it, it seemed to her as if she'd watched what happened next but hadn't really been a part of it. She saw herself move to the door to block the path of a man who looked like Jeff but couldn't be Jeff, because Jeff would never behave this way. She heard this awful new Jeff whisper in her ear, as he tried to force his way past her, that she was the only thing that mattered to him now, that he couldn't lose her too. And she heard someone— a Gwen who was also unrecognizable— say that please, he mustn't do this. And the Gwen who wasn't really Gwen pushed hard at the Jeff who wasn't really Jeff until she was off balance and when he stepped back, she fell to the floor. There was a popping sound as if something had snapped. And then Gwen wasn't watching from a distance anymore, because that was when the pain came. It shot through her hand to her wrist and up her arm in a white hot streak, and the dizziness that accompanied it made her mouth water with instant nausea. She looked up at Jeff as the tears sprang to her eyes. She was on the floor, his expensive loafers—a fine, buttery soft leather—were inches away from her face. He had to see how badly she hurt. Foolishly, stupidly, she waited for him to help her to her feet.

"You slut!" he spat at her. "You tease a man, you let him think . . . well, to hell with you! To hell with all of it." He turned on his heel and strode away.

Chapter Thirty-five

Gwen wasn't sure how long she stayed on the floor. But eventually the first screaming pain died away and she was able to get to her feet and close the door. Gingerly she tried moving her fingers—she'd heard somewhere that she wouldn't be able to do that if her hand was broken. The test was a success—if agonizing. The fingers were mobile. What she had was nothing more than a nasty sprain. There was a bucket of ice in her room; she stuck her hand in it and kept it there until it was numb. The wrist was swelling but the pain had become a dull throb. She had some aspirin in her purse and she swallowed a couple of tablets. Slowly and painfully she set about the process of gathering her belongings and putting them in her overnight bag. There was no way in hell she was staying in this room tonight.

*   *   *

The road was curving and Jewel was driving way too fast. She knew it and she didn't care. She had to get away from Langham, had to get away from the vision of her husband kissing Gwen's hands. Gwen Girard! No, get it right, damnit, she was Gwen Wright! Forget the blue-collar loser she had married. She was Cassie Wright's spoiled brat daughter who always got everything she wanted. Now she had Jewel's husband, and . . . The curve ahead was sharp and the divider in the middle of the road suddenly loomed up from out of nowhere. Jewel slammed on the brakes and felt the car swerve first to the left and then, out of control, to the right. The back wheels lost traction, the car spun, the divider was coming nearer. Helpless, Jewel could only wait to see how hard the crash would be when the car smashed into it.

At the last second the car righted itself and stalled. Miraculously, it had stopped inches away from the divider. If there had been anyone else on the road, if the car had just pulled a little more to the right . . . Shaken, Jewel started the engine and drove slowly and carefully to the nearest exit. She kept on going until she found an all-night diner, where she pulled in between two trucks, and sat shaking, as she replayed in her mind the close call she'd just had. She could have been killed. And it was all Gwen Wright's fault. Dull, boring Gwen who had managed to steal Jewel's husband. Tears started down Jewel's cheeks; they came faster and faster as little animal cries of pain emerged from her throat. With trembling hands, she dug her cell phone out of her purse and dialed Wrightstown information.

* * *

Stan was waiting for Gwen to call. By now she'd have finished her reading, she'd be in her hotel room. She had to know how sorry he was that he wasn't there with her. She had to know how much he'd want to hear from her. She was always the one who made up first when they had a fight. She'd call. She would. And when she did, he was going to say he could have been wrong about Jeff Henry—even though he didn't believe it. But Gwen still hadn't called. He looked at his watch; he'd give her five more minutes and then he'd call her. He started for the kitchen to get a drink of water, and the phone rang.

"Gwen!" he said joyously into the phone. "Gwen, darling . . ."

"If you want to know where your darling wife is, try my husband's room at the Langham Inn," gasped a voice that was vaguely familiar.

"Jewel? Is that you?"

"Yes," Jewel cried. "He said he was working. I went there to see him. I thought things were going to be better. . . ."

"Jewel, where are you?"

"He put the damn house in my name!" She choked out the words through sobs. "He put most of his portfolio in my name. A man wouldn't do that if he was going to leave—that's what I thought."

"I don't know what you're talking about—"

"Jeff!" she screamed. "And your perfect little wife. They were up there together. I saw them in the parking lot of the hotel, and they went up together in the elevator. God knows how long they've been meeting like that. . . ."

"Jewel, you've got it wrong, Gwen was in Langham for a reading—"

"I don't care why she was there! I knew he was leaving me for someone. She's the one. If it had been anyone but her! Anyone else! I could have—"

But she got no further because Stan cut her off. "I've got to go, Jewel," he said and hung up the phone. He paced for a moment trying to clear his head. What Jewel had said was absurd; until that day, he had been the one who was going to Langham with Gwen, so there was no way she'd planned an assignation with a lover. Even if he'd thought

Gwen was capable of doing such a thing. Which he didn't. But Henry was a different matter; he was capable of anything—including following Gwen to her reading and trying to seduce her while she was alone and vulnerable. And she would have been very vulnerable in that hotel in Langham by herself. . . . He ran to grab his car keys off the sideboard. There was the sound of scratching at the front door as if someone was trying to unlock it, then the doorbell rang. He answered it.

Gwen stood in the doorway. Her hair was dripping wet from the rain, and her face looked drained and white. She was carrying her overnight case in her left hand, and there was a large bulky towel wrapped around her right wrist. It appeared to be damp.

"You were right!" she said. "I'm so sorry. You were right!" Then as he moved to take her in his arms she said with a little gasp of pain. "My hand!" And she started to cry.

It took a little time for him to get the whole story out of her. Then she had to convince him that there was no need to see a doctor because it really was just a sprain and he had to scold her—very gently—for driving home instead of calling him to come and get her. And she had to explain that she'd been so upset that driving with a hurt wrist—and after all it was her right wrist and she was left-handed—was easier than staying in Langham another second. He'd threatened to find Jeff Henry and kill him, and she'd begged him to let it go because it had been partly her fault. And he'd stopped talking about it because she'd looked like she might cry again, but he'd promised himself that he would have a meeting with Mr. Henry very soon. Then he had to take her into the bathroom and stand guard while she took a hot shower, and dry her off himself with the biggest towel he could find and put her to bed and lie down next to her and listen while she told him about the reading and the good part of the night, before Jeff had appeared in the parking lot of the library. And sometime after that she drifted off to sleep with his arm around her—placed very carefully so he wouldn't hurt the injured wrist—and then later, not wanting to disturb her, he fell asleep at her side still fully dressed.

Sometime in the middle of the night, the pain in her wrist woke her and he got up to bring her an aspirin, after which he undressed. As he was climbing into bed next to her, he sat up with a jolt. He'd just remembered something that had been gnawing at the back of his mind. He hadn't really registered it because so much else had happened, but now it came back to him. It was something Jewel had said.

*   *   *

The next morning Stan awoke while Gwen still slept and dialed his mother-in-law's phone number. Cassie was an early riser, and she answered on the second ring.

"I have a problem and I don't know where to go," Stan said. "I think something's happening at JeffSon." He told Cassie briefly about the numbers that hadn't added up, the way he'd been treated after he'd reported his discovery, and the final scene with Jeff Henry in which he had quit.

"It does sound suspicious," she said thoughtfully. "But it could have been a legitimate mistake."

"I tried to tell myself that too," Stan said. "But then I heard that Jeff Henry has been moving all of his assets into his wife's name."

There was a long silence on the other end of the phone, then Cassandra drew in a breath he could hear. "It's probably better if you don't say anything more about this until I look into it," she said. "I'll let you know what I find out."

"I'll wait to hear from you."

"And Stan?"

"Yes."

"Do you own any JeffSon stock?"

"No. I never bought any when I had the chance."

"Thank God."

* * *

The collapse of the JeffSon Corporation was a clap of thunder on a mild afternoon.

Very few people could possibly have imagined what had been happening in the sleek glass and chrome offices in

Texas, New York, and Wrightstown. And perhaps if there had been more time, the bailouts from Tokyo, London, or Dubai might have come through and no one would ever have known. But there hadn't been enough time—or luck—and soon the shock waves were roiling through the business community. It had started, said the Wall Street pundits, in a little backwater town in New England. Cassandra Wright, the low-profile but powerful CEO of Wright Glassworks, had somehow gotten wind of something that didn't smell quite right at JeffSon and she'd alerted Tommy Rubin, the stock analyst who had a popular radio talk show dealing with finances. Tommy began poking around, and three weeks later he was advising the public to unload its JeffSon stock. The house of cards that had been JeffSon came tumbling down soon after, and the rest, as they say, was history. Teachers in Georgia and civil servants in California suddenly found that retirement was out of the question—their pension funds, which had been invested in JeffSon stock, were now worth pennies on the dollar.

Senior citizens who had placed their trust in the company's promises would not have an independent old age; they would be living off the kindness of their children. And parents who had believed that Jeff Henry's dream company would secure their children's college funds were now facing their high school seniors empty-handed. Most of the men and women who had worked with Stan at JeffSon and taken the stock options were wiped out. Jeffery Henry was one of the most hated men in America.

Inevitably, the investigations followed. And the lawyers. "Get yourself the best, you're going to need them," the head of the New York accounting firm advised Jeff. That was before his own lawyer convinced him to take a deal and cooperate with the authorities in their investigation of Jeff. Mark Scotto had already taken his deal.

In her big mausoleum-like house Jewel panicked. Once she'd thought that the worst thing that could happen to her would be an affair between her husband and Gwen. She'd accused him of it, and he had denied it so vehemently that she had actually believed him. And she'd breathed a sigh of relief because she'd faced her biggest fear, found out it was nothing, and she was home free. There was nothing more life could do to her. She'd thought. Now it seemed that she'd been terribly, horribly wrong. "What do you mean?" she screamed at her husband. "What the hell are you telling me? That they're going to put you in jail?"

He had taken off his jacket and, sweating in his shirt, had sunk into the chair nearest the door of the huge living room. He rubbed his head as if it ached.

"Haven't I explained it to you at least ten times? Haven't I? For God's sake, what more do you want me to tell you? I'm not in prison yet, for Christ's sake. Calm down!"

"But I don't understand what this is."

"Don't shriek at me. Of course you don't understand it. What do you know about the law? What do you know about money? All you know is how to spend it."

There he sat. His legs were sprawled, while one hand wiped his forehead and the other dabbled in the bowl of nuts on the table beside his chair. The nuts made a revolting sound as he crunched them. She kept staring at him as if she were trying to recognize and remember some stranger's face and name. Jeff's tie was loosened and lay on his heaving chest.

"I would have been all right," he said. "I could have claimed that I didn't know anything. I was on the road hyping the company. I didn't pay attention to the day-to-day operations. I didn't know about the offshore accounts. . . . I was innocent. . . ." He trailed off. "But she found out. That bitch Cassandra Wright found out I was transferring assets to you . . . that was what started it all. . . ."

And Jewel remembered sitting in her car after she'd nearly run off the road because she'd just seen her husband kissing Gwen's hands. Jewel remembered the rage that had swept over her. She remembered wanting to make Gwen—lucky, pampered, undeserving Gwen—pay for once in her life.

So, blinded by jealousy, without thinking of the consequences, Jewel had called Stan Girard to tell him that his wife was no better than her birth mother who had been a whore. She had also told Stan Girard that her husband had just put their house in her name.

Jewel looked around the room, at the tall window that framed a suddenly frightening vision of an eternal, limitless, empty sky.

She turned back to Jeff and demanded in a voice that was low and hoarse, "Why didn't you tell me this before? Why didn't you let me know what was going on? If I'd known how bad it was, about the courts and prison . . . Why the hell didn't you tell me?"

"Might as well ask a man from Tibet why he doesn't have a conversation with a Bulgarian. They don't speak the same language, that's why!"

She felt oddly disconnected. Her mind flitted through crazy split seconds: The curtains in the room looked like something in a funeral parlor. What was going through Jeff's mind at this minute? His features were the same, the firmness of the mouth, the way the eyes looked at you as you spoke to him and as he measured you . . . but he was a different man now. He was bankrupt. He was going to jail. And overriding everything else was the thought she could not get out of her mind, the thought she knew would be with her forever: She had helped bring about his downfall. It wasn't all her fault, she knew that, but it had taken just one tiny moment of jealous rage to begin the process that had led her husband to the indictments he was now saying he could not beat. One sliver of a second. Now Jewel was left with a meaningless and yet frightening mingling of words about quarterly losses, retirement accounts, lost jobs, millions of dollars, lawyers, more lawyers—all things she neither knew anything about nor understood. And somewhere in the muddle of guilt and fear that filled Jewel's head was an unexplainable, queer kernel of bewildered, awful pity for Jeff, who had once loved her so much.

Chapter Thirty-six

The Lamborghini was worth every dollar
it had cost, Jeff thought for the hun-
dredth time. The seat was just right for
his long legs and back. The graceful
simplicity of its lines and the bright triumphant glint of its yellow paint, the soft
silky leather of the interior—all were
so absolutely right. He took his seat,
pressed the accelerator, and the car
leaped forward as if he had spoken to it,
as if it had understood his mood, the

strange mood that he himself could not possibly have described.

He had driven to his father's house, to the neighborhood that was quietly decaying next to the river. He had gone to see the old man for . . . what reason? To obtain absolution? To explain? But there had been no way to make his case with Father—no more than he could with the investigators or the judges, or the lawyers. No one seemed to understand that he had not meant for any of this to happen. JeffSon was not supposed to die like a great gasping beast crashing through the forest, taking everything in its path with it.

"There was nothing I could do, Dad," he had said as close to tears as he had been since he became an adult. "When everything started going south, I couldn't stop it. It was like . . . drowning . . . or a car wreck. Everything spiraled out of control."

"Faustian bargains, Jeffie," the old man had said, shaking his head. That had been it, that had been the only comfort his father had offered—"Faustian bargains."

And so Jeff had walked out of the house where there was no comfort to be had and started driving his beautiful, triumphant car. Not south, not back to Wrightstown, for there was no comfort there, either. The river appeared at his side; the road ran parallel to it. He thought about the picture that hung in his office, the one of the little girl who was all alone and looking out over this very river. Walter Amburn had painted it and Jeff had bought it. Was that only a few years ago? It felt like a million. Jeff had seen the painting and known he had to have it. That was before he'd gone to Gwen Wright's birthday party, before he met Jewel who encouraged him to make his millions—and his Faustian bargain.

So, now go, Jeff. Just go to any place that is different. Not to the next town. Not, most of all, to a city. He had seen enough cities. He had seen the world's cities, from Paris to Shanghai, and he was tired of them. He was tired of people, too, of their faces, their voices, and their unending talk. Their predictions and opinions: *Today you should do this. If you do this today, you will get that. If you get that, you will be able to get some more.*

I don't want any more. But maybe I do? Only, I don't know what. I know I don't want to go back to that house— my house. To the house that used to be mine. And I don't want to go back to the woman in that house. The other woman, the woman I wanted, fought to get away from me. She was on the floor at my feet looking up at me with horror in her big smart eyes. I don't want to go back to the place where she lives. That I do know.

The road was following the river into a gap between two hills in a low mountain range whose name Jeff couldn't remember. The river sparkled like one of the diamond tennis bracelets he had bought for Jewel back in the days when it still delighted him to see her joy at his presents. Back when he still cared what happened to him.

But God! He didn't want to sit in a cell, like a bear at the zoo. In a cage for years. But the appeal . . . he could afford it, so the lawyers said. Oh, sure! And if it didn't work? It would be two years, two years of courts, of fear, of sick stomach, dry mouth, staring, cold eyes, so curious. People judging him. Two years. Two years.

But look ahead, the road is curving up onto the hill. Below it is the sparkling river. All this is so beautiful . . . beautiful America . . . At the top of the hill the road stops at a crossroads; if you go to the north or the south you will find a small city. Like the small city you are trying to escape. To the east is another road and yet another city. But to the west . . . the river will turn, curve, and race away from this place to the real West. The West of beautiful America. Fly to the West with the river, Jeff. Enjoy the day. Love the day. Press hard with your foot. Race. Feel the cool wind through the wide-open windows of the Lamborghini. Let the sweet air flow in. So cool, so fresh. Faster. Faster.

On the turn, the car leaps over the embankment, plunges, and comes to a final stop in the river below, and there it lies. In the silence, in the silent water.

And the car, with all it contains, lies still. Broken, crushed, and still.

Chapter Thirty-seven

Jeff Henry's funeral was mercifully simple. For once, it seemed that Jewel had
decided to be restrained.

"I'm glad," Gwen told Stan. "For Jeff's
sake." Her husband was silent. "I think
about how much Jeff loved music and
books . . . the way he'd talk about history and philosophy . . . he had such a
fine mind. And you have to admit that he
was generous; look at that shelter he
started for homeless families. He en-
dowed it so it can go on for years."

"Good. Maybe some of the people who lost their homes when they discovered their JeffSon stock was worthless can live there." Stan's lips tightened in the way Gwen recognized well.

"Do you think you'll ever be able to forgive him?" she asked.

Stan brushed his hair out of his eyes and fixed her with a steady look. "I'll work on it. But I can't make any promises."

*　　*　　*

Gwen thought that was the last of the conversations she would have about Jeff Henry. But one afternoon there was a knock on her door. She opened it to see Jewel standing in front of her—a changed and different Jewel. Gone were the gold and diamond bracelets and the big dangling earrings that Cassie said were vulgar. Jewel was dressed in a tweed skirt and cashmere sweater. Her face seemed changed too; there were circles of weariness under her eyes, and a hint of a wrinkle on either side of her mouth. Her hair was still a shiny ebony but she'd bundled it into a knot at the back of her head instead of letting it flow gloriously over her shoulders.

"May I come in?" she asked. Gwen nodded silently and led her into the living room.

"I wanted to say good-bye," Jewel said, taking over the conversation, as she had the first time she and Gwen met.

"Are you going somewhere?"

"I'm leaving Wrightstown—the house is already sold—and I'm going home. Back where I grew up. Two of my sisters are still living there. Peggy's husband left her after their third baby was born so I'm going to buy a place and she and the children will come and live with me."

"That sounds very . . ." Gwen struggled for a word and finally produced one. "Practical," she said.

"I won't be alone anymore," Jewel said. "I realized the other day that I've never really put down any roots in Wrightstown." Then she laughed her big warm laugh. "Hell," she said, "why did you think I'm here saying good-bye to you? You and Patsy Allen are the only

people I know well enough. That's pa-
thetic."

Gwen laughed to keep her company.
Then Jewel sobered up.

"Do you think he did it on purpose,
Gwen?" she asked softly. "I keep telling
myself he wouldn't, that it was an accident, but you knew him so well, better
than I did. And I think . . ."

"Don't think!" Gwen interrupted, and
the command in her voice surprised
both of them. "My mother always used
to say 'let sleeping dogs lie' and it used
to make me so mad. Now I know that
sometimes that's the only thing we can
do. Just live your life and don't look
back, Jewel."

Jewel nodded and turned as if to go.
Then she stopped. "Being jealous is a
terrible waste, isn't it?"

"Yes," Gwen said. "It is."

Jewel turned again and Gwen walked
with her to the door. "If you're ever up in
my neck of the woods," Jewel said,
"check out my new shop. I'm opening a
branch of Times Past."

Epilogue

❧

Cassie drove down the quiet street in Brookside. The little town had been one of the first suburbs of Wrightstown; a blue-collar community built for the workers at the glassworks. The streets were laid out on a neat grid, with rows of simple, matching houses, interspersed with an occasional row of mom-and-pop stores, and then more rows of matching houses. The stores were not fashionable, and the homes were not new. But the lots on which the houses were built were good-sized, and there was a park with hiking and bike trails nearby.

Cassie reached the house that was her destination. As she always did when she pulled into the driveway, she shook her head and sighed. There were dandelions all over the front lawn, which had gone at least three weeks without being mowed, and a few weeds were spreading on the side of the narrow sidewalk that ran between the house and its immediate neighbor. If it had been Cassie's place, she would have been on her knees at that moment pulling up the offending vegetation. But the house wasn't hers. It belonged to Gwen and Stan. Cassie sighed again. Stan did his best to pay attention but after three years of home ownership, in his heart he was still a city boy. He thought like a tenant who rented his home and waited for his super to do the necessary maintenance on it. But if that didn't bother Stan's wife, Cassie told herself firmly, then his mother-in-law wasn't going to say a word. She and Stan had come a long distance; Cassie wasn't going to do

anything to jeopardize their new en-
tente. For one thing, Walter would scold
her if she did.

She could still remember the day—it
had been about six months after the
collapse of JeffSon and Jeff Henry's accident, at least, that was the official
word on his car wreck, although some
people had their doubts—when Stan
had asked if he could come to her office
to talk. He'd paced around nervously for
several minutes before he'd come to the
point. Finally he'd plunged in.

"There's a house," he said. "Gwen
wants it very much. And I'd like it too,
now that we . . ." He stopped himself.
"But I'll let Gwen tell you our good
news. The fact is, we'd like to buy this
house. It's in an old neighborhood, but
it's been very well kept up and all the
real estate people say it's a good investment and we wouldn't lose our money
. . . ." He drew in a big breath. "But we
can't afford it. I'm going to go back into
business for myself and that's going to
take all the money I got when I sold my
shop. Gwen's book is doing well, but
it takes time to build a writer's career

and we want to move in the next few months, before the . . ." He stopped himself again. "But Gwen'll tell you about that. Right now," he went on, "we can't get a mortgage because I'm not making enough. So I was wondering if . . ."

And she'd broken in happily. "I'd love to give you and Gwen the money to buy whatever house you want, Stan."

"I was hoping you'd let us borrow the money," he said.

She had learned a lot about this man, because she hadn't argued that the money would be nothing to her and it would be foolish for them to strap themselves for no reason. It had only taken her a second to say, "Did you want to draw up a formal contract with lawyers or can we just shake hands?"

*   *   *

Cassie stopped the car in the driveway. One didn't have to enter Gwen's home in order to know that there would be very little of either mahogany, Persian rugs, or silver inside. For one thing, people who own such things seldom tolerate weeds and dandelions. The only thing that might possibly link this house to the one in which Gwen had grown up was a line of small red maples at the edge of the front lawn. They seemed to be thriving, Cassie noted as she got out of the car.

The front door of Gwen's house opened and a small bullet propelled itself across the front lawn to throw itself into her arms. "Grandma!" shrieked two-year-old Stanley Girard, Jr.—aka little Stan.

At the same time, Gwen said from the doorway, "We'll just be another minute. Big Stan has a new camera that he wants to try today and he's still fussing with it." She disappeared again, and little Stan began lobbying Cassie for ice cream.

"A cone, Grandma," he said. "A cone!"

"You're incorrigible," Cassie informed him as she knelt down to hug him. But Little Stan was not to be deterred. He wriggled out of her grasp. "Ice-cream cone," he said sternly. And even though she knew she shouldn't encourage him, Cassie started to laugh.

"All right, you win," she said. "We'll get an ice-cream cone."

"Chocolate," Little Stan specified, wreathed in smiles.

"He plays you like a fine violin," said Gwen as she joined them. Behind her Big Stan, as he was now called, was walking and fiddling with the camera. The three Girards and Cassie headed for Cassie's car.

"Walter will join us at the glassworks museum," Cassie told Gwen. "He just finished painting the background diorama two days ago and he was afraid it wouldn't be dry in time for the unveiling of the exhibit. But he called me as I was driving over here, and he said it's fine. He and the curator are setting the figurines up in front of it right now."

"I loved the sketch he did; it looked exactly like my little refuge on the hill," Gwen said.

"That's what it's meant to be," said Cassie.

Gwen linked her arm through Cassie's. "Thank you for doing this, Mother," she said. "Thank you for exhibiting the New Orleans Group."

"The figurines are beautiful, people should be able to see them," Cassie said. "And it's time for me to grow up."

Little Stan had run ahead of them, and he'd reached the young red maples at the edge of the property. "Honey, that's far enough!" his mother called out to him.

He turned, planted himself where he stood, and fixed his mother with a quizzical gaze as if he was trying to decide if he wished to obey her. There was something in that strong little stance and the determined tilt of the little head that reminded Cassie of her father and her grandfather—never mind that there was no direct blood line connecting them all. She could see Little Stan someday taking his place as the head of the Wright Glassworks, and living in the Wright house. Neither of those options would ever be right for his mother; Gwen had found her own way. But this little person standing in front of them all . . . well, now, he was a very different story.

Little Stan had decided to comply with his mother's wishes. He ran to Gwen, who scooped him up in her arms and swung him high. The air was filled with the sound of their laughter.

Cassie watched them. *Gwen's come such a long way,* she thought. *Such a long, long way.* Looking at her now, it was almost impossible to remember the diffident, unhappy girl who had once been jealous of flashy Jewel Fairchild. In spite of herself, Cassie felt her eyes well up.

"Cassie, stand with them," Big Stan commanded, his camera at the ready.

Cassie blinked back her tears and smiled as she moved close to the child she had rescued so long ago, and that child's child. The two women, with Little Stan in Gwen's arms, stood together in the bright morning sunlight. In front of them was Gwen's house and the husband who was so very right for her. Behind them were the red maples Gwen had planted with loving memories of the gardens and forests of her old home.

There was a mechanical whir as Big Stan began taking pictures, freezing this slice of time into pictures which could be copied onto some tangible substance like paper and saved. Over the years, with all the joys and sorrows that would inevitably come, the pictures would be a reminder of this perfect moment.

But Cassie knew she would never need pictures printed on paper. The laughter, and the sunshine, and the love were already tucked away in her mind—and in her heart.

About the Author

BELVA PLAIN lives in northern New Jersey. She is the *New York Times* best-selling author of *Evergreen, Random Winds, Eden Burning, Crescent City, The Golden Cup, Tapestry, Blessings, Harvest, Treasures, Whispers, Daybreak, The Carousel, Promises, Secrecy, Home-coming, Legacy of Silence, Fortune's Hand, After the Fire, Looking Back, Her Father's House,* and *The Sight of the Stars.*